BAGHDAD NOIR

EDITED BY SAMUEL SHIMON

BROOKLYN, NEW YORK, USA
BALLYDEHOB, CO. CORK, IRELAND

Published by Akashic Books
©2018 Akashic Books

Series concept by Tim McLoughlin and Johnny Temple
Baghdad map by Sohrab Habibion

ISBN: 978-1-61775-343-5
Library of Congress Control Number: 2017956562

All rights reserved
First printing

Akashic Books
Brooklyn, New York, USA
Ballydehob, Co. Cork, Ireland
Twitter: @AkashicBooks
Facebook: AkashicBooks
E-mail: info@akashicbooks.com
Website: www.akashicbooks.com

ALSO IN THE AKASHIC NOIR SERIES

ATLANTA NOIR, edited by TAYARI JONES
BALTIMORE NOIR, edited by LAURA LIPPMAN
BARCELONA NOIR (SPAIN), edited by ADRIANA V. LÓPEZ & CARMEN OSPINA
BEIRUT NOIR (LEBANON), edited by IMAN HUMAYDAN
BELFAST NOIR (NORTHERN IRELAND), edited by ADRIAN McKINTY & STUART NEVILLE
BOSTON NOIR, edited by DENNIS LEHANE
BOSTON NOIR 2: THE CLASSICS, edited by DENNIS LEHANE, MARY COTTON & JAIME CLARKE
BRONX NOIR, edited by S.J. ROZAN
BROOKLYN NOIR, edited by TIM McLOUGHLIN
BROOKLYN NOIR 2: THE CLASSICS, edited by TIM McLOUGHLIN
BROOKLYN NOIR 3: NOTHING BUT THE TRUTH, edited by TIM McLOUGHLIN & THOMAS ADCOCK
BRUSSELS NOIR (BELGIUM), edited by MICHEL DUFRANNE
BUENOS AIRES NOIR (ARGENTINA), edited by ERNESTO MALLO
BUFFALO NOIR, edited by ED PARK & BRIGID HUGHES
CAPE COD NOIR, edited by DAVID L. ULIN
CHICAGO NOIR, edited by NEAL POLLACK
CHICAGO NOIR: THE CLASSICS, edited by JOE MENO
COPENHAGEN NOIR (DENMARK), edited by BO TAO MICHAËLIS
DALLAS NOIR, edited by DAVID HALE SMITH
D.C. NOIR, edited by GEORGE PELECANOS
D.C. NOIR 2: THE CLASSICS, edited by GEORGE PELECANOS
DELHI NOIR (INDIA), edited by HIRSH SAWHNEY
DETROIT NOIR, edited by E.J. OLSEN & JOHN C. HOCKING
DUBLIN NOIR (IRELAND), edited by KEN BRUEN
HAITI NOIR, edited by EDWIDGE DANTICAT
HAITI NOIR 2: THE CLASSICS, edited by EDWIDGE DANTICAT
HAVANA NOIR (CUBA), edited by ACHY OBEJAS
HELSINKI NOIR (FINLAND), edited by JAMES THOMPSON
INDIAN COUNTRY NOIR, edited by SARAH CORTEZ & LIZ MARTÍNEZ
ISTANBUL NOIR (TURKEY), edited by MUSTAFA ZIYALAN & AMY SPANGLER
KANSAS CITY NOIR, edited by STEVE PAUL
KINGSTON NOIR (JAMAICA), edited by COLIN CHANNER
LAGOS NOIR (NIGERIA), edited by CHRIS ABANI
LAS VEGAS NOIR, edited by JARRET KEENE & TODD JAMES PIERCE
LONDON NOIR (ENGLAND), edited by CATHI UNSWORTH
LONE STAR NOIR, edited by BOBBY BYRD & JOHNNY BYRD
LONG ISLAND NOIR, edited by KAYLIE JONES
LOS ANGELES NOIR, edited by DENISE HAMILTON
LOS ANGELES NOIR 2: THE CLASSICS, edited by DENISE HAMILTON
MANHATTAN NOIR, edited by LAWRENCE BLOCK
MANHATTAN NOIR 2: THE CLASSICS, edited by LAWRENCE BLOCK
MANILA NOIR (PHILIPPINES), edited by JESSICA HAGEDORN
MARRAKECH NOIR (MOROCCO), edited by YASSIN ADNAN
MARSEILLE NOIR (FRANCE), edited by CÉDRIC FABRE
MEMPHIS NOIR, edited by LAUREEN P. CANTWELL & LEONARD GILL
MEXICO CITY NOIR (MEXICO), edited by PACO I. TAIBO II
MIAMI NOIR, edited by LES STANDIFORD
MISSISSIPPI NOIR, edited by TOM FRANKLIN
MONTANA NOIR, edited by JAMES GRADY & KEIR GRAFF
MONTREAL NOIR (CANADA), edited by JOHN McFETRIDGE & JACQUES FILIPPI
MOSCOW NOIR (RUSSIA), edited by NATALIA SMIRNOVA & JULIA GOUMEN
MUMBAI NOIR (INDIA), edited by ALTAF TYREWALA
NEW HAVEN NOIR, edited by AMY BLOOM
NEW JERSEY NOIR, edited by JOYCE CAROL OATES

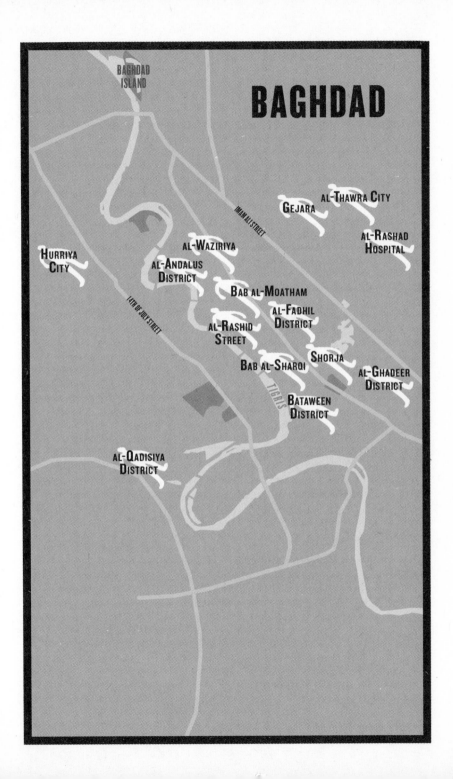

TABLE OF CONTENTS

13   *Introduction*

PART I: MURDER IN THE FAMILY

23   **MUHSIN AL-RAMLI**   al-Fadhil District
I Killed Her Because I Loved Her

36   **NASSIF FALAK**   Hurriya City
Doomsday Book

55   **SINAN ANTOON**   al-Rashad Hospital
Jasim's File

69   **AHMED SAADAWI**   Bataween District
A Sense of Remorse

PART II: WHERE IS THE TRUST?

91   **SALAR ABDOH**   Gejara
Baghdad on Borrowed Time

116   **HADIA SAID**   al-Qadisiya District
Post-Traumatic Stress Reality in Qadisiya

150   **HAYET RAIES**   al-Waziriya
The Fear of Iraqi Intelligence

168   **MOHAMMED ALWAN JABR**   Bab al-Sharqi
Room 22

PART III: WAKE ME UP

183	**SALIMA SALIH** *The Apartment*	al-Ghadeer District
197	**HUSSAIN AL-MOZANY** *Empty Bottles*	al-Thawra City
213	**DHEYA AL-KHALIDI** *Getting to Abu Nuwas Street*	Bab al-Moatham

PART IV: BLOOD ON MY HANDS

227	**ROY SCRANTON** *Homecoming*	Shorja
254	**ALI BADER** *Baghdad House*	al-Rashid Street
279	**LAYLA QASRANY** *Tuesday of Sorrows*	al-Andalus District

293	**Acknowledgments**
294	**About the Contributors**

For Hussain al-Mozany and Maggie Estep

INTRODUCTION
GARDEN OF JUSTICE, CITY OF PEACE

In the aftermath of the British invasion of the Ottoman Empire in 1917 and the period of the British Mandate, modern Iraq came to consist of three provinces: Mosul, Basra, and Baghdad. After Iraqis rose up against British rule, Faisal I was crowned king of the Hashemite monarchy, with Baghdad as its capital—a city with a long, rich history that was founded by the Abbasid caliph Abu Jaafar al-Mansur in the year 762, and which he named Madinat al-Salaam (City of Peace). Since that time, Baghdad has remained a nexus of Arab culture, commerce, and learning, positioned literally in the cradle of civilization itself on the banks of the mighty Tigris River, within the area that once comprised Mesopotamia. When the modern Iraqi state was established in 1921, its population was barely three million; today, the population is approaching forty million—with nearly ten million people residing in Baghdad alone, making it the second-largest city in the Arab world, behind Cairo.

Historically, Iraq has been one of the world's most ethnically diverse countries. In the more distant past, before Arab tribes emerged on the scene, it was the land of the ancient Sumerians and Assyrians. Then, as the center of the Islamic Caliphate for a thousand years, it attracted various commingling nationalities. Until relatively recently, marriage by Iraqis to Circassians, Turkmens, Kurds, and Iranian people was commonplace, along with intermarriage between these groups. If

we add to this the many Mughal, Turkic, and Iranian con-
quests of Iraq, and the innumerable pilgrimages to the Shia
holy sites by various ethnic groups over the centuries, we are
confronted with a picture that makes it impossible to counte-
nance the idea of a singular national ethnic identity.

Although the Arabic language is dominant, Kurdish, Turkmen, Assyrian, Armenian, Syriac, and Persian are also spoken
across the country. And these diverse ethnic and linguistic
groups likewise reflect a multitude of religious beliefs. (Officially, Iraq remained a secular country from the establishment
of the monarchy until the fall of Saddam Hussein's regime after
the American invasion of April 2003.) The majority-Muslim
population is divided between Shia and Sunni adherents—
and while there are no official statistics, it's generally pre-
sumed that the number of Shia outnumber the Sunni. There
is also a significant population of Kurds (majority Sunni Mus-
lim) and Turkmen who are concentrated in the north, particularly around Kirkuk. Many Iranians settled around the holy
sites in Najaf and Kadhimiya, as did Mandaeans in Basra and
the greater south. The robust Christian population within the
country comprises a variety of origins and denominations,
forming a large part of the population in the north, while the
Yazidis mostly settled around Mount Sinjar. Yet the once-
vibrant Jewish community in Baghdad (and many other Iraqi
cities) had mostly left for Israel by the end of the 1940s.

From amid this melting pot I commissioned fourteen brand-
new short stories: ten written by Iraqi authors and four by
non-Iraqis. Among the non-Iraqis, one author is American,
another is Iranian, and two are Arab women from Tunisia
and Lebanon. However, the latter four have all spent time in
Baghdad and know the city well.

It proved to be a tough task to assemble the stories in this collection. In the Arab world we are not fully accustomed to the concept of commissioning stories around a specific theme or of a specific length—and in this case even set in a specific location—then working with the author on revisions. In general, Arab authors are not familiar with the editorial process found in the West, which posed some challenges. More significantly, given that this is the first collection of Iraqi crime fiction that I am aware of, few of these authors had previously tried their hands at writing noir literature.

In general, the development of the modern novel is a relatively recent phenomenon in Iraqi literature. Most people consider *Jalal Khalid* by Mahmoud Ahmed al-Sayed, published in 1928, to be the first Iraqi novel. Structurally, the book takes the form of a memoir by an Iraqi man in his twenties who moves to India in 1919 to escape the British Occupation, and ends up marrying a Jewish woman he meets during his travels. After World War II, Iraqi writers grew more influenced by the giants of American and European literature, whose works were translated into Arabic—though many would also read them in English. Some of the pioneers of Iraqi fiction include Abdul Malik Nouri, Ghaieb Tuma'a Farman, Fouad al-Tikerly, and Mahdi Issa al-Saqr, who were then followed by well-known names like Fadhil al-Azzawi, Lutfiya al-Dulaimi, Muhammad Khudayyir, and Abdul Rahman Majeed al-Rubaie, Mahmoud Saeed, among others. Their short stories and novels explored Iraqi society and the matters of everyday life: love, revenge, romance, illness, and isolation. In more recent years, some of these works have even adopted formal aspects of magical realism and existentialism.

The Iraqi novel became much more ubiquitous after the US invasion in 2003 and the fall of Saddam Hussein's regime. In less than fifteen years, close to seven hundred nov-els have emerged from the country (more than had appeared over the entirety of the twentieth century), including works that deal with contemporary topics such as the UN-enforced sanctions, the Iraq-Iran War, the Iraqi occupation of Kuwait, and, of course, the US invasion of Iraq. As reflected in these pages, the literature has condemned both the US occupation and barbaric destruction of Iraq, as well as the former dicta-torial regime. Others have written about and criticized the dominance of religious and sectarian militias which largely control the streets of Baghdad today. The top Iraqi authors writing now (many of whom appear in this collection) include Ahmed Saadawi, Nassif Falak, Betool Khedairi, Ali Bader, Inaam Kachachi, Dheya al-Khalidi, Sinan Antoon, Muhsin al-Ramli, Duna Ghali, Dhia al-Jubaili, and Shahad al-Rawi, among others. Many of their works have been translated into other languages. Ahmed Saadawi's *Frankenstein in Baghdad* won the International Prize for Arabic Fiction and is a best seller in the United States.

While all Iraqis will readily agree that their life has always been noir, the majority of the stories in *Baghdad Noir* are set in the years following the American invasion of 2003, though one story is set in 1950 and three are set in the 1970s and 1980s. Yet it is this recent history of Iraq—over the last few decades—that serves to inform its present.

I fled the country mere months before Saddam seized power in July 1979. Back then, before the regime declared war on Iran, the Iraqi dinar was worth $3.60 US—today one dinar trades at $0.00084—and the country was at the height of its prosperity, boasting an international workforce and an upwardly mobile middle class. Upon arriving in Damascus, I was immediately arrested by the Syrian secret police for being a Jewish spy. This happened for two reasons: firstly, because of my name (I am actually of Assyrian descent); and secondly, when I explained that I was heading to Lebanon to look for work, one of the officers looked at me in disbelief and shouted: "How do you expect me to believe that, when everyone dreams of working in Iraq!"

The Iran-Iraq War was the beginning of the end for Iraqi civil society, with half a million soldiers and half a million civilians killed on each side, effectively wiping out an entire generation. Unfortunately, most of the literary production of that time glorified the war effort against what were known as the Iranian *Magi*—and, of course, very few other writings were allowed to be officially published in the first place. Cementing the destruction of Iraqi life was Saddam Hussein's invasion of Kuwait in 1990. The seventeen days of bombs falling on Baghdad and other cities, dropped by the US-led military coalition in defense of Kuwait, and the subsequent thirteen years of crippling economic sanctions took Iraqi society back to the stone age. But that was hardly the end of Iraq's noir story. In April 2003, the US invasion, though it precipitated the end of Saddam's dictatorial rule, killed off any possibility of a secular, modern Iraq once and for all.

To help guide the authors in this collection, I turned to one of the first books in Akashic's Noir Series, *Queens Noir*. In particular, I found the story "Alice Fantastic" by Maggie Estep to be a quintessential noir story, so I asked the publisher for permission to have it translated into Arabic, then sent the translation to most of the authors to show them an example of good noir—one of the best I've ever read, one without a Monsieur Poirot–type character taking center stage. The author Hussain al-Mozany loved Maggie's story and, after reading it, wrote his own tale, "Empty Bottles." Unfortunately, "Empty Bottles" was the last story he ever wrote, as he died after a heart attack in December 2016 at the age of sixty-three. (Maggie also passed away far too soon in February 2014, at the age of fifty.)

The three stories set during the Saddam era tell readers about Iraqi life over the last fifty years. In "The Apartment" by Salima Salih, appearances may be deceptive when an old lady living alone is found dead after apparently hitting her head in a fall. "Tuesday of Sorrows" by Layla Qasrany and "The Night Sabah Disappeared" by Hayet Raies capture the atmosphere and climate of fear in Iraq in the 1970s, when Saddam Hussein was ruthlessly consolidating Baathist power. "Baghdad House" by Ali Bader is a tribute to Agatha Christie, who famously lived in Iraq during the 1950s.

The random kidnappings and abductions that have terrified Iraqi families since 2003 feature in the story "Room 22" by Mohammed Alwan Jabr; meanwhile, in "Getting to Abu Nuwas Street" by Dheya al-Khalidi, a story set after the American troops left Iraq, the protagonist wakes up in a living nightmare, held captive by schoolchildren in an abandoned workshop. "Homecoming," by former US soldier Roy Scranton, is a dog-eat-dog tale of brutal savagery set in Baghdad just before Daesh occupied Mosul, in which an Iraqi soldier takes revenge against militia leaders; while "Jasim's File" by Sinan Antoon is based on the true story of patients from al-Rashad mental hospital escaping en masse after the Americans invaded—but with a crucial difference. In "Baghdad on Borrowed Time," Salar Abdoh writes about an Iranian war veteran and private detective who is tasked with investigating a series of murders of regime conspirators.

A prominent theme in the collection is family, and specifically the deteriorating relationship between parents, children, and even siblings. In "I Killed Her Because I Love Her" by Muhsin al-Ramli, two beautiful sisters are murdered by someone close to them in a whodunit that asks *why?* as it reveals the terrible fracturing of post-2003 Iraqi society. Nassif Falak's "Doomsday Book," set during the time of UN sanctions, unearths dire warnings, disappearances, secret directives, and riddles that end in assassination, ordered by mujahideen as "the express will of God" and all recorded in a ledger, line by line. Hadia Said's aptly titled "Post-Traumatic Stress Reality in Qadisiya" is a skillful portrayal of the unraveling of a man's mind as he returns to Iraq from abroad and encounters his destroyed and deserted family home. In "A Sense of Remorse" by Ahmed Saadawi, the protagonist Jibran combines a detective's curiosity with pragmatic and persistent inquiry as he uncovers the surreal story behind his brother's apparent suicide.

Taken as a whole, the stories in *Baghdad Noir* testify to the enduring resilience of the Iraqi spirit amid an ongoing, real-life milieu of despair that the literary form of noir can at best only approximate. Yet the contributions here manage to hold their own as individual *stories*, where the rich traditions of intersecting cultures transcend the immediate political reality—even while being simultaneously informed by it. Much like the diverse tapestry of cultures that join together on the banks of the Tigris to form the City of Peace, *Baghdad Noir* reveals that there's nothing monolithic or ordinary about the voices of its writers.

Samuel Shimon
June 2018

PART I

MURDER IN THE FAMILY

I KILLED HER BECAUSE I LOVED HER

BY MUHSIN AL-RAMLI

al-Fadhil District

We found Qamar's body in the courtyard—it was half past five in the morning, and her mother's screams echoed throughout the old Baghdad house in the Fadhil District. Qamar had been the most beautiful girl in our neighborhood. Now her arms were still and lifeless, her legs splayed open, and her luxuriant hair framed her face like the dark moon suspended in the sky above us. From the second-floor balcony where I stood, Qamar looked like she'd been crucified.

The old landlord approached the body. When he saw that there was no blood he took her pulse at the wrist and neck, then announced that she was indeed dead. He pulled a slip of paper from her fingers. It said: *I killed her because I loved her.* He adjusted his glasses and read it again, then went to the main gate of the building to inspect the padlocks and bars that had been installed after the Americans came. He found them all firmly locked—just as he secured them at ten every evening when the curfew came into effect. Then he went to his room to call the police.

The police, good for nothing except taking bribes, just sent over a sergeant and two patrolmen, who gathered us together. It was the first moment we had all been in the same place at the same time. The patrolmen had brought a folding table and two chairs. The sergeant sat on one of the chairs and asked us one by one to sit on the other. He told us to write the sentence, *I killed her because I loved her*. Meanwhile, two other cops wrote down the details from our identity cards. They dipped our fingers in ink and pressed them for prints, collected all the papers in a file, and departed—never to return. We were left to our fears—and our suspicions about each other.

The building, like most old Baghdad houses, was built around a square courtyard. It had two stories and eight large rooms—four on each floor. Some of the rooms had been divided with wooden partitions, and each floor had a communal bathroom and kitchen.

My friend Rafid and I rented a room on the upper floor. We had moved to Baghdad from al-Haqlaniyah, our village in western Iraq, to study at the university, and we hadn't found anywhere cheaper or closer to our school, which was in the Bab al-Moatham District, just a twenty-minute walk away. The area was down-market and right in the middle of Baghdad—close to the large al-Fadhil mosque, Maidan Square, Rashid Street, and the Central Bank. Kifah Street ran alongside the hospital, and nearby were markets of all sizes, coffee shops, cheap restaurants, public baths, spice and cloth merchants, pet stores, bakeries, hardware stores, and people who repaired old appliances. Arabs, Kurds, Turkomans, Muslims, Christians, and Mandaeans mixed together in relative harmony. The residents were simple, unpretentious, generous, brave, patriotic, and sentimental. They respected strangers who came to visit or rented houses.

The neighborhood seemed to have been forgotten since it was founded in Abbasid times, or timeless with its narrow, smelly alleys. The streets were pocked with potholes, noisy with the clamor of children playing and the clattering of peddlers' carts. The smoke from piles of putrid, smoldering garbage mixed with the scent of grilled meat and spices. The houses, built of old bricks and planks of wood, leaned precariously against each other—the only reason they didn't collapse was because there wasn't enough space on the ground between them. Some houses bore signs of shelling or bullet holes from past battles between the Americans and groups of gunmen.

The tenant in the room across from ours was Adil, a university student from another village. A Baghdad policeman, his wife, and their son with Down's syndrome occupied one of the rooms between us. The officer, a fat man with a bushy mustache, spent most of his time drinking and waiting for his retirement. The landlord stored wool that he sold in a fourth room, with a door that hung off its hinges. Rafid used it as a hiding place for his nocturnal trysts with Qamar—they had developed a close relationship under the pretext of studying English together. It may in fact have been she who told him that the house had a room available. In the wool storeroom everything had to be done furtively, since it was right above the landlord's room. He had chosen the room closest to the stairs and the front door so that he could keep close watch over the building and its tenants, locking the front door himself each night. The landlord's widowed daughter and her two children lived across from him, and a married couple occupied the other room down the hall. They were civil servants with two sets of twins—teenagers and infants. They were a poor, conservative, and quiet family; we rarely saw or heard them, except for the infants' crying. Qamar's mother and her three sisters lived next to the civil servants. Qamar was the middle daughter. The mother had named the oldest Fadhila because she had been born here in the Fadhil District. Fadhila had studied English too and graduated, but she was out of work and growing desperate, as no one had asked to marry her yet. The youngest daughter, Sahar, was still in high school. She spent most of her time talking to boys or listening to loud music. Their father was an Egyptian who had failed to persuade their mother to stay in Egypt. They tried living there for two years after Fadhila was born, during which time Qamar and Sahar were born, but their mother longed for Baghdad.

Their Egyptian grandmother had chosen the girls' names: Qamar after the moon, because on the summer night that Qamar was born, their grandmother had been looking out from the balcony when she saw the moon shining serenely in the sky, reflected in the waters of the Nile. Their mother liked the name because it reminded her of the *takiya*, or Sufi lodge, of Sheikh Qamar, one of the greatest Sufi masters in the Fadhil District. Students of Islamic learning traveled there from all over the world, and in the nineteenth century, Sheikh Muhammad Said al-Naqshabandi emerged to lead the famous Naqshabandi order in Baghdad. His grandson, Sheik Bahaa'eddin, inherited the role. Qamar's mother told her daughters about the times her father took her to the *takiya* as a child—the dervishes beat their drums, mesmerizing her as they chanted and danced endlessly in circles. When the youngest granddaughter was born, their grandmother peered out from the balcony and thought the dawn looked magical, and so she named her Sahar.

Their mother returned to Baghdad with her daughters, saying she couldn't bear to live away from Iraq, even if the country was falling apart. Here she had been born—and here she would die. Her grandfather had fought against the British occupation and her father was an officer who had helped transform Iraq from a monarchy to a republic. She'd ignored all her husband's pleas to stay in Egypt. Even though shelling had destroyed the roof of the house she'd inherited in Baghdad, their mother was relentless. She rented a place nearby, insisting she would rebuild the old house once the American occupation ended.

Four days after Qamar's death, at six in the evening, the policeman next door came to visit our room. I was alone and had just come back from class. Rafid was late as usual; he sometimes slept out. He was so gregarious that he had managed to develop an extraordinary network of friends in less than a year. He knew all the people who owned restaurants, shops, and cafés, both in our neighborhood and around Maidan Square and Bab al-Moatham. Through these connections he could solve any problem, whether it was a food shortage or a lack of kerosene for cooking lamps. He also knew most of the regulars at the Umm Kulthum café and the pimps in the Haidar Khana District. And he did well in school despite barely studying. The policeman next door would sometimes come to our room to hang out with Rafid, who smuggled him alcohol whenever the cop couldn't find any. They would stay up late together playing chess, smoking, and chatting about their lives. They did each other favors and gossiped like old men.

That evening, the policeman sat on the edge of Rafid's bed and sighed. "Poor Qamar," he said. "What do you think happened to her?"

"I don't know," I said.

"I think she was definitely murdered. Probably strangled or poisoned. I don't know yet, but I'll find out. This case is going to be my final assignment before I retire."

This news made me uneasy. "Shall I make you some tea?" I asked him.

"No thanks," he said. "Does Rafid have any booze in here?"

"Under the bed," I told him.

He reached under the bed, pulled out a bottle of whiskey, and poured himself a glass. "Where's Rafid?" he asked.

"I don't know," I said. "He's probably at university or at the Umm Kulthum café."

He took a sip of his drink. "I know he had an intimate relationship with Qamar. I know all about their secret trips to the storeroom."

I couldn't think of anything to say except: "I don't think so . . . I don't know."

"My son told me he saw them sneaking in there several times."

After a pause, I said: "Even if it's true, I don't think Rafid had anything to do with her death. There's no way he would harm anyone—we've been friends since we were children back in the village. Her death was a shock to him, as it was to all of us."

"I know, I know," the policeman said. "Rafid's a good guy and treats everyone well. He's not my only suspect."

I was somewhat relieved by his words, although I didn't get the feeling he was being completely honest. "Besides," I said, "the killer left a handwritten note on the body. The police are bound to figure out who the killer is once they compare our handwriting."

"That was just a routine procedure they do to cover themselves. That's why they've given me the assignment. I've been a policeman since I was your age and I know they won't do anything, especially under these chaotic conditions. There are no labs, no real investigations. They'll just put the report in the archives along with hundreds or thousands of other files, as bodies pile up in the streets every day. Besides, what makes you think that the killer didn't deliberately leave behind that piece of paper in someone else's handwriting to throw us off his track?" He paused. "The killer must have come from inside the building. The landlord locks the front gate every evening, and he checked the door himself the night before Qamar was murdered. Do you suspect anyone?"

"I don't know," I said. "I'm as puzzled as you."

"I'll find a way to get to the killer." He looked like he was getting drunk. "What do you make of our neighbor Adil . . . the other student? He's young and he lives alone, and I've seen him ogling Qamar. He's a little mysterious. Do you know him well?"

"I know him a little. Sometimes we walk to the university together or we meet in the library. I don't think it could be him. He's a decent, easygoing kid who's only interested in his studies. He's very religious."

The policeman snorted. "Don't let appearances deceive you. Most crimes are committed in the name of religion."

Rafid came in at that point and the two of them embraced. Rafid sat down next to the cop and poured himself a drink, then topped up the policeman's glass.

"Where have you been?" the cop asked.

"I was with Adil at the Umm Kulthum café," Rafid said.

"Since when do you guys hang out together?"

"He's upset about what happened. He asked me if he should look for a new place to live," Rafid said. "He told me he hasn't been able to concentrate on his studies. He sees Qamar's body every night in his dreams."

"Aha!" the policeman exclaimed, turning to me. "Didn't I tell you not to trust religious people?"

Rafid reacted with his usual assuredness: "It's because he's squeamish. He says it was the first time in his life he's ever seen a dead body. Hard to believe—this is Baghdad, after all."

Rafid offered to play a game of chess with the policeman, but he declined, saying he was tired. Tomorrow would be a busy day.

Once he left, I told Rafid everything the policeman had said earlier, but he brushed it off, which surprised me. He just sat back on his bed and smoked. Then he said: "Don't bother with him. He's stupid. I'm sure no one assigned anything to him. At the very most, maybe someone told him to be on the lookout just in case he notices something. Who knows, he might even be the killer—or his sick son, or his wife. Qamar herself told me he's harassed her several times. One night he was drunk, and started shouting and blocking her path. His son snooped on Qamar too. Sometimes he touched her arm in the hallway, and once he tried to touch her breasts. He's a young man with raging hormones. So why couldn't it be him? Or even his mother—maybe she wanted to keep Qamar away from her son and her husband? He was probably threatening to take a second wife, or blaming her for the deaths of their other kids at a young age."

I was surprised at Rafid's words. "Listen," I told him, "we have to move out of this building as soon as possible—we won't be able to live and work in peace here any longer."

"Don't you be stupid like Adil," Rafid scoffed. "Anyone who moves out of the building now will immediately become a suspect. They might pin the murder on anyone—just so they can close the case."

"So what should we do?"

"First we have to find out who the murderer is," he said, "and then we can think about moving out. I'm going to investigate on my own. This murder is personal. I loved Qamar."

"I didn't know you cared about her that much!"

"Yes," Rafid admitted softly, "we were very much in love. But we couldn't keep it a secret. Qamar told me her sisters figured it out. They slept in the same room as her, and they caught her sneaking out in the middle of the night or coming back from meeting me in the storeroom. Her older sister told her off. She was jealous that Qamar was prettier and more intelligent, and that she had a relationship with me. Fadhila had tried to approach me when we first moved here, but I wasn't interested—I mentioned that to you at the time. So maybe Fadhila killed her. Even the younger one could have done it, although I'm less suspicious of her. Sahar was always arguing with Qamar, threatening to expose her, since Qamar wouldn't let her go out with the neighborhood boys."

"Did their mother know all this?" I asked.

"No, the mother's a sad case. She's too busy trying to make money to pay rent. She goes out early to buy fish and then spends most of the day doing the rounds, selling to restaurants and private homes. She can't get money from her family in Egypt, ever since the banks closed after the invasion. That's why Qamar sometimes worked as a translator for the Americans. She brought her older sister documents to translate. They need money for their personal expenses too. You know how much Qamar spent on her appearance—all the perfumes and makeup, the bracelets and necklaces, the latest clothes."

Rafid lit a cigarette and went on talking as if to himself: "The landlord gave them a very hard time whenever they were late with the rent, often threatening to evict them. Qamar told me he tried to persuade her mother to divorce the Egyptian and marry him, or to have one of her daughters marry him, and in return he would register half the building in his new wife's name. He offered the same deal to anyone who might marry his daughter. But ever since Qamar's mother rebuffed him, there's been lots of tension. Who knows? Maybe he's the murderer—besides his temper, he hates that they haven't paid rent for three months. Or what about his daughter? She's a young widow, tied down by two children and an overbearing father. She might have believed that Qamar was sabotaging her chances of finding a husband. All the men who came to the building were only interested in Qamar once they saw how beautiful and pleasant she was. Or maybe the father and daughter worked together as part of a larger feud between their family and Qamar's. I know the two families are always disagreeing, arguing, and causing trouble. Maybe the conflict goes back even further. Both families come from the Fadhil District, and families here inherit everything—even their feuds."

For a whole month, Qamar's murder was all Rafid and I talked about. We spent the evenings remembering additional incidents and situations, analyzing everything we discovered or noticed, going over everyone who lived in the building one by one. Because we spent so much time pinning down the minute details and reviewing every shred of evidence, we were sometimes convinced that this or that person was the murderer, including the civil servants downstairs. Rafid said the twin boys had some sort of relationship with Sahar, that there was an unspoken rivalry over her affection. Qamar had intervened several times to stop her sister from hanging out with them. She'd even warned the twins to stay away. So maybe one of them murdered her—or both of them, or even their parents— to prevent a scandal and to protect their family, for which they toiled night and day. About Adil, Rafid commented: "One day he took Qamar aside at the university and tried to persuade her to dress, talk, and behave properly, and not to do things that are forbidden in Islam. He even offered to marry her if she would turn religious like him."

In our conversations, we eventually went so far as to suspect one other.

"You knew the most about my relationship with Qamar. You warned me about it at the start, then you tried to stop me. You also said you envied me, that you found Qamar attractive," Rafid said. "When I came back from the storeroom you used to asked about her body and what we did in there."

"If anyone's a prime suspect here, it's you," I shot back. "That's what your friend the policeman thinks, as well as everyone else in the building."

Apparently all the people in the other rooms, and maybe even the people in the neighboring buildings, were having the same conversations, either among themselves or in their own heads. The whole place was a minefield, highly charged with tension and suspicion. Everyone was watching and snooping, weighing every word anyone said, every move they made. We all felt like we couldn't breathe, as if the situation might blow up at any moment, for any reason—and no one could predict what the consequences of the explosion would be.

Forty days after the murder, we woke up again to Qamar's mother screaming in the courtyard. Rafid and I ran to the balcony and saw the body of her oldest daughter, Fadhila, lying on her back, her arms and legs splayed, her hair framing her face, the spitting image of Qamar.

She too looked like she'd been crucified and nailed to the ground. The landlord approached her, and when he saw there was no blood he took her pulse at the wrist, and then the neck, before announcing that she was dead. He took a slip of paper from between her fingers. It said: *I killed her because I loved her.* He adjusted his glasses and read it again, then went to the main gate of the building. He checked the padlocks and bars, and found them all secured, just as they had been the previous evening. So he went back to his room to call the police.

Soon after, American soldiers broke down the main gate. More than thirty of them burst in, alongside the three police-men who had come to investigate Qamar's murder. Through the broken gate we caught sight of an armored vehicle parked in the street. The American commander strode into the courtyard and stopped right next to Fadhila's head while her mother clung to her body, sobbing. The man waved his arms and barked out orders in English. The soldiers dispersed in groups, breaking down any doors that were locked, turning everything upside down, searching everywhere.

Rafid and I stood paralyzed, trembling in fear in our pa-jamas. Adil, also in his pajamas, was there too, mumbling prayers and curses. The policeman next door was standing there in his undershirt with his paunch hanging out. Next to him was his son, so drowsy he could hardly stand, drooling and rubbing his eyes. The women were in their nightdresses or wrapped in cloaks.

The soldiers assembled in the courtyard. One of them sa-luted the commander and spoke to him. I looked quizzically at Rafid beside me. "He's saying they didn't find any weapons," he whispered.

The commander said something else, then two soldiers ran over to lift Fadhila's mother off the corpse. They twisted her arms behind her back and tied her hands together, then carried her out toward the vehicle.

"It's me who killed her, because I loved her!" the mother

suddenly shouted out. "It's me who killed her, because I love her, and I love Iraq!"

She kept shouting until she and the soldiers and the vehicle had all disappeared. Our policeman neighbor approached us, clearly embarrassed, dragging his feet. "I knew she was working with some of the insurgent groups, and that she disapproved of her daughters working with the Americans, but I never imagined she would go as far as to kill them," he said. He put his arm around Rafid's shoulders and added: "Forgive me, my son. All my suspicions focused on you—we were even planning to arrest you on Tuesday. I must admit, I've failed my last assignment. I'm looking forward to retirement more now than ever, so that I can build myself a new home, far from here, and finally relax."

Translated from Arabic by Jonathan Wright

DOOMSDAY BOOK

BY Nassif Falak

Hurriya City

With tigerlike grace, he slunk his way past everyone and into my room. He snatched up the jewelry box containing my wife's gold, and stuffed it into his jacket pocket. Good-looking and smart, he left the house through the front door. Spots of sunlight fluttered like innocent moths around the flame of his face that September morning. The wonderful cool season really began that day— the clouds were arguing: *Should we rain or not?*

I went out after him without even brushing my teeth or rinsing out the bits of hard-boiled egg and dark bread—black as the days we were living. I knew straightaway he was the house burglar—my teenage brother, Abdullah. He had us all in a tizzy when valuable things started going missing at home. We didn't accuse anyone. Would someone rob himself? Impossible . . . unless you're a pathological thief. Everything in those days, no matter how worthless, had its value and price, thanks to the sanctions the United Nations had imposed on Iraq due to Saddam Hussein's obsession with war.

I walked behind Abdullah at a distance. This wouldn't arouse his suspicions even if he looked over his shoulder and spotted me. I usually headed out to work at that time—to the Shorja Market near the Church of the Virgin Mary. I had a stall there where I sold all kinds of stuff, including socks, baby bonnets, and trashy silver jewelry.

I saw him cross the road without stopping and climb aboard one of the long yellow buses. I hurried after him before he vanished. The main road of Hurriya 2 was always packed with lines of long yellow buses that went to the Imam al-Kadhim mosque. Those buses were a curse on Hurriya City, the latest curse since the Baath Party and Saddam; they were piles of scrap, roughed up, out of date, out of service, though they had once taken kids to school in America. Arab businessmen could not let the buses enjoy a peaceful retirement, instead shipping them off to Iraq, to Baghdad, and to Hurriya City in particular, filling life here with more death. I always imagined them as large multiple-occupancy coffins, and us the corpses, going to our final resting place in the graveyard that was Baghdad.

My brother got on one of the yellow buses heading to the nearby Hurriya 3—it was so close that we would usually walk there. Another bus came speeding by, which was unusual, as we rarely saw a fast yellow bus. I got in and kept watch on the bus my brother was riding. He might get out, then my wife's gold would be lost along with all the other goods he had stolen. I had to know where he was selling the jewels, and to whom. He didn't buy any expensive clothes or other material objects for himself, so where did the money go? The few passengers on his bus got out by the Hurriya 3 yellow buses, and I saw him head to the main street of the Dolai neighborhood. It didn't appear that he was planning to catch the bus to Dolai; I walked a few paces behind him, worrying now that he would see me if he turned around.

He passed the al-Farouq mosque, which had been built in a rush, as though God were about to lock the gates of Heaven and Earth and did not want another mosque disturbing him with the call to prayer. I saw Abdullah put his hand in his pocket, as if to make sure the jewelry box was still there, as he entered the improvised Dolai market. Traders were scattered around the pavement, hawking fruit and vegetables, and I saw spring onions spread on the ground for the first time since their disappearance during the long summer months. Now, they were back in season. From amid the crush of passersby and shoppers, there was little chance my teenage brother would notice me.

He soon left the market, having seemingly readied himself for something significant. He walked more cautiously as he approached the Rasoul Bakery on the corner. He looked left and right before turning down a side street. I sped up so as not to lose him. A small girl ran past me; the poor child tripped and dropped her black plastic bag. Her steaming fresh bread had fallen on the ground. I looked hesitantly at her, then at the bread, but I didn't have time to help. I stopped at the top of the street and peered around the corner to observe Abdul-lah's movements. He stood in front of a green metal door and glanced in my direction. His eyes met mine but he quickly turned away. *No, he didn't see me. I just imagined that.* Oddly, my brother didn't knock on the green door; he just pushed it open and entered like he was family, like he went in there every day.

I moved at a brisk pace. The house was the fifth on the right. It had a small front garden filled with dead plants; I peered at the dried-up bitter-orange leaves and the leafless branches of the acacia and castor oil trees. Scrap metal, tools, and junk were piled up. The door to the house was not prop-erly closed, and there was a gap I could peek through. With a shock, I saw a man with a florid face who looked just like Izzat al-Douri, dictator Saddam's vice president. The man's mustache had the same red tint as his face, mixed with a few white hairs, and he sported a bushy red beard. The hair on his head was thin and did not fully conceal his red scalp. Bizarrely, he was sitting behind a green ping-pong table beneath the inner balcony; Abdullah was sitting directly opposite him on a small metal chair.

The street was empty apart from a few children. At nine in the morning, most people were busy with breakfast. I could hear the clang of spoons stirring glasses of tea, ringing like the school bells of a distant childhood. I could smell the eggs frying in their pans. I would not attract anyone's attention here, as I stole glances through the narrow gap in the doorway. I saw my brother put his hand in his jacket pocket, take out my wife's jewelry box, and set it reverently in front of the florid-faced man, as if my brother were paying off some sort of debt. I could not hear exactly what the florid man was saying to him, but he spoke like he was dispensing King Solomon's wisdom. My brother nodded his head in agreement at what was being said. Then the red man handed my brother something wrapped in a blue rag. Abdullah took it and quickly stuffed it in his pants pocket as he continued to listen. It appeared that the meeting was ending, so I hurried up the street and went into the Rasoul Bakery. I joined the line of men waiting to buy bread, but turned toward the outside window, waiting for my brother to walk by. He sneaked past the bakery, stealthy and lithe, like a tiger about to pounce on its unsuspecting prey. I watched him kneel down underneath a palm tree on Dolai's main street to tie his shoelace, and at that moment I remembered that I had buried a hand grenade under the palm tree at our house.

I left the bakery and hid behind a fruit seller's wooden stand, afraid that Abdullah had sensed my presence or spotted me. At that moment the blasted hand grenade leaped into my mind again—a grenade that might explode at any time and cause a catastrophe at home.

My friend Hamza and I had often talked with anger and excitement about how to resist Saddam's dictatorship and the fascist Baath Party. But we didn't have concrete plans, and our enthusiasm remained mere talk, until one no-good Friday.

Baghdad was melting in the heat that burning summer day; asphalt stuck to our shoes and we could barely step out of the viscous tar. We took refuge in any patch of shade, no matter how narrow or weak. The sun would have hard-boiled an egg in three minutes, as my friend Hamza put it. "The sun in Iraq," he stated with unshakable certainty, "is the wet-nurse to tyrants. Our summer is the world's biggest factory for dictatorship, violence, and crime. We have to overthrow summer before Saddam and the Baath Party."

We had a short and enigmatic meeting at the Tobji Café that sizzling Friday. I couldn't have known that it would be our last—I can't even remember what Hamza was wearing on that no-good day. He came into the café drained of color, glancing around like an Iraqi sparrow, his eyes darting in every direction. He sat down across from me. On the table between us were some dominoes. The waiter put a glass of tea down in front of Hamza, but it remained untouched on the table. He uttered a terrifying command: "Leave this café and never come back. I've come to warn you—I've been wanted for the last two days, and the security guys have turned the neighborhood upside down trying to find me. Take this bag and look after it for me. In a few days I'll come and pick it up. You mustn't tell *anyone* about me or the bag."

When I got home, no one sensed my confusion and worry. I crept straight to my room and opened the black bag.

I was shocked when I saw a hand grenade, which emanated a foul smell. Cold sweat started streaming down the back of my neck, despite the intense heat. In the middle of the night, after everyone was asleep on the roof, I went back down to my room and put the hand grenade and its black bag inside an empty tub of Polyfilla. I dug up the soil under the only palm tree in our yard and buried it, expecting Hamza to come get it in a couple of days. But a week went past and he didn't come.

That had been a year and two months earlier, and since then there had been no trace of my friend anywhere in Hurriya City, Iraq, Asia as a whole, perhaps even the whole world. The hand grenade remained buried. Then I searched for it the night before my age group was called up for military service. *I'll put the grenade in my blue backpack with my food and other stuff,* I thought to myself. *On my way to al-Shorja on al-Shuhada'a Bridge, I'll throw it in the Tigris along with its black bag.*

I dug up the earth around the palm tree but couldn't find the empty tub of Polyfilla. I had no idea where the shifting soil had taken it, or when it was going to explode once the firing pin had been corroded away by rust.

My brother straightened up after tying his shoelace beneath the palm tree. He didn't look around him, confident in an invisible bodyguard, or as though he were under some sort of spell. I did not want to spoil the results of tailing him before I had discovered where this mysterious morning would take us. I didn't care about losing a day's pay, and didn't think about my colleagues with stalls near mine.

My brother went back the same way he had come. I watched how he ignored the people, the shops, the houses, the trees, and the cars—oblivious to everything. He walked the surface of the Earth alone. Handsome and elegant, he moved through the market, shrugging off the crush of shoppers and passersby who bumped into him. He did not hear the jumble of singsong voices from dozens of traders calling out to attract customers. He did not smell the hundreds of scents and fragrances wafting around the market. He walked unaware of his steps and in pursuit of his shadow. He passed the al-Farouq mosque, recently built but on the verge of collapse, like a defective fetus. He crossed over to the other side of Hurriya 3 Street, where the yellow buses were lined up blocking the view of the barbers, the herbalists, the cobbler, the hardware store, and a number of secondhand shops. It seemed like Abdullah didn't care what these shops sold, that he didn't even notice the sparks flying off metal being welded in a nearby workshop. He soon reached the al-Moshahda mosque, one of the landmarks of Hurriya 3. My father used to pray there before he got arthritis in his knees. My brother continued down the street, leading to the large market of Hurriya 2 without hesitation or confusion, apparently unconcerned that anyone he knew might see him. He walked with confident steps. I was stunned by the poise of this teenager; shocked by a brother who I was seeing for the first time as a stranger. Even some kids playing soccer stopped running after their ball when they sensed him coming.

He did not go into the market, but veered into a backstreet and toward the gateway of the gas cylinder depot, which overlooked Hurriya 2 Highway, opposite the schools. Abdullah stopped and stood in the middle of the street in front of a small shop with *Elegance Tailor* written on the window in large red letters. He stood with his back to the wall of the gas depot; I watched how he looked the place over, as if he were making sure he had the right location, then took out the blue rag the florid-faced man had given him and burst into the tailor's shop.

I heard a single shot. People jumped and ran off in every direction. Terrified, strangled voices cried out, and heads disappeared into shoulders and behind doors, windows, and fences. All I could see were feet running desperately. A three- or four-year-old child fell over and was swept up by his mother as if by a magnetic pull. She carried him inside another shop and shut the door. A woman on a rooftop next to the tailor's shop shrieked and abandoned the wet laundry she was draping over the fence. Another woman left her gas cylinder to roll, clunking along as she fled through an open doorway toward the end of the street. Everyone ran away—not a head in the area was raised because there was still the threat of another bullet. At that point, my brother came out of the tailor's just as he had gone in, calmly and confidently, as though he had just met the proprietor to discuss the finishing touches to his wedding suit. He was empty-handed, no blue cloth or pistol. He walked at the same pace as he had on our street and in Dolai, gracefully and handsomely, still with those innocent butterflies dancing around the flame of his face.

I remained rooted to the spot at the corner of the gas depot wall, trembling and nervous, and on the verge of throwing up all over my shoes. I was totally paralyzed, unable to move my arms and legs, while Abdullah made his way toward Hurriya 2 Highway with an eerie calmness. He stopped for a moment when a yellow bus came along. He climbed in and his face vanished among the passengers. I realized that his serenity was even worse than the murder I had witnessed; the unawareness of someone who kills in complete serenity with no compunction in his heart or mind; someone who kills a human being as though he had simply plucked a hair off his face—unaware that he had poisoned the wellspring of life. Such people have murderous ideologies, but my brother had no such creed. He didn't even know how to pray. Was he from a new generation of killers—one whose members had no ideology or motive?

A crowd formed in front of the tailor's shop. Heads emerged from shoulders, from doorways, windows, and rooftops. The workers at the gas plant came running. I also started to move again as I awoke from my paralysis. As I walked on heavy legs, I glimpsed a man covered in blood behind his sewing machine. His head had fallen onto his right shoulder, and I was stunned by the great similarity between him and the red man who sat behind the green ping-pong table at the desolate house in Dolai.

I got home just in time to prevent myself from vomiting. Everything seemed normal, like any other day. It appeared that my wife had yet to miss her jewelry box. I was crushed, however, as though I had to carry the corpse of the tailor on my shoulders. I asked my mother about Abdullah. The word *brother* had become odious and discordant, an antonym of itself. Should I say: *my teenage enemy?* The calamity was that he was my brother, whether I wanted him to be or not; no matter what he did, in the end, he was still my brother.

"He hasn't come back since the morning," my mother answered.

What should I say to my family? To my mother and father? *Your son is a dangerous criminal. He's the burglar who stole the Kashan rug.* Which was my father's favorite carpet; he practically sanctified it, and didn't allow anyone to so much as touch it. It reminded him of precious immaterial values: a fire had erupted in a big carpet shop on al-Nahr Street, and my father had picked up a hose and forced his way through the fire. His fellow firemen had pulled back in fear of the flames and smoke that consumed everything they came across, incinerating the surfaces while writhing serpents of steam coiled up into the air. My father, though, had raced straight to the source of the fire and put it out. The pillars of smoke dispersed and al-Nahr Street erupted with applause and cheers for the heroic fire-slayer. The shop owner arrived carrying a Kashan rug that he gave to my father. My mother would repeat to us: "Your father is a ball of fire, with a God-awful temper. He gets angry and worked up about the stupidest things. He's the ball of fire that puts out fires . . . I've never seen another fire put out flames."

The Kashan rug disappeared like the Japanese juicer, which had remained in pristine condition because it had never been touched; we didn't use it and didn't drink any juice. The economic sanctions on Iraq had squeezed the juice out of every last one of us. How on Earth could we drink fruit juice?

My brother stole the juicer too; he prevented us from selling it, even though we could have lived off the proceeds for a week or more. We still did not know the scale of his other, as yet undiscovered thefts.

I could sense the hand grenade creeping about under the rooms in the house. The safety pin had been corroded away by rust and the thing was about to explode.

Abdullah was surprised when I invited him to the Tobji Café. I had forgotten Hamza's warning not to go to that café, but where was *he* now? It had been over a year since all trace of him and his name had been wiped from space and time; as though he had no place on the tree of life; as though his mother had neither carried him in the womb nor given birth to him.

My brother and I stood on Hurriya 2 Street in front of the Working Men's Café, crowded as usual with yellow-bus drivers. I had never been inside and hated its name, which harked back to the early Baathist era, when words like *fighter*, *revolutionary*, and *working man* meant the opposite. We got into one of the yellow buses during the afternoon rush hour, when the streets were at their most crowded and walking was quicker than driving. But I was exhausted, enfeebled, and violated in body and mind. I didn't know where to start with my brother or how to present him with all the tangled threads of the riddle. Barely able to keep my composure, I somehow maintained a facade of calm. The person sitting next to me was a murderer with blood on his hands, and the lives of all these pedestrians, shoppers, and strollers bumping into each other on both sides of Hurriya 2 Street and Bata were in jeopardy. No one knew who the next victim would be—maybe someone dictated by the florid-faced man in Dolai, whose instrument of death was sitting next to me. There were so many people on the street; it looked like everyone who lived in Hurriya City had gone outside.

We got off the bus at the edge of Hurriya City on Rabie Street. I saw a drab-colored mass of Baathist comrades carrying machine guns and looking fiercely into people's faces. We dodged the mud-colored group by slipping behind a tractor trailer hulking over the pavement. I spotted the Tobji Café, where customers were still sitting outside despite the cold breeze, and shouting at each other as they played dominoes.

We sat down in the same place that I'd had my final meeting with Hamza. The waiter set two cups of tea down on the table. Without preliminaries, I surprised my brother the moment he put the cup to his lips so that I could clearly see the tremor in his hand. "Abdullah, why did you kill the tailor near the gas depot this morning?"

He stammered, but his face seemed flushed with innocence. It would have been hard to condemn him had I not seen him kill the tailor myself. Could I deny the evidence of my eyes? He didn't drink his tea, only put the cup back on the tray. Then, with an astonishing lack of artifice, he answered: "Me? Kill? I try not to accidentally step on ants! Kill? How? Why?"

I slapped him with another accusation in a voice hoarse with rage: "Earlier this morning, I saw you steal my wife's jewelry box, and discovered that it was you who stole the Kashan rug and the juice machine! Do you deny that too?"

"If I didn't love you, I'd think you were an enemy, not a brother," he said sweetly, his voice dripping with sadness and pain. "In the blink of an eye, I've turned into a killer and a thief. God knows what's next."

Abdullah's eyes glistened and the tears flowed. It was enough to break my heart. Suddenly, he stood up and quickly fled the café. My eyes followed him as he disappeared among the people and houses. I stayed sitting, confused and unsure what to do. Night had fallen and the lights had turned on, but the darkness inside me remained thick and black.

Sometime later, I too stood up and left. My feet stumbled in the darkness and I sensed that I was in danger. I had woken the sleeping monster. My brother would tell the florid-faced man in Dolai; I sensed that he obeyed that man's every command and would carry out all his orders, even if it meant killing those dearest to him. I had recklessly rushed to accuse Abdullah, who now knew I was onto their secret. They would never leave me alive. God, where to run? Going home meant going to my death, but the house was my only refuge: *que será, será!*

* * *

I went home. My brother was sleeping. I stepped into my room and comforted my wife over the loss of her gold. We agreed that she wouldn't tell anybody it was stolen.

Later, I decided to monitor the entrance to the red man's house in Dolai. I saw lots of guys the same age as my brother going in and out. I also saw a few older men, but the strange thing was the comings and goings of women and girls, all of them carrying bags or household objects. I realized that the florid-faced man's front was his old business—buying and selling secondhand goods.

In the following days, I heard talk of murders in a number of parts of Hurriya City. The most horrific was in the Dabbash District, where a mother found her child crucified on his wooden cot with a pacifier still in his mouth. The killer, it seemed, had stuck it there *after* crucifying him—a final touch to the scene of the crime.

On that same Tuesday as the crucifixion of the child, I came home late at night and my mother pressed me with questions about Abdullah. He had not come home yet, which was unusual. I told her not to worry; he was probably with his friends or at work, and would certainly return. I tried to persuade her to sleep, but she continued to moan and sob. She carried on like that during the days we spent searching for my brother at hospitals, police stations, security offices, the morgue, and any conceivable place he might've been. But he had vanished, disappeared in an instant, just like Hamza, despite the enormous differences between the two of them.

The world turned black once I was certain that my name was on the red man's death list. I was a dead man with only a short reprieve set by the red man's ideological clock. Should I just wait for my demise? Fine! If I was dead according to that

man, should I act like a corpse without emotion or feeling—
without a heart or conscience?

Now it was Wednesday, and the clock of fate might as well
have been showing ten minutes to doomsday. Cloudy before
sunset, a chill wind blew between my feet and up to my head
as I walked, carrying an Aladdin paraffin heater. I crossed the
street, imagining that I was holding the body of a tiger about
to be born into the world from the womb of the days to come.
I didn't look in the direction of the Working Men's Café and
didn't notice the rows of yellow buses perched on either side
of the street. I paid no attention to the crowds of people coming out of the isolation of their homes. As calm as an invisible
man, I rode in a long yellow coffin that soon disgorged me
in front of the Hurriya 3 buses and then turned back toward
Hurriya 2. I crossed the street by the al-Farouq mosque and
immediately climbed aboard another long yellow coffin heading for Dolai Road. Many familiar faces assailed me: Hamza,
the tailor, my murderous brother, my mother, my wife, Vice
President Izzat al-Douri, and many anonymous others, all
striking at once in furious pandemonium. The bus was almost
empty and I took a seat in the last row—always my favorite
choice. From my left-hand jacket pocket I took out a piece
of white cloth. I tore it into two pieces of the same size and
wrapped one piece tightly around my right hand, and the other
around my left. From my right-hand jacket pocket I took a
length of thin wire and wound it over the cloth on my right
hand. I got off the bus near the market and headed toward
the Rasoul Bakery. I walked slowly, with the dark closing in
around me, until I reached the street of the terrifying house
where that man dispatched death. The heater weighed heavy
in my right hand, but I could not switch hands in case the

wire should uncoil. I passed the Rasoul Bakery and then finally arrived. The big green iron door was still half open and the street empty. I looked through the gap and saw him as I had become used to: seated behind the ping-pong table, scowling. I pushed the door open smoothly and walked in as gracefully as a tiger with retracted claws. Unlike my brother, I did not sit down opposite him on the small metal chair. With all the skills of a hardened veteran, I set the Aladdin paraffin heater down in front of him, and like lightning I was behind him uncoiling the thin wire with my left hand. In a trance and half blind, I strangled him. Immune to the sting of his blood that had soaked the cloth and my hands, I had not realized that I had cut his throat from vein to artery; I did not hear him kicking the heater onto the floor or perceive his panic-stricken gasps. The shock of being strangled killed him. He had never anticipated someone would have the electrifying courage to take his life. He was above the law of mortals, far removed from death. The time of his garroting was not written on the clock of fate that he held in his hands; he believed that the purveyor of death could not die.

I jolted out of my trance after my palms started burning, as the thin wire cut into them and caused some bleeding. My semiblindness lifted and I saw him lying on the floor by the heater. His eyes were bulging, but they were not asking for mercy. I wiped the blood off my hands onto his dark-brown trousers, grabbed the heater, ran over to the green iron door, and shut it with the large bolt. Seeing as I was unsure whether the house was empty, that was as stupid as trying to make a getaway down a dead-end street.

I saw an arched entranceway leading to a large room built to look like a mosque—it had a prayer niche, a small wooden lectern, and an untidy heap of prayer mats alongside a small table piled with ten or so copies of the Koran. I noticed five wooden doors leading off to smaller rooms. Each room had its own distinct style of couches and beds, but they were all like wedding suites, arranged and decorated to evoke scenes of Paradise. The furniture gave off an otherworldly scent of perfume, the likes of which I had never inhaled before. But I ignored all the opulence of the rooms and their perfumes; I was looking for something unknown, something that would guide me to itself and clear up the enigma of this house full of mysteries. I ascended the cement steps and found more rooms in the same sensuous style upstairs. I was not reckless enough to continue up to the roof. I rummaged through the rooms, searching without success for that unknown thing. I was afraid someone would knock at the door, or that a visiting murderer such as my brother would show up. So I decided to abandon everything and go back out to the street and to the world.

I slipped as I hurried down the stairs. I would have fallen if I hadn't grabbed ahold of the metal banister. At that moment, I spotted a closed door under the stairs with a bunch of keys hanging from a padlock. I opened the door in a hurry, and everything leaped out at me: different kinds of pistols, packs of ammunition, bundles of cash, a large ledger, a green telephone, sticks of incense, *miswak* toothbrushes, boxes of musk and ambergris perfume, and other small and valuable things piled on top of each other. I stuffed my pockets with cash, then picked up a large black pistol and stuck it in my belt— after checking to make sure it was loaded. I grabbed the ledger and went back through the arched entranceway toward the metal door and out onto the street.

I carried the heater with my injured hand, as my blood dripped and mixed with the blood of the florid-faced man.

I took out my blue handkerchief and wrapped it around my right hand while I walked calmly like Abdullah had done after killing the tailor. Once I was beyond the Rasoul Bakery, I stopped a taxi driven by an old man wearing thick spectacles. I had him drop me at the front door of my house. As we drove, I conversed with him about the good times before the siege. I was well aware that the so-called good times were a lie, because our country had always been on a knife's edge.

I shut myself off from the world and threw myself into deciphering the massive ledger I had collected from the florid-faced man: the doomsday book. I quit working at the Shorja near the Church of the Virgin Mary; the fate of my friends with pitches and stalls was of no concern to me anymore. I abandoned my wife, my mother and father, everyone. I imprisoned myself in my room night and day, exploring the ledger's mazes. Monstrous symbols leered at me from the undergrowth of lines, frightening me. They snarled in my face, bearing the promise of destruction. I unearthed the symbol for my brother: A.J.M. –> *Afghanistan.*

Here were my brother's initials, with a list of the gifts and donations he had offered up for the victory of the mujahideen: the juicer, the Kashan rug, and my wife's gold. I also noticed a section titled *Cleansing the Righteous Path*—cleansing it of stones, weeds, and filth. There was a drawing of five brooms, including one for the tailor—implying that my brother had committed five crimes. The encoded tragedy was that the tailor was the brother of the florid-faced man; I unraveled the mystery of that riddle after I devoted myself to analyzing and deciphering the signs and symbols. It became clear that the florid-faced man had cleansed the righteous path of all his family. He had uprooted the weeds represented by his four brothers and eleven nephews—among them, the child who had been crucified on the wood of his cot with a pacifier in his mouth—dispatched by the florid-faced man himself. By dissecting a few lines and pulling the veil off the words, I learned that the florid-faced man's family had kicked him out; his tribe had kicked him out as well. He wanted them to obey him and execute his orders, because in his mind they were orders from God. His family had removed him once they gave up hope of curing him: he was sick with the plague of religious perversion. He intended to completely finish off his brothers and the rest of the names on the list—including his other family members—uprooting them from the Righteous Path. All the murders were carried out with the express approval of God. They were divine, holy murders chosen with absolute care to aid the establishment of the Caliphate.

I saw many sets of those same initials with an arrow pointing to Afghanistan. That's where my brother was then, educating himself in the universities of jihad, while I was a confused mess. What lessons did he learn? What degree would he get?

By chance, I stumbled across the solution to the riddle of the rooms from Paradise, with their perfume-wafting couches and beds. I cracked it when a page fell out of the ledger. It was a description of Paradise, with symbols for sixteen dark-eyed virgins and the names of those taking part in a mass wedding, whose bridal suites were those chambers. The wedding date was not far off—I guessed that enticing teenagers into an earthly Paradise would make them hot with desire for eternity in Heaven.

I sunk up to my nostrils in the quagmire of the ledger, then dived deep between the lines and signs, enigmas and runes. I trembled in terror when I discovered that the florid-faced man was just one among hundreds of others like him, spread across cities and neighborhoods, from one end of the country to the other; all of them working night and day to rip out the weeds and cleanse the Righteous Path of stones and filth. They all received orders from the Caliph, who accepted them directly from God. With great reverence and piety, they were working to institute the Caliphate—God's state.

I trembled and dived back into the horrific ledger holding my breath. As soon as I turned a page, I was sprayed with the stench of blood from the clouds of lines. I smelled the foulness of corpses wafting from the paper—their ghosts rising from the ink, in search of their unknown killers. What hole have I slid into? Wading through mazes of blood and forests of bones, I read and shivered. Tears welled up in my eyes as I sat in my room above a grenade set to explode at any moment.

Translated from Arabic by Raphael Cohen

JASIM'S FILE
BY SINAN ANTOON
al-Rashad Hospital

I. Jasim Goes Home

The Americans kind of liberated me. They were looking for WMDs, I guess, and stormed the place like cowboys—cowboys with iron horses. There was a slight problem, though. There were no Ws—only MDs! The medical doctors! But there weren't many; their number had dwindled in the last few years. They ran away, leaving that place and the whole country in droves because of the embargo. That's what I'd heard at least. Anyway, the Americans drove right through the wall thinking it was a military camp or a weapons depot. Instead, they figured out right away it was nothing of the sort, and then went through another wall. I didn't see any of that myself. I was asleep.

Abu Hinich, the toothless old bastard whose bed was next to mine, woke me up. "They're here! The Americans are here!" he yelled.

He'd been saying that since the bombing started weeks before. So I told him to leave me the fuck alone, as I usually did.

"They're outside!" he said. "People are escaping!"

That last bit got my attention. I'd heard a lot of noise and distant screams, but reckoned they were part of the normal soundtrack of my nightmares. I'm (still) not a deep sleeper at all, but I'd managed to sleep soundly the night before. Thanks to the sleeping pill I'd won playing cards with some guys from the adjacent ward. I sat up. Something was off. The ward was almost empty. Except for Garo, the Armenian engineer who stood by the window, looking outside. I ran over to see what the hell was going on.

Some of the inmates were roaming around like terrified sheep. But there were outsiders too. I could tell, since they weren't wearing those silly blue uniforms. Some of them were dragging beds and chairs out of the other wards, and others were trying to unhook the air conditioners from the windows.

"Uncivilized bastards," Garo muttered.

"They're wrecking the place," I said.

Abu Hinich ran up to me, joining us by the window. "I told you. They're here."

"The Americans are already gone," Garo pointed out, in his usual unfazed tone.

"Come on, let's get the fuck out of here," I suggested.

Garo said he was staying put: "We'll get killed. I am not going anywhere for now."

"Are you fucking crazy?" I shrieked.

Then I remembered that he *was*. Otherwise he wouldn't be here. The guy had gone to California to study engineering in the late 1970s and was crazy enough to come back during the war with Iran. He had inherited the family's business—a Jell-O factory—but psychosis too, and ended up here.

"Well, I'm leaving. Wanna come, Abu Hinich?"

Abu stood there nibbling on his index finger with his toothless gums. I don't know why I asked him. He would've been a liability, and I was already wasting my time. I ran back to the dresser next to my bed, took off the sweatpants I was wearing, and put on the only pair of jeans I had. They were a bit loose; I'd lost a lot of weight. The food was so crappy here.

I put on my black leather jacket and sneakers. I had saved some money from winning at cards, and kept the cash in my underwear. I took out a few bills and stuffed them in the inside pocket of the leather jacket. That should get me home. I'd memorized the address after I took a peek at my file—the shrink assigned to me had been busy answering a phone call from his chatty wife. He left the folder open, and I read: *Hayy al-Khaleej, Street 43, House #13*. I thought about getting my file before leaving.

I put everything I had inside the locker (some underwear, T-shirts, and a *ghutra*) into a plastic bag, and added the sweatpants I'd taken off.

"Good luck, guys," I told them.

"Yeah, you too, buddy," Garo replied, without even turning around. Maybe he thought I wasn't serious.

Abu Hinich just took his fingers out of his mouth and waved.

There was no guard at the door. Once I got out to the yard, I saw three men approaching our ward. One of the MDs on shift, a young guy from the south, was yelling at the looters and telling a guard to lock the other ward, so I ran to the main administration office. I slipped by the tall lieutenant who was performing his daily ritual (jumping up and down, singing 1980s war songs) as if nothing had changed. I saw a kid wearing slippers come out of the main door carrying a large floor lamp. The three men were trying to get a huge leather couch out of the door. I looked through the window. The cabinets were gone; the files were scattered all over the floor. Then I heard gunshots coming from the women's section. I ran to the main gate—it was locked. The looters were entering from the east, so I ran in that direction and saw the opening in the wall.

II. Cousin Jasim Comes Home

I heard banging on the door. I got up and drew the curtain just a bit. There was a man in his midthirties with very short black hair and a mustache, wearing a leather jacket. Dad was asleep on the couch. He barked at me when the man knocked again: "Who is it?"

"Dunno. A man in a leather jacket," I said.

He got his gun from the cabinet next to the TV and came to see for himself. "Good God," he mumbled, "he's back."

"Who?"

"Your crazy cousin."

"That's him?" I asked, nodding toward the door.

"Yes," Dad answered, sounding annoyed. "Go tell your mother. Lock the corridor door and don't come out unless I tell you to."

I went and told Mom, but I was scared. I stood behind the corridor door and put my ear to the cold wood to listen in. I heard Dad greeting him with forced joy. Then they talked about the photographs on the wall. Dad asked him if he was hungry or thirsty. I didn't catch his answer, but I heard Dad yell: "Madiha, Umm Madiha! Where are you? Come say hello to Jasim and make some tea!"

III. Jasim Comes Home

A fat man with an unshaven beard, wearing light-blue pajamas and holding a gun in his right hand, opened the door.

"Jasim! What a surprise! Welcome back, son," he said.

He sounded a bit nervous. We hugged and he kissed me on the cheeks (very bad breath). I asked him who he was.

"I'm Uncle Abbas."

Seeing how puzzled I was, he added: "Don't worry, I know

about your condition. Come on in, please. It's so good to have you back."

I glanced at the gun he was still holding in his right hand. I'd felt it against my back when we hugged.

"It's very dangerous these days. You never know," Abbas said apologetically.

I took off my sneakers and left them next to the door; I waited for him to show me the way. He led me to what looked like the living room. I wondered why the bastard had never visited me. Not even once.

"So did they release you?" he asked.

I lied: "Yeah, they said those of us whose condition wasn't serious are better off at home. They're out of food and supplies."

"Oh, I see," Abbas murmured.

I wasn't sure he bought it.

"We moved in a few months after the accident to take care of the house. You still don't remember anything?"

"No."

A few framed family photographs hung on the wall across from where I sat, right under one of Saddam in civilian attire. I got up to look at them, and asked him: "Do you have any pictures of my parents and siblings?"

"Yes, we have an album somewhere. We put them away. It was too sad, you know."

He approached and pointed out a photo of his wife and three children, two of whom were married and living with their own kids. The youngest, a girl named Madiha, was still here. I nodded but couldn't muster any genuine interest.

"Did they catch him?" I asked, as I went back to the couch.

"Who?"

"The bastard who killed my family."

He hesitated a bit before answering: "No. They didn't. By the way, are you thirsty? You must be."

Before I even answered, he called out to his wife and daughter to come and greet me. The mother was in her late forties, heavyset, and wearing a veil, even though there wasn't much worth covering. She didn't even shake my hand, just said: "Praise the Lord for your safe return."

The daughter, Madiha, had wavy black hair, big hazel eyes, and luscious lips. Her breasts were already budding beneath the green blouse she wore. I extended my hand to shake hers. She couldn't look me in the eye. "Hi there," I said. But she didn't reciprocate. They both left, and then Madiha came back fifteen minutes later carrying the tea tray. Her hands were shaking and the clinking stopped only when she set the tray in the middle of the table. Was it the cold? Or was having an amnesiac cousin terrifying? I guess it wasn't just amnesia. There was the depression too. Once one goes to al-Rashad, even for just a week, they're considered insane. I stayed there for eight years. Even if you are sane, they add the *in* to be sure.

The remainder of the day was weird—there were long stretches of awkward silence in between talking mostly about politics. What were the Americans planning to do? Where did Saddam go? My uncle claimed that they'd wanted to visit me and had done so a few times. But the doctors told them that it would affect my treatment negatively. I laughed when he said that.

"What treatment? It was more like psychological torture," I said.

"I'm sorry."

He was probably lying anyway. I had a feeling he was a scoundrel. He was probably worried now that I might start charging them rent or just kick them out. But I wasn't going to do any of those things. Not right away, at least. I needed time to think and figure out how to put my life back together.

The wife was a decent cook. Her eggplant *tabsi* was yummy. It was my first homemade meal since I was committed. Well, actually . . . the best ever, since I can't remember a fucking thing before that. I slept on a comfy mattress in the guest room and jerked off thinking of Madiha's mouth milking me dry.

IV. Jasim Stays Home

When I woke up the next morning, they were gone. Just like that—no car in the garage. I couldn't understand why. Was I that scary? Maybe he saw the way I was looking at his daughter and was afraid I'd knock her up. They left some food in the pantry. Cans. The fridge was empty. I remembered him telling me that they'd emptied and unplugged it on account of their having no electricity. They took the generator with them. But they left so much stuff here. Well, I wouldn't know if it belonged to them or my family.

I spent the next few days in the house. I found a small radio and some batteries, and listened to the news every once in a while. No one knew what had happened to Saddam. There was chaos and looting.

I found an album in a box in the storage room and studied the photographs, but I needed someone to tell me who was who. I went into what I'm sure was Madiha's room. She'd left some of her clothes and underwear behind. I slept in her bed. It smelled good. I used her panties to jack off.

V. Jasim Goes Out

After three days, I ran out of food and had to go out. I had seen a bakery and some stores five blocks away the day I came back. Everything was closed that day, but I was sure the bakery would be open. The streets were slightly busy and I saw a crowd of about ten men outside the bakery. I waited and bought two bags of pita. I also got some cheese and corned beef from the shop next door. On the way back, I heard someone calling my name. When I looked I saw a man about my age in the driver's seat of a black four-wheel-drive. He stopped the car and got out. He was dressed in all black, had very short dark hair, a neatly trimmed beard, piercing coffee-colored eyes, and a broad smile.

"Jasim, it's you, isn't it?" I took a step back. Yet he moved in and hugged me tightly. "It's Zayn, man! Hey, buddy! I've been asking about you since I got back."

"Sorry, but I don't—"

"We went to school together," Zayn said. "We used to hang out and play soccer all the time. So, what they're saying is true . . . amnesia . . . and what happened to your family?"

"Yes."

"Sorry to hear that. That's heavy. No worries, I'll tell you everything you need to know about me," Zayn said, laughing. "Come on. I'll give you a ride home."

I was going to tell him that my house wasn't far, but I got in anyway. The car was clean and relatively new. There was a green ribbon tied around the rearview mirror and a sticker showing the face of a turbaned cleric on the dashboard; *The Islamic Brigades of Iraq* was printed in tiny letters under the image. Zayn saw me looking at it.

"You don't even remember the martyr, do you?" he asked.

"Not really," I told him.

"That is al-Hasani—Saddam executed him back in 1980," Zayn explained. "Right around the time he executed my father, deported our family, and threw us across the border, claiming we were of Iranian descent. But the fucker is gone now." He paused and then asked the inevitable question: "So is it true that you were committed to the loony bin?"

"Yes. I had a nervous breakdown and couldn't remember anything."

"Man! When did you get out?"

"Last week, but tell me about you and me," I urged, wanting to fill in more of my memory.

"Well, we were best friends. Went to the same school and hung out and played soccer all the time. Man, I can't fucking believe you don't remember any of it. Are you sure you didn't fake this amnesia stuff so you'd avoid going to the army or something?"

I didn't answer him so he thought I was offended.

"I'm sorry, man. Just kidding."

"No worries."

After twenty-three years he still remembered where our house was, and stopped the car in front of the gate. I invited him in for tea.

He told me how the Baathists took them one night and drove them to the border, after separating them from their father. They later learned that he died in prison. They confiscated their house and turned it into the local branch of the Baath Party. He, his mother, and two siblings stayed in a camp on the Iranian side, near the border, for three months, before being moved to another camp and later to cheap housing on the outskirts of Tehran. His mother married another man, an influential figure in the Iraqi opposition—also a sadistic asshole who beat Zayn and his siblings. He enrolled in school in Tehran, learned Persian, and later volunteered and joined the Brigades. He went through their military training, which was his ticket out of misery. The Brigades had entered Iraq from the south just a few days ago and drove up north to Baghdad. He was staying at a hotel in al-Jadiriyyah, but was planning on returning to his family's home here in the neighborhood after fixing it up.

"The Baathist cowards ran away, but I'm gonna find them," Zayn promised. He then took the last sip of his tea and stood up to leave. "Listen, I've got to head back, but I'm so happy that I saw you. If you need anything, here's the number of my hotel." He took out a hotel business card and wrote down his room number.

"But the lines are down," I reminded him.

"Shit, I forgot. Keep it just in case. They'll be fixed sooner or later. I'll be back tomorrow or the day after. Do you need anything?"

"No thanks."

VI. Jasim Has a Job

Zayn came back two days later, and brought shawarma sandwiches and cans of Pepsi. We sat down to eat, and with a bite of food in his mouth, he asked: "What are your plans?"

I thought about that for a second, but couldn't find an answer. "I don't have any yet."

"Do you wanna help out and make some money?"

"Sure, but how?"

"I need someone I can trust."

"To do what?"

"Watch my back and stay by my side," Zayn said. "We have a lot of unfinished business."

"What kind of business?"

"Catching the Baathist rats who are hiding."

"But what about the police and security services?"

"Are you fucking kidding me?" he hissed. "There is no police or security now. Plus, they were all criminals themselves."

"So you're just going to catch every single Baathist?" I asked. "How?"

"Not every single one—just the bigwigs. We have a list."

"And then what?"

"Have the Angel of Death interview them," Zayn said. He smiled and pointed to the gun he was carrying. "I'll get you one, of course."

"I don't know how to use it."

"Very easy. You'll learn in half an hour."

"But why me?" I asked.

"Why you? I vouched for you, because I trust you. You're the perfect candidate. No past. Well—sorry for being blunt—no *access* to the past. No sentimental attachments. And I'm sure you wanna get back at them for killing your folks."

"I'm still not sure who did it."

"We'll find out," Zayn assured me.

I ate the last piece of pickled beet that came as a side with the shawarma and took a sip from the cold Pepsi can. "Okay, I'm in," I said.

"Great! You'll start out on a freelance basis for a couple of weeks, and then I'll introduce you to my commander and we'll make it official."

It was the first time I'd been excited about something since I came home. I was getting bored sitting around doing nothing. I still had no idea what I was going to do with my life.

Before leaving, Zayn gave me five $100 bills and said: "Here's an advance. We'll get you a sturdy but comfortable pair of shoes, and some new clothes too."

VII. Jasim Is Trained

The next day, Zayn picked me up and we drove south on

al-Qanat Highway for half an hour. I was surprised that we didn't have to go through an American checkpoint. He said that was precisely why we went this way, then added: "I have a special permit that would get me through their checkpoint. We'll get you one soon too."

Zayn took a sharp right onto a dirt road and we drove by some orchards. The spot he chose for practice was close to where his father's cousin used to have a farm with a small house.

"We would come here on holidays. Roam around and play. I checked things out a few days ago. There's no one here. The house is abandoned. Just some stray dogs."

"And where is your relative?"

"Last I heard, he's in Syria," Zayn said. "He took his family there in the late 1990s."

He parked the car under two tall palm trees that stood in front of the house. Their low fronds had withered. Three bunches of dried dates were dangling from one of them. He went back and opened the car trunk and took out a leather bag. A couple of pigeons flew from the roof of the house. It looked deserted. Most of the windows were broken and the front door had come unhinged.

"We're not going inside," Zayn explained. "The spot is in the back, behind the house."

I followed him as he went to the left and around the house. I could see through the broken windows—there was some graffiti on the walls: *Raad is a faggot . . . Tayaran League Champions . . . Asshole . . . Real Madrid . . . I fucked your mother . . . War . . .*

There was a wide-open space behind the house that led to the river. Zayn placed the bag on the ground and took out a plastic bottle filled with water; he walked about thirty feet to a giant mulberry tree and set the bottle at its trunk. He walked back and took out a gun from the bag.

"This is a Beretta 92," Zayn said excitedly, as if he were introducing me to a friend of his. He gave me a quick rundown about the parts, how to load and empty the magazine, the best posture for firing, and how to attach the silencer and shoot.

"Go ahead and give it a shot," he told me, handing the gun over.

I missed the target the first two times, but hit it the third time, and the bottle was blown away.

"You're doing great, man. Very steady. Are you sure you haven't done this before?"

"I might have. I wouldn't know."

We both laughed.

"Okay. Take off the silencer and do it raw. It's good to hear the sound to appreciate the power of what you're carrying," Zayn said. "Just aim at the trunk of the mulberry."

I fired two shots in a row. They were deafening.

"Go ahead and empty the whole cartridge."

VIII. Jasim Works

Zayn had a list with names and addresses of the "comrades." We would drive around a neighborhood, park near a house, and wait until the target came out. I watched how Zayn did it: two shots to the head and another two in the chest after they fell. Then we would drive away. It was two weeks before I got to finish a comrade by myself. He was a university professor. It felt good.

IX. Jasim's File

While Jasim was settling into a rhythm and helping Zayn go down the list, the officials at al-Rashad Hospital had secured help from the newly formed local militia to protect the building. The damages were being assessed and windows fixed. Some inmates returned voluntarily, while some families brought others back. The outside world was too chaotic. Fifteen miles away, near the outskirts of Baghdad, a boy was going through the heaps of trash that had been dropped off for the first time in weeks. He found a piece of paper, and tried to read the first few lines: *Jasim Hamza Khidir . . . Place & date of birth: Baghdad, November 9, 1969 . . . Amnesia . . . Killed his entire family.* The boy threw the piece of paper away and went on looking for something valuable. One of his three goats ate it.

This story was originally written in English

A SENSE OF REMORSE

BY AHMED SAADAWI

Bataween District

Jibran's room was dark and dingy, stuffy from the stale smell of old furniture and the thick layer of aromas from the flavored tobacco he had smoked in his *shisha* during his nightly ritual of drinking alone. His younger brother Yasser believed the room, by helping to isolate Jibran from his family and neighbors, suited a man who had grown increasingly depressed as the years went by. But could Yasser really have any insight into his brother's behavior and temperament?

Yasser wasn't in the habit of visiting Jibran's house. Even when Yasser first heard his brother was dead, he hadn't been able to like him. Jibran had been bad-tempered, overbearing, and foul-mouthed. During his childhood and early youth, Yasser had suffered greatly at Jibran's hands. He had managed to put that behind him, but only when he moved to his own rented house in the Bataween area—in the center of Baghdad— where the rest of the family lived. Jibran had stayed with his wife and children in the big family house, with its damp walls and broken floors.

Out of compassion, Yasser racked his brain to remember the details of his last meeting with his older brother, but he couldn't come up with anything important. He managed to dig up a few incoherent fragments, including Jibran's sad, wrinkled face—the face of a man who had been greedy and rigid in the past, yet in more recent times was no longer happy about that history. Yasser remembered a short conversation he'd had with his brother about drinking:

Jibran was sitting on a wooden chair, leaning on the small square table he had set against the wall in his room. He placed two ice cubes in a glass of arak and stirred it a little before taking a sip. A song by Saadi al-Hilli was playing softly on an old tape player on the same table. Jibran didn't want to listen to Saadi al-Hilli at that moment, but rather the words of his younger brother, who now, after years of living on the sidelines, had become a police officer working in the criminal investigations department. He told Yasser he didn't feel any remorse, and that this annoyed and depressed him. He spoke vaguely about mistakes he had made in his life but he didn't tell his brother what they were.

"Why don't you feel any remorse?" Yasser asked.

"I don't know. Perhaps there's something wrong with me. I don't feel like I'm a normal person."

"No, you're a normal person who drinks too much. That's all."

"Drinking doesn't bring remorse, but I've gotten used to drinking now, even without remorse."

Yasser suddenly felt sad, as he remembered the conversation. He sympathized, but at a very late stage, with a brother who had ruined his own life and caused problems for everyone. Perhaps he was just unlucky. Yasser kept repeating those words in his head as he walked around the room. He examined the contents of the room, and despite the daylight that flooded the space, he shone his flashlight at everything. He went up to his brother's body, but he couldn't bring himself to touch it, though seeing corpses was nothing new to him. He looked at the bottle of arak that was still sealed and set in the middle of the table, at the plate of mezes garnished with cu-

cumber and yogurt. It didn't look like Jibran had even started his evening. He had gone to his death without a final drinking session. Yasser examined the glass next to the limp arm stretched out to the middle of the table. Jibran's head, with disheveled hair, was resting next to it, and he noticed some gray powder at the bottom of the glass. He glanced around and saw a small, crumpled piece of paper that had been thrown under the table. Yasser smoothed out the paper and saw traces of something black. He quickly guessed that it came from the same substance as the powder in the bottom of the glass.

The autopsy in the forensic department later showed that Jibran had taken a mixture of poisonous herbs—a strange, rare mixture. According to the doctor who examined the body, this meant that Jibran had probably committed suicide.

Yasser kept the suicide theory to himself, and instead told the family that Jibran had suffered a heart attack—which many people expected, since he'd been drinking so much in recent years. He had finished off three-quarters of a bottle of Asriya arak every evening. His family's attempts to make him cut down on this lethal intake had come to nothing. *Cause of death: drinking.* It was the logical conclusion.

Jibran's suicide remained a personal preoccupation of Yasser's. He didn't share it with anyone, not even his closest friends. He didn't tell his other brother Tahseen, who was Jibran's partner in a car repair shop on Sheikh Omar Street, close to Bataween.

Tahseen had been having problems with Jibran over their stake in the workshop. Yasser thought they were both greedy and it was hard to see how either of them was more in the right than the other.

At the funeral, Tahseen looked relaxed—no sign on his

face that he was upset or grieving his eldest brother's death. To Yasser, he almost looked relieved to be rid of a nuisance, though in recent months Jibran hadn't really been annoying Tahseen as much as he annoyed his wife and children at home. He'd been spending a lot of time at home just drinking, and would often wake up with such a hangover that he wouldn't stir till midday.

Several months after the funeral ceremonies ended, Yasser was the only person who was still troubled by Jibran's death.

Jibran's family—his wife and daughters—didn't waste their time. The sixth week after Jibran's death, his wife knocked down the front wall of one of the rooms in the old house in Lane 7 and turned the room into a shop. Her teenage daughters sat in the shop till late at night—selling cigarettes, sweets, chewing gum, and other things that neighbors often needed.

There was every reason to expect Jibran to fade gradually from Yasser's memory, especially as he was busy at work, where he heard stories that were much more horrific; stories of vendettas and revenge killings and the strange crimes that began to take place in Baghdad after American forces occupied the city in April 2003. Murder in its many varieties was commonplace.

Yasser was so busy with the killings, which could strike anyone at random, that the mystery of Jibran's death did gradually recede into the background. After weeks of thinking about it, and trying to analyze the little evidence available on whether a crime had been committed, Yasser had not reached any definitive conclusions. Then something happened that revived his interest in the question of whether or not Jibran had been murdered.

Yasser had read a succession of reports about similar

deaths by means of the same substance that killed his brother. The people who died were generally old, some of them older than Jibran. There were no young people among the dead. *Could it be that certain old men are prone to some form of suicidal depression?* he wondered. Was it because of the war and the chaos?

"These are crimes, and we don't know how far this will go," Yasser's boss said, as he flipped through the autopsy reports on seven bodies. The bodies had turned up in recent weeks in circumstances roughly similar to the ones in which Jibran's body had been found. They had died in bed or at tables where they drank. One of the victims was found kneeling at the door to his house, as if he were trying to knock but couldn't because of the effects of the poison.

With help from two of his assistants, Yasser questioned the families of the victims but couldn't identify the source of the poison. Most of the families were unaware that the powder even existed.

One man had told his wife about the powder and how effective it was, but he hadn't told her where he had obtained it. The man's widow was living alone in a dilapidated house near the Jewish synagogue in the middle of Bataween. She was morose, spoke curtly, and was unenthusiastic about dealing with strangers. Yasser kept trying to persuade her to open up, and eventually she told him something interesting.

"He used to say that he wanted to feel remorse, and that this was a medicine that would make him feel remorse," she revealed.

"Why did he want to feel remorse?"

"He'd had problems in the past that he didn't want to tell me about," she said.

Yasser left the old woman to her memories and the darkness of her run-down house and went out into the street with his assistants. He had the distinct impression he had put his finger on some clue. This old woman's husband had died in much the same way as Jibran, and probably for the same reason: a desire to feel remorse. It was a clue, but it wasn't clear where it led. He put aside the reports, which concluded that these were merely cases of suicide by poison. But the cases weren't completely closed as far as Yasser was concerned—not until the evening he met Hannoun al-Saher—also known as Hannoun the Magician.

Jumaa al-Nouri was a childhood friend of Yasser's. He was an intelligent and adventurous young man, and everyone expected him to use his intelligence to improve his social and financial position. But he kept taking risks and engaging in unsuccessful commercial ventures; he ended up an alcoholic, living in a miserable room at a lodging house called the Happiness Motel—waiting for miracles. Despite the political turmoil that transformed the face of the country after April 2003, Jumaa didn't change at all. During the day he worked as a clerk for a shipping company, and he spent the afternoon drinking in his room, sitting with his next-door neighbor, Hannoun the Magician.

Hannoun's situation wasn't any better than Jumaa's. He was a man in his fifties, and one of his legs had been amputated below the knee due to a disease he had contracted in prison, where he had spent more than ten years. His time in prison ended suddenly when the United States prepared to attack the regime—for mysterious reasons, Saddam Hussein had felt compelled to set all the prisoners free, emptying out the jails before the invasion began. When Hannoun emerged from prison, he found that his family had dispersed and his only son had left Iraq. Even the house where Hannoun had lived for years was no longer there. Yet Hannoun seemed un-moved; perhaps he already knew his family had fallen apart and that he wouldn't find the house where he had grown up.

Hannoun had been sentenced to prison for helping people avoid military service. He used to make amulets and talismans that supposedly saved soldiers on the run from arrest by the military police or by Baath Party members—who took on se-curity functions in the towns. At the time, his case was blown out of proportion and Hannoun was held responsible for many soldiers deserting. The soldiers had supposedly believed that with Hannoun's help, they would be able to escape, and soon the bars on Abu Nuwas Street and the nightclubs on Saadoun Street were full of young men avoiding the war, clinking glasses instead of shooting at the enemy. Hannoun was portrayed as a very dangerous man. Although he denied he was responsible for a single soldier's desertion, the authorities sentenced him to life imprisonment.

His reputation had reached the prison before he arrived, and he found the other inmates hovering around him, curious to discover what this extraordinary man could do for them. They all asked him to help them escape by giving them amu-lets that would prevent the guards from seeing them as they climbed the high concrete walls or slipped through the barbed wire. He didn't want to give them the real reason why that was impossible: if he had had such powers, he wouldn't have stayed trapped with them one minute longer. One old prisoner came up to Hannoun and sat in front of him as though he were a god or some highly influential imam. "I've been wait-ing for you," the old man said. "You haven't come to prison in vain. You've come in answer to my prayers to God."

As far as that man was concerned, Hannoun was a divine

envoy, as he was for others—even the guards and cooks in the prison canteen. Everyone expected salvation at his hands—but he didn't have anything real to offer them. The most he could do was help them imagine life outside prison. In the absence of more realistic options, this delusion was perhaps a good solution, especially for those serving long sentences. Jumaa al-Nouri spoke about Hannoun at great length to Yasser, and it was clear that he admired the man and was fascinated by him.

"You could ask him who killed your brother," Jumaa said, without expecting Yasser to react to the offer. Maybe Jumaa had gotten the wrong end of the stick since his life was so chaotic; maybe he couldn't think straight and believed the nonsense of soothsayers—but there was no obvious explanation for why his friend, a police officer, would believe such things. To put questions about a police case to a fortune-teller was clearly ridiculous.

Yasser was sitting in Jumaa al-Nouri's room, subjecting himself to blasts of warm air from the ceiling fan and looking at the flame from the small kerosene heater that kept sputtering because of the draft from the fan. Jumaa picked up a teapot from beside the heater and poured two small glasses without stopping his chatter.

"He's here in the room next door," Jumaa told him. "People come and see him every day. He was well known before he went to prison, and when he came out, he soon regained his reputation. Someone like that couldn't possibly just be telling lies, or else how could he be so popular?"

"People will believe anything," Yasser said. "Reading the future and discovering people's secrets are like conjuring tricks."

"Let's go and say hello to him before the weather cools down and people come flocking to see him."

* * *

Jibran was killed by someone close to him.

This sentence, attributed to Hannoun, stuck in Yasser's head for many days. Jumaa al-Nouri, despite Yasser's refusal, had taken the initiative to put the question to Hannoun, to try to find out who killed Jibran.

Hannoun was well aware of the story and he didn't wait long—to think, for example—before making his interesting pronouncement: "Jibran was killed by someone close to him."

Yasser couldn't ignore this remark, although it seemed illogical to him. He thought it must be his brother's wife. She had slipped some poison into his glass that night and made him quietly breathe his last at his table. Or it was his other brother, Tahseen, who wanted to get rid of him to obtain sole ownership of the workshop.

He went back to Jibran's house, sat down with his wife, and started a new round of questioning. Jibran's room had been turned into a storage space for furniture and there were other changes to the house, making it livelier than it had been. The wife, deferential and composed, didn't provide any new information. When Yasser looked deep into her eyes, he sensed she was telling the truth. She hadn't done anything to her husband. She had suffered from his angry outbursts and the way he mistreated her, but she didn't hate him. How could she hate the father of her children?

Interrogating Tahseen didn't work either. Nothing new. Hatred doesn't lead directly to murder. Not as easily as that.

The weather was changing. The summer heat was rapidly easing off and the nights were becoming milder. Hannoun was drinking with Jumaa al-Nouri. Saadi al-Hilli's tormented singing played in the background. Hannoun was less reserved than on previous nights. He chatted cheerfully, telling jokes and laughing at anything Jumaa said.

Hannoun told Jumaa that for the previous ten years he'd been afraid of dying, but that now he wasn't afraid of anything. All he could do was breathe in and breathe out, no longer wishing that the foot he had lost would come back, or that he could go back in time and be young and strong again. He no longer had a desire for women, and his body was letting him down more and more. He would probably die in his sleep in this miserable lodging house—but that in itself didn't upset him or frighten him. He was now prepared to die, more than at any time in his past.

"Why do you say that? We were just laughing and singing. What changed your mood?" Jumaa asked.

"No, my mood hasn't changed or anything—I'm just talking with you frankly."

"Really?"

"I was afraid of dying before my enemies died."

"Do you have many enemies?"

"Not many, but I did, though now they're gone," Hannoun said.

Jumaa thought that his friend was a little drunk. He had knocked back more than usual, and since he was speaking so openly it didn't seem right to interrupt him or leave the room before he had finished.

Hannoun explained that he had found out who'd written the security report that sent him to prison. They were from his part of Bataween—two people from the ruling party—and after all these years, he'd also managed to find out the name of the officer who had questioned him and the name of the judge who had sentenced him.

One of the Baath Party members who'd helped write the

security report had been ambushed one night by a group of young men who were sons of his victims. They sprayed him with bullets, and his mangled body was found the next morning, thrown in front of the large Armenian church near Tayaran Square.

The other Baathist was the original informer, and the person that Hannoun hated most of all. The man was an old neighbor of Hannoun's family. He remembered the time when he used to play dominoes with the man in local coffee shops, or when they would help each other unload gas cylinders from the trucks that drove around selling them. He was almost a friend, though they didn't exchange many words, and Hannoun had no idea why the man had dared to write that report about him helping people to escape military service. Perhaps he was jealous, or perhaps he desired Hannoun's young wife. The name of that horrible Baathist was Jibran.

Yes, he wanted to marry Hannoun's wife—that's why he had him sent to prison.

The officer who had questioned him had lost his job in the de-Baathification campaign, but came back later under a political deal that reinstated a large number of junior officers. Unfortunately, this officer had also died before Hannoun could get to him. A car bomb had exploded close to the officer's vehicle while he was standing outside his office, and his body was blown to pieces.

The judge was just an old man, and he too died before Hannoun could take his revenge.

Jibran was the sole survivor at the time, though deep down, he had hoped someone would kill him—pull the trigger and blow his head off with a single shot—rid him of his frustration and distaste for life.

Hannoun had been absolutely sure about two of them:

the security officer who interrogated him and the judge who sentenced him. But it wasn't till later that he found out about the two Baathists who had written the report that led to his arrest.

One evening, before Jumaa al-Nouri moved into the Happiness Motel, Jibran suddenly came into Hannoun's room. He greeted Hannoun and sat down opposite him like any other customer coming to have his fortune told or to get an amulet that would ward off the evil eye, secure a livelihood, divert stray bullets, or any other purpose that preoccupied people in Baghdad. It took Hannoun a long time to recognize the person sitting across from him, and when he realized it was Jibran, he treated him like a friend. He shook his hand and smiled at him, but Jibran didn't smile back. He looked like someone who hadn't been able to smile for ages. His face was frozen. He looked awful. He wasn't at all the way he had been in 1980—smart and clean-shaven, with gelled hair, fancy aftershave, and expensive Italian shoes. Now he was just a rickety skeleton, more like a beggar or a tramp.

Hannoun talked to him at length and found that his old neighbor was in a bad way—on the verge of madness. Jibran told him stories about how his old Baathist comrades in the area had been assassinated, then suddenly moved on to talk about how long his grandfather and father had lived. They were both over a hundred when they died, and he didn't want to live to that age. He was afraid it might be hereditary. There wasn't much that he wanted in this life. Even drinking was no longer enjoyable. Quite simply, he was an old man who wanted to die, and that's why he had come to Hannoun.

"I sent lots of people to the front in the Popular Army," Jibran told Hannoun. "I wrote hundreds of reports that led people to their graves. I did lots of horrible things. Why doesn't anyone take revenge on me?"

Hannoun didn't know how to reply, and he didn't know why Jibran was telling him about his death wish.

"I want to feel remorse," Jibran continued, "to cry about the terrible things I did, but it looks like I'm hopeless. I'm a demon, and I'll admit to you right now that I enjoyed doing what I did. It was fun. It gave me an amazing sense of power and control. Is that what a normal person would say?"

Hannoun remained quiet, waiting for Jibran to finish.

"I think you'd be interested to know that it was me who had you put in prison," Jibran confessed. "It was me who wrote the security report, with help from a comrade in the party. The two of us had you put in jail for fifteen years. Aren't you going to hate me now?" He saw the signs of shock on Hannoun's face.

Hannoun hadn't expected to find other men to take his revenge on, and yet a monster had appeared in front of him; by the logic that had governed him for many years, he had to take his revenge on Jibran. This was his opportunity. But how could he do it? He was an old man with an amputated leg. He didn't have a gun with which to shoot Jibran. He couldn't get up and strangle him. Even if he tried, he probably wouldn't be strong enough to strangle him properly. *What does this madman want?* he wondered. Perhaps he was lying; perhaps he was just looking for someone to kill him and had chosen Hannoun at random.

"Either you kill me or you make me feel remorseful," Jibran demanded.

"How could I make you feel remorseful?"

"Cast a spell on me, or give me some magic potion. Treat me. Make me cry a lot and feel guilty!"

"That's impossible. There's nothing that can make someone cry unless it comes from inside—from deep inside."

"If the person's empty inside, what can we do then?" Jibran asked.

"I don't know—and I don't believe you wrote the report. No one would do that and then come to confess."

"You have to believe me," Jibran begged. "I don't have any proof for what I'm saying, but I'm your main enemy. You have to hate me and try to take revenge on me. I wish you would do it tonight—right now, if you like."

"I don't know. I'm tired and I need a drink."

"I don't really enjoy it that much, but shall we have a drink together?"

"As you like," the magician agreed.

They drank until midnight, and then Hannoun gave him a poisonous herbal mixture. He told him it would kill him instantly, as soon as he mixed it with water and drank it. Jibran thanked him profusely and went home happy. At home, he found that his wife had set his table. She had bought him a full bottle of mastic-flavored arak from Abu Edward the Christian's store on the main street in Bawateen. She had prepared the *jajiki* for him and had put on the Saadi al-Hilli tape. She was as obliging as a slave-girl. She waited for him to sit down at his table and made sure he didn't need her for anything else before heading to bed. Jibran mixed the dark herbal mixture with water in the glass and drank it. It took a few minutes before he became drowsy; he either had drunk too much with Hannoun or the poison was working. He put his forehead on the table and stretched out his arms on it, then sank into a lethal coma.

The last thing Hannoun had said to him was: "If you're incapable of feeling remorse, this stuff will kill you. It's a serious test." It appeared Jibran wasn't capable of feeling remorse.

Hannoun told the whole story to Jumaa, who listened in amazement, but he also added some magical elements to his account. He told Jumaa that he had sent a kind of djinn to the judge—to strangle him in his bed. Then he cast a spell that forced the officer to stay seated behind the steering wheel of his car—until the car bomb drove up and exploded next to him. Hannoun told him that he continued to summon all his enemies—the ones who tortured him in prison, spat at him, and even slapped him just once during an interrogation or in detention. He had counted eight enemies in total. The magician swore that he contacted them one by one using telepathy, and by taming the djinn. He slipped them the herbal powder—the same powder that provided a sense of remorse to those who were capable of feeling it and killed those who weren't. One man managed to pass the test, and after that, he spent most of his days weeping and wailing near the tomb of Sheikh Abdel Qader al-Gilani, a twelfth-century holy man. Hannoun's other seven foes died.

That one man who passed the test was Jibran—and now Hannoun believed his life was over. He hadn't expected to take his revenge so quickly.

"Haven't you ever thought, even for a moment, that perhaps they didn't deserve to die?" asked Jumaa.

"I didn't kill them. They killed themselves. Deep down they didn't want to feel remorse."

"You gave them a poison that killed them . . . so *you* killed them. Don't you have any pangs of remorse?"

"No, why should I feel remorse?" Hannoun argued. "It's only fair."

"I feel guilty now, because I sat and listened to the story." Jumaa paused for a moment. "You're a criminal, Hannoun. I should tell the police. But then I'd be betraying you as a friend, and as my neighbor in this lodging house. And if I don't tell them, I'll feel guilty because I'll be covering up for you, and you might commit more crimes—"

"No!" the magician interrupted. "First, I'm not a criminal; and second, the story's over. I'm telling you because it's over."

"You've implicated me, Hannoun. You shouldn't have told me anything. We used to just laugh, sing along with Saadi al-Hilli, and drink Zahlawi arak and wine. Why did you raise this bizarre subject? How will I be able to sleep now?"

"I could give you a herbal mixture that might help you sleep . . ."

"No, I don't want anything from you."

Jumaa went through a real ordeal after this. He was convinced that the man he'd been socializing with for a long time was deranged. But he wasn't deranged in the normal sense. Apparently, the most severe forms of madness are those where the victim looks like an ordinary person with placid features.

Two days after Yasser questioned his elder brother's wife in their house, his brother's youngest daughter—the most adventurous of Jibran's daughters—came to visit him. She sat in the reception room and, before drinking the juice that Yasser's wife put in front of her, she told Yasser that she knew how her father had died. She didn't want to tell anyone about it for fear of the scandal it might cause.

"They were herbal stimulants, sexual stimulants," she said. Out of modesty and shame, she didn't look into her uncle's eyes. Then she told him that her father hadn't had any problems—no suicidal tendencies, no sense of despair or frustration. He was an ordinary person who enjoyed his simple pleasures, especially sitting at the table and drinking. But his wife used to nag him about the trouble he had getting an erection and his lack of interest in sex. So, along with the nagging, she advised him to go and see a man in the area who was famous for selling a herbal mixture that helped to treat erectile dysfunction. That man was Hannoun the Magician. She had heard about him and his expertise from some women in the neighborhood. Since it wasn't far away and he wanted to keep his wife quiet, Jibran went to Hannoun and drank the herbal mixture that very night, but instead of curing his impotence, it killed him.

Yasser remembered what Hannoun had said to him: *Your brother was killed by someone close to him.* Yasser had just corroborated this version of events. Yes, Jibran had been killed by his stupid wife, but without her intending it, of course. That was the whole story as far as Yasser was concerned—and in the police files, the case had already been closed for weeks.

Even so, he wanted to be doubly sure, so he went back to Hannoun to ask him about the herbal mixture that had killed his brother.

When Yasser went into Jumaa's room as usual, his friend seemed surprised by the visit. Jumaa didn't look comfortable; in fact, he looked uneasy and put out. They chatted awhile about the mild weather, about how the summer had ended so soon, about the news reports on victims of the terrorist attacks, the new transitional government, and how the Americans were arresting young people accused of terrorism. But what caught Yasser's attention was that Jumaa then paused. He offered to get a *shisha* ready for Yasser to smoke, but Yasser declined. Jumaa went to the brazier and turned over the glowing coals, choosing a big one that he then put at the top of the *shisha*. He sucked deep on the pipe several times until thick white smoke came out. Yasser told his friend the latest developments in the story of his dead brother.

Jumaa was silent for a while, but after smoking the *shisha* for a bit, he felt brave enough to tell his friend what had been happening with Hannoun over the previous few days. Yasser was surprised, and grew convinced that Hannoun was a damaged man who had killed his brother and others by the same method. Now he just needed to prove it.

The two of them went to see Hannoun shortly before sunset and found people sitting around, waiting to receive their amulets, their spells, or their folk medicine. When the room was clear of customers, Yasser explained to the magician that he couldn't feel the sensation of remorse, and wanted some type of treatment for it. From behind Yasser's back, Jumaa made a gesture that Hannoun understood—that it would be best to get rid of this man before he exposed him.

"Here's a herbal mixture. It's like a test: if you're incapable of feeling remorse, it will kill you," Hannoun told him.

"How can I tell whether I'm capable of feeling remorse or not? I don't want to die."

"You have to be ready to face death in order to feel the remorse that you want to feel," the magician explained.

"Yes," Yasser replied, as he took the paper packet that contained the dark herbal powder.

He went straight to the police lab to have it analyzed to see if it matched the substance that was found in the possession of the seven dead men—and in the bottom of Jibran's glass.

Jumaa was sitting with Hannoun when night fell. They were

confident that no more customers would come in. Jumaa poured a fresh drink into Hannoun's glass.

"What's this?" Hannoun asked. "It tastes strange."

"This is *mao-tai*. The Chinese national drink."

"Where did you get it?"

"My boss brought it today and gave me a bottle."

They drank the *mao-tai*—then Jumaa looked at the old magician. He was about to say something. He felt . . . sorry for him.

Hannoun noticed his intense expression. "Is something the matter?" he asked.

"Yes, I'm waiting for you to get drunk," Jumaa joked.

"You'll have a long wait."

"Did you realize that Yasser, the young man who visited us today, is a police officer? He took that herbal stuff from you to have it analyzed in the lab."

"Why would he do that?"

"Because it might be poisonous. What kind of idiot would drink something when he doesn't know what it is?"

"We're all idiots. Life's a big trick that's been played on us," the magician muttered.

They chattered away, slowly sinking into a stupor of mild intoxication.

"I told you: my life's over now. I've taken revenge on all my enemies. That was what mattered most to me. Now, whenever death comes, I'll welcome it."

"That's crazy talk. What kind of idiot would throw his life away?"

"You're talking a lot about idiots tonight, but you're one of them," Hannoun replied.

"Of course I'm an idiot. I've wasted my life on stupid things. I haven't done anything honorable."

"If that's how it is, then don't talk about idiots," Hannoun warned, an edge to his voice.

"You don't want me to talk about idiots because I might upset the big one—which is you."

"Do you have any regrets, Jumaa?" Hannoun suddenly asked, his eyes glistening as though he were about to cry.

"Yes, I regret my whole life . . . everything in my life. It's just been one mistake after another."

"Great!"

"Why do you say that?"

"Because while you were bringing another piece of charcoal for your *shisha*, I slipped that herbal powder into our drink—the *mao-tai*," the magician whispered.

"What do you mean?"

"Well, we can now find out together what it tastes like for the first time—a taste mixed with the powder of remorse."

"You're crazy! How could you do that?"

"It's the only lesson I can give you," Hannoun said. "As for me . . . I don't feel remorse and it seems I can't. I'm very proud of what I've done and I don't want to go through hell in prison again because of your friend the detective. I've experienced enough torment. I probably won't wake up tomorrow morning. But you—if you're sure you can feel remorse, you'll be a new person tomorrow morning. Cheers!"

And with that, Hannoun swallowed what was left in his glass.

Translated from Arabic by Jonathan Wright

PART II

WHERE IS THE TRUST?

BAGHDAD ON BORROWED TIME

BY SALAR ABDOH

Gejara

I was tired of the artist types who needed my services. The trouble was, they were the ones neurotic enough to want to pay for those services in the first place. Either a husband suspected a wife or a wife suspected a husband. There was hardly a variant to this. I would've had to shut my business down if I told them the truth: *If you suspect it, it's probably not your imagination.*

They could not believe that there was an actual private detective agency in this city. They imagined themselves to be playing a role in a film. And to get on my good side, they'd say exactly the same thing, every time: "Have you ever read Raymond Chandler and Dashiell Hammett? I love those writers . . ." It was always in that order: Raymond first, Dashiell second—not the other way around. It was their way of saying they understood my world. It was silly. And because I didn't want to give them a lecture on the million sentences that had been added to the craft since those gentlemen wrote what they wrote, I would simply state my exorbitant daily rate, plus the very hefty extra expenses, and watch them swallow and pretend to be considering it before they said yes. It wasn't like I had a whole lot of competition in my line of business here.

So imagine my surprise one day when in walked a guy who spoke Persian with an Arab accent. I knew him for what he was right away—reluctant military. Retired now and ready to forget all the corpses he'd seen in his life.

"What brings you to Tehran?" I asked him.

"This," the military man said, softly. He laid a blown-up photograph on the desk.

It was an image of the sort of thing you saw back when Saddam attacked Iran in the 1980s—a wall of names and inept political propaganda: *Long live Saddam Hussein. Our leader, and father, and friend. President of the lionhearted people of Iraq.* Beneath the dedication were a half-dozen names.

I looked up at the man. "You are . . . ?"

"Abu Habiba."

"You spent the war on our side, I assume."

"I fought against Saddam," he said. "If that's what you mean."

"Badr Brigade?" I asked.

He nodded. "Seventeen years of it. I went back to Baghdad when that accursed man finally fell."

There was so much fatigue in his voice, so many lost years. Not a drop of relish in mentioning the dictator's inglorious demise. He seemed too tired to relish anything. Abu Habiba's eyes roamed a bit, finally resting on my window overlooking Karim Khan Avenue. I had rented this hole-in-the-wall office for its centrality, but all you could really see from here were cars swooshing over the bridge and honking their horns.

"I researched you," he admitted. "You've been to Iraq. Do you know Baghdad well?"

When there's no reason to lie, tell the truth. It takes less effort. I knew Baghdad just enough. A decade earlier, the family of an Iranian MIA, going back two decades, had hired me to go to there and look for their missing boy. The *boy* would be older than me now, if, by some chance, he were still alive.

This had been in 2006, and Baghdad back then was a nightmare you wouldn't wish on your worst enemy. The Americans were receiving a bloody nose from the insurgency every day. It was a dogfight, neighborhood by neighborhood. One time, on a side road off Umreidi Street, I came face-to-face with my own mortality. After that, I wasn't sticking around. Why? Because as my driver and I turned the corner, we almost drove headlong into an American Stryker vehicle that had its gun trained at the building thirty feet away from us. The arrival of our taxi in the middle of an about-to-go-down gun battle between the Americans and the Sadr militia makes for a good tale in retrospect, but back in those days, it was just about the worst thing that could happen to you in Baghdad.

I want to give you a complete picture of those moments, so you'll understand why at first I wasn't keen on going back, even ten years later: the beastly looking armored carrier sat there idling, then its gun turret slowly turned until my driver and I were dead center in its line of fire; the wind raised swirls of garbage off the street; shattered windowpanes dangled precariously from crooked frames of crooked homes; flapping doors squeaked like the cry of the devil; if one side or the other didn't kill you, the heat would. It was a *High Noon* moment, I thought. Gary Cooper or John Wayne could've walked out of that building with a shotgun and a six-shooter. Instead, I looked to the building and saw one of the Sadr militiamen staring at me like a demon: *What the fuck are you doing here, you fool?*

That was when I softly called my driver's name: "Haider!"

Haider was frozen. We were about to be blown to pieces in a corner of Baghdad, and Haider seemed to be having a stroke.

"Haider!" The guns of the Stryker were still trained on us.

They also seemed to be saying the very same thing—*Are you mad? This is a gunfight. Get lost!* Then I saw the drip of sweat rolling off Haider's face. He wasn't dead—he was in shock and couldn't speak. "Easy, brother. Just back the car out slowly and get us away from here. Don't make a sudden move. Don't turn one way or another. Don't plead for our lives. Just back the car out the same way we came. That's it . . . There you go. Slowly does it. Nice and slow . . ."

And that was the last time I was in Baghdad. It was enough for a lifetime. All the money in the world couldn't get me back there again—or so I thought. But I was bored with all the adulterers of Tehran and ten years had passed, after all.

I brought my attention back to Abu Habiba. "I don't come cheap," I warned.

"Do it for your heart," he said.

It wasn't the Baghdad I'd known in 2006. In Karrada, I went back to Abu Ali's and had myself a *teman wa marag*. Iraqi men tore into flatbread and rice, while posters of Imam Hossein and Ayatollah Sistani watched over them. This was a thoroughly Shia establishment, and had been targeted at least twice that I knew of. Once by the Americans and once by al-Qaeda associates who had eventually been caught a little farther north in Diyala. I didn't think Abu Ali would recognize me after so long. But he did. He still looked like the grand old uncle of the entire world. Flowing white beard, honest eyes, and a great big smile that exuded unshakable faith.

"You didn't find your missing Iranian all those years ago, so you decided to abandon us altogether!" Abu Ali shouted, his voice hard.

I loved this man; he had a selflessness that was infectious. You never went hungry at Abu Ali's, no matter how much money you had or didn't have. He was Iraq at its best—stoic, solid, kind, and given to moments of ecstatic anger that was pure art. You haven't seen anger unless you've seen an angry Iraqi—I admit, it is kind of beautiful to watch. It is so all-encompassing and passionate that you too wish you could get angry that way. It turns you into a believer.

"My heart will always stay in Baghdad. You know this, Abu Ali."

We looked at each other for a while. Silent. There are things that are unspeakable. Men don't talk about it—at least not inside a dining joint off a side street in Karrada, Baghdad. There had been a war once, and I'd run to it, because I thought that if I didn't, the war would end, and I wouldn't have my glory. I was sixteen and stupid. It didn't take long before I was in an Iraqi prisoner-of-war camp. I spent twelve months there, until the eight-year war between us and the Iraqis ended, and it was another six months before I got home.

Suddenly I was a hero. I looked around and saw all the mothers holding pictures of their missing sons. Everyone wanted to hear good news from a boy like me. They wanted me to tell them I'd seen their sons in a camp or, at the very least, that I'd seen them die in front of me. The worst thing is the not-knowing. You stare into a mother's eyes and you wish you could give them 100 percent proof, but you can't. Maybe that was why I had accepted the MIA case ten years earlier. I was trying to make up for all the good and bad news that I couldn't provide before.

I'd learned to speak Arabic in the camp. I'd learned that some of the guards were sadistic sons of bitches, and others would have given a sixteen-year-old boy the food off their plate if they could be sure they wouldn't get in trouble for it. I'd come home, finished high school, studied for college, and began reading books and watching films only in English. After a year of college, I dropped out. That one year in the camp had made it hard to sit still. You'd think it would be the opposite, but it wasn't. Why did I start reading only in English? After a while, I ran out of detective books to read in Persian translation. There were only so many of them. *Dashiell Hammet . . . Raymond Chandler . . .* I swear I could have taken my clients' heads off when they asked if I'd read those writers. They were hitting a nerve, but for all the wrong reasons. After ten years of trying my hand at everything else, the day I announced I was opening a detective agency, my mother thought I had finally lost my mind. She had been watching some foreign TV show and called it post-traumatic stress.

Then, after two months, some guy from the municipality showed up and said exactly this: "Who do you think you are to open a . . . what? Detective agency?" He laughed in my face. "You were never even on the police force."

Was there a law that said I had to be a police officer before becoming a private detective? The guy had no answer to that, and at the end of the day, I was a war hero—wasn't I?

"You need a license," he said.

"Is there such a thing here?" I asked.

"No," he replied. "But I'll make you one if you like."

We agreed on a sum to get him and the municipality off my back, and therein was the beginning of my career as a PI in Tehran.

Now, back to Baghdad. Abu Ali was asking: "How can you leave your heart in a country that almost killed you and put you in jail?"

"Oh, Abu Ali. In my book, a man doesn't salute a badge, he salutes the man underneath the badge. My heart is right here, in Iraq still."

He smiled. "What brings you here then, aside from your heart and my *teman wa marag?*"

"I have a case that disturbs me," I said.

"Shouldn't they all?"

"No. Most are just about jealousy and boredom and greed. This one . . . I don't know. It eats at me."

"Let's have it."

I laid out several postcard-size photos that Abu Habiba had given me after our first meeting. It's not my style to share the details of a case I'm working on with anyone. But this was Baghdad, not my native territory, and I needed all the help I could get. I could rely on Abu Ali.

He looked up at me questioningly. "Why are you chasing after some writings on a wall from a war that ended almost thirty years ago?"

"A man came to see me in Tehran."

"An Iraqi?"

I nodded and told him the story, or as much of it as I'd pieced together from the photos and Abu Habiba's words. Men had started getting murdered around Baghdad about a year earlier—strangled, necks twisted, laden with explosives and blown to pieces, burned, chopped up, faces melted by acid. The list went on. There was no shortage of murder in Baghdad the past thirteen years, but these were different. There was an MO. This was the work of a serial killer with a purpose. Each time, he (and I could only assume it was a he) left a calling card: a photo of a graffitied wall with the names of the Iraqi soldiers who had left their mark there. One of the names always belonged to the victim. The killer had thirteen on record so far. He made sure his handiwork was discovered.

"And the police?" Abu Ali asked.

"Abu Ali! You know better than me how many bombs went off in Karrada just this past month alone. How many dead? Sixty? A hundred? Two hundred? Even if the Baghdad police have the resources to go after a serial killer, which they don't, I doubt they have the stomach for it right now."

Abu Ali glanced outside. There was a roadblock just fifty meters down the street. There were so many roadblocks in Baghdad, you would have thought this was the safest city in the world. A roadblock, though, is a sure sign of weakness. It stops nothing. It is only decoration. A suicide bomber would not be deterred by that decoration.

"Who brought this case to you?"

"A man named Abu Habiba," I told him. "He lives over by the Souk al-Gejara in Sadr City."

"And this Abu Habiba travels all the way to Tehran to bring you his case? Why is this so important to him?"

It was the most obvious question in the world, and I realized I didn't have an answer to it.

Abu Ali got up to attend to some customers and I continued staring outside. Next door at the café, Anwar Little was serving no less than nine cups of tea at the same time. Anwar could pour tea with his eyes closed; he could pour while standing; he could pour while upside down or with his arms wrapped around his torso and legs; he could make a tea glass roll off his side and land on his thigh, then proceed to pour with his teeth. A TV station from Dubai had once made a short documentary about him, then one day, while watching satellite television in Tehran, I'd seen that the famous Anwar Little of Karrada had been burned in a bombing. Now he was here again, with a half-scorched face that still did not stop smiling. He tossed four tea glasses in the air, caught them neatly on a tray, held the tray behind his back, and began pouring with the other hand. Not a drop of tea spilled. You had to love this country. And feel its pain.

It was why the Americans never stood a chance here.

Over the next couple of weeks I tried to see if I could find a pattern in where the killer had struck. It wasn't hard to figure that all the victims had been staunch Saddam supporters. The writings on the walls literally said it all. When you came across something like, *Saddam is the hammer and we are the nails—commandos of Tikrit Police—Ali al-Marsouli, Luay al-Toogh, Najmeddin al-Bakr*, you knew these were not men who went grudgingly to war. They no doubt received every kind of bonus Saddam's Baath Party regime offered in those days, and God help anyone who ran afoul of them. However, Luay al-Toogh was dead. He had been killed in the Mansour District, a Sunni neighborhood. Yet neither his name nor where he was killed told me anything of consequence. There was one guy from another photograph who had been killed in a staunch Shia neighborhood, Hayy-Ur. And I couldn't figure out if the killer had lured the victims into these places (I didn't think so), or what kind of access the killer had to so easily move into such wildly different neighborhoods. There was a third question too: where did these photographs come from?

While I contemplated my puzzle, I also familiarized myself with where I was living. Abu Habiba had set me up near his place, in an apartment overlooking the souk. I had a bird's-eye view of Gejara from my window and spent the mornings watching the quarter slowly come to life. Everybody knew each other; the section I was closest to was mostly stalls selling household plastic goods from Iran, and clothes and shoes from Turkey. Abu Habiba would visit me each morning and we'd have the same breakfast of bread with fresh cream, hard-boiled eggs, and tea. Only once did he ask if I was making progress with my research. Otherwise, he left me alone and went to visit with one of his two wives; one lived on this side of the souk and one on the other side. Another time, he took me to the mechanic's shop he partly owned, deep in the bowels of Sadr City, where for dozens of blocks in each direction there was nothing but car graveyards and repair shops. Two of his sons were there—tough-looking young men who smiled encouragingly and tried their hands at speaking in stumbling Persian.

As it turned out, being in Baghdad was also an opportunity to simply run away from myself. I could get lost in the sounds of this long-suffering city. Twice in the last year, female clients in Tehran had told me in no certain terms that they wanted to sleep with me. Maybe they thought if their husbands could have extramarital affairs, so could they. And who better than the guy you hire to find out the truth? I disliked myself for saying no to them, and disliked myself equally for thinking that I should have said yes. Business had been getting better over the past couple of years, but I went to the office with a dread of some sort—that maybe one day I'd wake up and have to settle for a *real* job. Maybe my mother had been right, and I had trauma of some sort from the war and the incarceration. In Baghdad, there were so many men who had either been in a recent war or were still at war right now—to think about these things was ridiculous. It was like wondering why you didn't get your after-dinner dessert when everybody around you hadn't had a proper meal in two months.

I needed an ear to speak to and went back to Karrada to find Abu Ali. Even as I turned onto the street, something was not quite right. Soon I was standing in front of the shell of what had been the restaurant. The teahouse next door where

Anwar Little had worked was also just a skeleton of half-burned debris. No point asking what had happened. I hadn't been watching the news and no one needed to tell me—just another bombing in Karrada. Maybe my face betrayed something, because just then, a regular came up to me and said: "He didn't make it. Not this time."

"Who?" I asked.

"Abu Ali."

"What about Anwar Little?"

"They didn't find even a pinkie."

I walked away.

Why had I come to Baghdad? The money I was getting from Abu Habiba hardly covered my travel and food. What did I think I'd find here? The answer to a war I should have never been in thirty years earlier? I went inside Ridha Alwan Café and ordered one of their famous *bunduqs*. Writers and TV people sat at different tables with no care in the world— or more likely with *all* the care in the world. No sign that a few blocks from here Abu Ali's was no more. How did these people go on? I couldn't figure it then, and I can't figure it now.

On my second *bunduq*, I laid out the photos on the table and examined them for the hundredth time. They were pictures from a book—but this was the first time I caught that. In the bottom right-hand corner of one of the photos, there was a very faint trace of a page number: *77*. This was negligent and amateurish of me; why hadn't I seen it before?

The next morning, I didn't ask Abu Habiba anything about a book, but spent several days roaming the weapon-sellers area of the Maridi Souk in Sadr.

"You never buy anything here, so why do you keep coming back?" The guy who asked this was an AK parts dealer who had a stall in the far corner of the weapons lane. He had the look of a sad middleweight boxer who knew he'd never graduate to the big leagues. He'd never sell a Glock pistol for $2,500, and had to settle for hawking refurbished parts of AKs in a half-hidden corner of the market.

The first thing I did was buy several grips, magazines, and rail side mounts from him. I paid twice what he asked for, and when his eyebrows furrowed and he came close enough that I could smell the onion from his lunch, I told him: "I have a few pictures I want you to look at."

The spare-parts dealer quickly confirmed what I'd begun to suspect—the murders had barely been reported. He said he'd know if they had been, and there was no reason not to believe him. The puzzle was changing. Why was Abu Habiba so hell-bent on discovering a killer no one cared about? In fact, most of the people in a place like this souk in Sadr City would have applauded the deaths of former Saddam lackeys.

The next day, I went by the Tigris and old Mutanabbi Street. The celebrated booksellers' quarter was bustling again. When I'd been here last, it was pretty much a no-go area. I have no other word for it, except to say it was heartwarming— to see books in the stalls and shops and on the sidewalks of this quarter of Baghdad—after dealing with Abu Ali's death. But I wasn't here to be a literary tourist. I started from one end of the street and worked my way down, showing the photos to every bookseller I found. Most just shook their heads and wouldn't give me the time of day, and I couldn't afford to buy something from each one so they might deign to give my pictures a second glance.

I was working my way back toward the old Shabandar Café when a young guy with an unlikely ponytail and devilish sideburns gave a long glance at one of the photos, then looked at me. "Yes, this is from a book," he observed. "But it's not a book that was printed here or that you'll find in Mutanabbi. I saw a copy of it at the Tehran Book Fair last year."

"Can you order me a copy?" I asked.

He said he could.

Abu Habiba was leafing through the book. The title said it all: *Memoir from the Neighbor*. An Iranian photographer had taken the pictures just after Khorramshahr had been liberated. The only things that had been left behind in that port city were heaps of war slogans and graffiti by Iraqi soldiers who had occupied the place for more than a year and a half. I had marked the pages that were related to the murders in Baghdad; it didn't take a genius to figure out the killer had picked his targets based on the men who'd written their names on the walls of Khorramshahr and were therefore a part of this book.

Abu Habiba took his reading glasses off and sighed. "You think the photographer killed these men?" he asked.

I smiled, almost embarrassed at how patently insincere the question was. "This book came out a quarter of a century ago. It was republished two years ago. The photographer . . . he died over a decade ago."

"Then . . ."

"Abu Habiba, when did you last renew your passport?"

He gave me a confused look. "Two years ago. Why?"

"Can you bring your passport tomorrow morning?"

His voice went flat: "Why?"

"I want to see your visa stamps for Iran," I told him.

"To prove what?"

"To see how many times you've been there in the past couple of years," I told him. "And to find out if you happened to visit a few bookstores or the book fair."

"Are you suspecting me?" he asked, clearly offended.

"No . . . yes."

There was a tray of our usual breakfast food between us, and we could hear the sounds of the souk down below. Birds chirped on a nearby roof, where a woman was laying out some laundry. I could see her silhouette from where I sat. I had thrown something into the wind, not at all sure if what I suspected was even remotely true. But now, suddenly, I was sure. It may have been the way Abu Habiba reacted—a combination of disingenuousness, curiosity, and something akin to pleasure at having been discovered. It was an odd moment, made all the more odd by Abu Habiba taking a Colt pistol out of his pocket and setting it between us.

"I served, like I told you, seventeen years in Badr. I can kill you right now for what you accuse me of. No one will know or care," Abu Habiba said.

"Why did you go all the way to Tehran and bring me here? This is what I can't understand. Do you have a copy of the book? Did you buy it in Tehran in the last couple of years?"

"As a matter of fact, I do have a copy of the book," he answered, standing up. He looked very tall all of a sudden— imposing, dangerous, yet strangely vulnerable and bewildered at the same time. I didn't know whether to fear him or feel sorry for him.

"Abu Habiba, what's going on?" I asked, bewildered myself.

He took his gun and walked out, leaving me with a long day ahead in a Baghdad that felt a lot less friendly than an hour before.

The next morning, when Abu Habiba came back with our breakfast, I had my bag packed.

"I booked a seat on the midnight flight."

"I can't let you go," he muttered.

"I have no idea why I'm here. I have a business I have to run back in Tehran," I replied.

"Here!" He threw another photograph onto the floor between us. I picked it up. Page 92. He hadn't even tried to hide the page number this time. Two names appeared in the photo: *Mahdi Kadhim* and *Osama Ben Zayd*. There was a nonsensical sentence below it that read: *The Fallujah people martyr path in heat.*

I stared into his eyes. "Which one did you kill?"

"Huh?"

"Which one?" I repeated.

It was as if he were speaking through a medium: "Mahdi . . . Mahdi Kadhim. May . . . he . . . burn . . . in hell."

I grabbed my bag and tried to walk past him, but he reached for my hand. "Do you not want to know where it took place? It happened yesterday, after I left you."

I raised my voice: "I don't give a damn where Mahdi Kadhim was killed or when! I'm leaving."

"I did it at Madinat al-Tib, Medical City. It was a beautiful job. The man had gone to get his eyes checked. So I started with his eyes."

I tried to release myself from his grip, but he was too strong. I realized in that moment just how broad-shouldered and powerful Abu Habiba really was. There was a mole on the side of his nose. He had a habit of squeezing it sometimes. He did it now. I kicked him hard. My foot caught him in the pelvis but he didn't budge.

"I can't let you leave. You have to catch this murderer," he pleaded.

Maybe this was all a dream, or I was losing my mind. Down below, on the street, the familiar song of the roaming gas-cylinder van settled into the neighborhood. I sat down.

My voice was tired, fed up: "What do you want from me, Abu Habiba?"

"Catch me. Please."

"No one cares about these murders," I said. "They care about the bombings in Sadr, in Karrada, in Bab al-Sharqi, in Zayouna. You hardly even make the news. Do you want to make the news? Is that what you want?"

"No. I don't want news. No news. I want . . ." Abu Habiba didn't go on and we sat in silence. Minutes may have passed before he blurted out: "They deserved to die! I was in exile seventeen years. Seventeen years I drank the blood of sorrow from Saddam and his men."

"How do you know that the men you killed were all Saddam's people? You could be killing innocents. Men who were nothing but conscripts back then, men who didn't want to be there at all."

"I know who they are. I do my research! I don't go after just anyone. I have files. I worked in the Ministry of Interior for six years after I came back. I worked in Defense too."

He sounded so logical when he spoke. As if his having been in the Interior Ministry absolved him of wrongdoing. I wasn't sure what to say or do. I was on thin ice and knew it. One wrong step and, instead of thinking of me as his confidant, he'd grab that pistol and kill me. Even if I managed to wrest the weapon from him, what then? This was his town. Everybody down there in the souk was probably his first or second or third cousin.

Also, to be perfectly honest, I didn't care. I didn't care if he killed another fifty of these men. Men like them had trapped me in an internment camp for a year. I'd been a dumb teenager and shouldn't have volunteered to fight. But they'd attacked us, hadn't they? Men like Abu Habiba had fought for our side, and now he had an impulse he couldn't control. I understood him. I understood his pain. They'd leveled Khorramshahr, and when they left it, there were only wild dogs remaining in that once-flourishing city—dogs and the piss stains of men like Mahdi Kadhim and Osama Ben Zayd. Why shouldn't Abu Habiba kill them? Let him! I had a mind to help him do his work even faster, with more efficiency— though he seemed to be doing quite a fine job on his own.

We just talked. We talked about cars, about Abu Habiba's children and grandchildren. We talked about the war, about my internment, about his years fighting to liberate his own country. We talked politics, the Sunni-Shia divide. We talked about the Kurds. We talked about women. We talked about the guns and cell phones we preferred to use. We talked about my work as a private investigator. We talked about what a shithole Saddam had left of Khorramshahr after the Iranians finally ran him out of there. We talked about what a perfect disaster Saddam had been. We talked about the disaster that followed Saddam, namely the Americans. We talked about Beirut and Istanbul, two cities that we both had a weakness for. We talked about the afterlife, and God, and the meaning of the martyrdom of Imam Hossein, peace be upon him.

When the muezzin's call for midday prayer came, Abu Habiba stood up to wash his hands and get ready. I did the same, because I didn't want him to feel alone. We prayed together. I could have taken him then, while he was praying. I was praying behind him, and there was nothing stopping me from grabbing the gun that he laid to the side, and then clobbering him over the head with it. But I didn't do that. Instead, I just prayed. And when we were done, we sat back down, facing each other once more.

"Is this why you called me here, just to share in your secret?" I asked him.

"No," he replied.

"Why, then?"

"I need you to do something for me."

"What?"

"Stop me. Please. Stop me from doing what I'm doing," he said, desperation rising in his voice.

"You think you're committing a crime?"

"No. Not a crime."

"What, then?"

He spoke softly, slowly: "I'm not sure God approves of what I do."

"I can tell you right now that He doesn't. I'm sure of it. So why do you do it?"

"Because I can't help it," he whispered.

"Just throw away the files from the ministry. You have a big beautiful family, Abu Habiba. You have grandchildren who adore you. You spent seventeen years in the wilderness and now you're finally home. Why do you want to throw it all away?"

"Nobody cares about those dead men," he murmured. "I can keep doing what I do."

"Then why are we having this conversation?"

"I want someone to stop me."

"How?"

He grabbed the pistol again and pushed it toward me.

"I can't kill you, Abu Habiba," I said. "You know that."

"Why not?"

"Because I don't make a habit of killing my clients."

"I'm not a client. I'm a murderer."

It was like speaking to a child. I took the gun, got up, and laid the thing back in front of him on the floor. "You'll have to stop yourself. I can't do it for you."

There were tears in his eyes. He'd had to reach way beyond his comfort zone to find someone like me. He had reached all the way to the country next door. I still didn't know exactly how he'd found me, but he had; and it didn't matter now. Nothing made sense. Why did Abu Ali's place have to go up in smoke while I was here? Why not last year or five years earlier? I had no luck when it came to Iraq. Being their prisoner had sucked away my youth, and coming here on the job had drained my spirit and reminded me of all the lives Saddam had wasted—including Abu Habiba's life, and my life, and even the lives of all those young Americans in uniform, who'd been sent here to die or go crazy.

As I closed the door behind me, I heard his whisper: "Please, my friend, your flight is ten hours from now. Talk to me still. I don't want to do this anymore. I will have to answer to God."

I hope you answer to someone—God will do! I thought to myself.

I imagine it won't always be this way, but in the year 2016, the year of my story, I got on my airplane at Baghdad International Airport only after passing through no less than seven security checkpoints, the first one starting a good few miles before I even got anywhere near the airport proper. Somewhere along the line I simply ran out of steam. My heart was not in it. How many more men was Abu Habiba going to kill? The crux of it was that I caught myself siding with him again; it wasn't the men he killed that I cared so much about, but Abu Habiba himself. I found myself worrying about his mental state. I'd known a few Badr guys in my time. Good men, fine soldiers. They'd given up every comfort, for years and years, just like Abu Habiba, to fight against a beast of a man who fancied Stalin as a role model. They'd finally won. It was a strange and roundabout win, because it had something to do with the Americans, who had subsequently reduced the country to an oil-pumping urinal. But, for better or worse, there it was! And Abu Habiba, this serial-killing granddad of fifty—I could not let him go on suffering. I truly cared about him. He was my man, not the victims. Fuck the victims!

I took a cab to Gejara. I was almost happy to be going back. It had felt as if I were betraying the Iraqis and Baghdad, and the memory of men like Abu Ali and Anwar Little, by leaving like that. There was unfinished business and it wasn't only about Abu Habiba. It was about myself: I'd been carrying a burden since I was sixteen, a love and hate for a people I'd fought against and who had imprisoned me. I'd been too young back then to know that I was suffering. But I was old enough now to know that Abu Habiba was. I had to do something for Iraq and Baghdad—and do it quietly—then take my leave. I didn't know what I could do; I just hoped that I would know when the time came to do it.

Hearing again the relentless sounds of the fruit hawkers in Jamila made me positively ecstatic, and I felt even better when I realized I still had the key to the place in Gejara in my pocket. When I opened the door, he was still there. The entire quarter's electricity was, as often happened, out. Abu Habiba was not using the emergency light, but a candle lit his lower chin, and he held a long knife in his hand.

"I knew you'd come back," he said.

"What do you plan to do with that knife?"

"Tonight's the night."

"Abu Habiba, last night was the night too, it seems. Can't you at least pace yourself?" As I kept up this ridiculous con-

versation, I wondered to myself what page in the book of photographs the next victim appeared on.

"This man tonight . . . do you know what he does? He
collects food and medicine for the men fighting up north right
now," Abu Habiba shared. "He pretends to be one of us. But I
know his history. I have read his file. I know what he did thirty
years ago."

"Let it go," I demanded.

"He is not even in that book of photographs. But I know
about him. He's like a disease among us."

"My friend, listen, you would have to kill half the men on
Earth if you keep going this way. No one is perfect. Sometimes
men do things and they are not proud of it."

"But this man . . . he will settle his debts tonight," Abu
Habiba vowed. "He's here—we don't even have to drive."

We traveled the maze of the souk in semidarkness. People were
closing up shop to head to the mosque for evening prayer. The
harsh sound of electric generators penetrated the alleyways.
Men greeted Abu Habiba and he greeted them back. I had
pulled my cap on as far down as I could, hoping in this low
light no one would know or recognize me. The strong diesel
smell of the generators turned my stomach, as always, and I
tried to imagine what it would have been like had Abu Habiba
and I fought side by side three decades earlier during the war,
instead of meeting only now—too late to repair any damage
and be of help to one another.

The back of the souk opened out to an area where men
grilled *masgouf* over a half-dozen flames. The fish made my
stomach growl. If I decided to turn back, I still had a good six
hours before the flight. But instead I followed Abu Habiba's
deliberate steps. We moved past the fish, and another small

mosque, and more closed-up shops and stalls, until we came to a quiet area where an idling pickup truck's headlights illuminated the back of a small government building, its wall flanked by a pile of garbage. Boxes of dates, bananas, apples, flatbread, onions, tomatoes, frozen chicken, and red meat were all stocked in the back of the truck.

"This man pretends to be one of us—helping our brothers up north fight Daesh scum," Abu Habiba whispered. "But he's not. He changed his name. He changed everything. He became another person and thought he could get away with it. But I have his file. I have it on me. I told you before."

"Where is he?"

"He'll come out."

I felt illegitimate. I had felt a lot of things in my life, but never that, not even when I first opened the detective agency without a clue how to go about it. "What if you're wrong?"

"I'm not wrong. I tested him," Abu Habiba answered confidently. "I told him I knew who he was. I told him that he must bring me money at this hour or I would inform on him. I told him I would leave a copy of his file in a safe to be opened by the police, and by my family, in case something happened. He is scared. He told me to meet him in this deserted place." Abu Habiba paused for a second and listened to the sounds around us. "Here," he said, giving me his pistol. Then he told me to move into the shadows.

Now I felt as absurd as I had felt when that American Stryker had trained its gun on us ten years before. I wasn't sure what to do. So I waited. And it didn't take long for our man to emerge. He was smaller than I had imagined he'd be. Short and thin, with a white shawl draped over one arm. He wiped his face with it and regarded Abu Habiba.

"I've done nothing wrong," the short man announced.

"Not lately," Abu Habiba said, with something of a sneer. I hadn't heard that tone from him before.

I expected an effort, the man pleading, telling Abu Habiba that times change and people change—anything—anything to get himself off the hook and keep Abu Habiba from committing another murder. I was rooting for this guy to make his case, make it for all of us. But he just stood there for a minute, and then started to put his right hand in the inside pocket of his coat. Abu Habiba walked swiftly over to the man, and I remained tongue-tied. I didn't see the knife or the strike. He seemed to be holding the man up with the blade of the knife thrust deep inside his flesh. Abu Habiba twisted it deeper as I stepped in closer, and the man uttered a barely audible moan.

"This is for all the martyrs who waited for this night," Abu Habiba hissed, pushing the man back until he fell to the ground.

The car was still idling. I felt exposed. I ran to the car and turned off the ignition. We were plunged into darkness. Way over where they were cooking fish, I heard the distant laughter of men. Abu Habiba's gun was still in my hand. I went up to him. He was kneeling over the dying man. "Here!" I tried to hand him the pistol back. He pointed his cell phone flashlight at something. The man had been taking an envelope out of his pocket.

"Money. This son of a whore was going to give me money. Take it!" He shoved the envelope of cash into my hand, and simultaneously I heard a sound that was something between a gurgle and a cough. The cell phone dropped to the ground but the flashlight remained on, shining away from us. I was momentarily blinded.

"Abu Habiba, we need to get out of here. Get your phone and let's go."

Nothing. I was struck by fear for a moment, then reached where Abu Habiba should have been. He was there, but horizontal, the gun by his side. I took out my own phone and flashed it. He'd slit his own throat—both carotid arteries, from the looks of it. It was the kind of deep, clean job that's nearly impossible to do right. But if you did it, your victim didn't stand a chance. It was said there were Daesh women up north who had been taught to do this with their teeth; they called them "biting women."

I heard footsteps, but they were distant, not coming this way. Abu Habiba remained prone, and there was still gurgling . . . but which one did it come from? I couldn't tell if it was the other man or Abu Habiba. I brought my ears closer. Nothing. How could a man cut himself like that? Surely it didn't come with practice! I stood still, in a desert of my own thoughts, not feeling much of anything, except that maybe it was time to leave Baghdad after all. Abu Habiba hadn't given me a warning, hadn't given me enough time to consider he was capable of killing himself with such fierceness. Had he only wanted me here as a witness to his last act? Or was I here to make sure this last act looked genuine? I put the envelope in my pocket, then took the shawl the man had worn and wrapped it around my hands. I rolled the two men into each other and my hand brushed against something thick underneath Abu Habiba's shirt. I knew what it was—the dossier he had on the man. It would be a hell of a stretch to believe that a single knife had killed them both in a struggle. But Baghdad needed its heroes, and Abu Habiba would be one tonight.

The private detective in me wanted to know a few things: One, how had Abu Habiba known I'd come back? And two, had I not come back, would he still have carried out this murder-suicide? Had the hour been fixed, or were we in some random loop of belated vengeance that wanted me to be the last man standing? There were too many variables, and because this was Baghdad, and all the security checkpoints in the city didn't mean a thing if your time had arrived, I chose to leave my questions for another day. Even if that day was never to arrive.

I went to the back of the truck and picked out a carton of tomatoes and bananas. I dumped the produce over the corpses, along with the knife and the gun. My clumsy way of creating a scene of struggle, I suppose. I'd have to get rid of that bloodied white shawl somewhere between here and the airport. Or, more likely, between here and the next checkpoint—plenty of time for my midnight flight. And if they ever brought me back here to explain what had happened (I doubted that they would, since Abu Habiba needed to be made a hero), I would just tell them that some of us have known the kind of pain that requires a few more killings before you're truly done.

This story was originally written in English

POST-TRAUMATIC STRESS REALITY IN QADISIYA
BY HADIA SAID
al-Qadisiya District

For Jalil and Sumer

The First Day

He said he's coming tomorrow and affirmed his arrival dozens of times by phone, on WhatsApp, and via that damn attorney. He asked me to trust him—and I want to. Indeed, I *need* to trust him, and not just him, but all the demons claiming a piece of this pie.

I know full well that it's my pie and that I'm the one who worked, struggled, and wore myself out constructing it from the ground up. The ground? No—sorry—from a rocky hole in the earth. I leveled the ground and built a foundation for a house, then added walls. Next came the roof, followed by an entire ground floor. After that, I added the upper story. All of this was accomplished by matching my labor with that of my unfortunate late sister, Nabiha. She saved up dinars from her paltry salary, while I exhausted my arms, time, health, and... what else?

Never mind. What matters is that he comes and that the final act of this comedy concludes—meaning the house in Qadisiya returns to its rightful owners.

Yes, yes, yes—you thieving relatives and strangers. You swarmed into the house like flies, after it became a paradise—

and we left like frightened mice instead of migratory birds. God forbid! I never was a mouse. Everyone knows that I held out steadfastly, till my grandmother said: "Go! Don't be afraid. I have the title to the house, and it will always be safe in my pocket or Nabiha's."

As she lay dying in the little room next to the stairs on the upper floor, she whispered to me that she knew the whole truth and that my mother and paternal uncle had no right to so much as a brick of our house in Qadisiya, even though everyone had lived in it and it had served as a haven for my siblings and other family members—some of whom were down on their luck, greedy, or even rogues. They would arrive whenever they were out of work, angry with their spouse, or embroiled in some deal with a shady party member.

They were nothing but phantoms when Nabiha's face shone on those evenings, caressed by summer's fleeting breezes as the garden lamp's pale light created a halo around her face and hair. In difficult times, following the countless family quarrels, she was like an angel arriving from the far horizon. She would smile, hold back her tears, and whisper her favorite phrase: "Brother, I would give my life for yours. No—don't worry."

I cannot believe that thirty years have elapsed since then. I was the last to leave Qadisiya, after my mother died and my four siblings departed. I fled with my paternal uncle and his wife, and then moved to my maternal aunt's house in the canal area. From there, we headed to Kurdistan in a truck driven by my aunt's son—a subcontractor hauling sand and asphalt for a project that would pave the Baghdad-to-Mosul highway. I didn't care what kind of life I would have subsequently, because a person is more than a life. I'm not referring to the life of this world and the next—the way some of my siblings and loved ones who have become eschatologists would refer to it, including Reem, my wife. She remained religious, even when she handed me a glass of wine and the mezes I love. Never mind. Now I'm in a different time, but back in my original space. That is what's important.

Time no longer concerns me. It's true that I've lost love, youth's vitality, and vigor; but in exchange I've become Amin. The rest of them have changed like chameleons and spread like cancer. Nabiha and I, however, remained resolute—like Qadisiya's earth and the stars in Baghdad's sky. After I left, Nabiha died and became a star that shined in every sky I saw. She was dearer to me than my mother, my wife, the whole world.

I'm in a different era now. Three decades later, and I'm waiting for a man who has a role to play in my history; I've got a lot to accomplish before he arrives. The most important thing is to find the key and the house title. Only Nabiha and I know where the title is.

Grandmother, when you were dying in the little room, before you took your final breath, did you foresee all the things that would happen to us?

I don't know. Your final farewell gasps reached Reem and me like wisps of love. While you were breathing your last breath and Reem was weeping, an overwhelming desire possessed me. I clung to Reem, and my hand hovered near her shoulder. I put my palm on her breast. She smiled slightly and moved away—as if she feared hidden desires. We said nothing as Nabiha shuttled back and forth between the kitchen and the bedroom, offering food to you; your face had started to resemble a child's. Then it went white, and you became a frightening ghost. The sound of your gasps grew ever louder, and you motioned for me to bring my face close to yours. I feared you would drag me along with you, wherever you were heading, then you whispered: "The title to the house is near my breast. Take it . . . take it . . . before your siblings come and wash my body."

Yes . . . I did indeed take the title to the house. Then I made love to Reem as if it were our wedding night. I was ecstatic when I woke the next morning. My grief flowed into a channel I knew how to hide and suppress. My demons and nightmares resurfaced only when I let them, at various times and places.

Yes . . . I managed to repress them, just as I managed to obtain the deed when I was alone with Grandmother. By God, I did not apply any pressure to her neck—as my demons suggested—even though, during our quarrels, which exploded from time to time over the course of thirty years, Reem would angrily say I had.

By God, my hand did not touch Grandmother's mouth. Instead, Reem wiped saliva away with her palm when it started to turn into revolting spume. Neither Reem nor I suffocated her, even though my worst nightmares suggested that I had—especially now, as I pulled the key to our house in Qadisiya from a hiding place I knew very well. It was strategically located at the base of the pomegranate tree, in a site not even the cleverest of surveyors could discover. There was a first hole some distance down, and then a cavity beside it. My hand descended and turned three times till I found the aluminum foil in which the key was wrapped. This was the key to the secret back door that no one knew about or had seen—except for two women, who were in the high heavens, and a third who has accompanied me, but at a safe distance.

I knew they'd changed the lock on the house more than five times during the past thirty years. Thieves belonging to the ruling party seized the house first. Subsequently, thieves from sectarian militias grabbed it. Some of them were crooked investors and realtors; others were creeps from intelligence agencies. The house eventually fell into the hands of a realtor allied with the regime. His boss rewarded him by installing him in the house. Now he wants to return it to its legal owners; he says that he has sincerely repented his sins and wishes to ensure that his life in this transitory physical world ends well.

One p.m. Typical October weather: breezes and dust. In twenty-four hours, I will meet with our contact. I need to leapfrog the thirty years I've been away from my Qadisiya. Where are my friends, neighbors, mother, Nabiha, and Reem? How have I reached this point? What decision will I make tomorrow?

He had offered me a choice: either accept an offer to sell the house to one of his relatives, who will pay me its price in cash as soon as I hand over the deed, or allow him to accompany me as I register the title with the current authorities—if I choose not to sell and prefer to return and settle here.

My God—will I stay in Qadisiya? Will Reem actually return so we can live together—after the experience of flight and migration from country to country devastated us? My mother and Nabiha were gone, and Reem was still vacillating between joining me, waiting for me, or leaving me, so who could I turn to for advice? In our last conversation, Reem said she would come. "Let the house in Qadisiya return to us; then we'll return to each other," she had whispered.

Would we really? I no longer knew anyone here. I didn't know how I made it from the airport to where I sat now, beneath the dusty pomegranate tree, using my small suitcase as a seat. My pack of cigarettes lay on the ground, together with the plastic bag that contained what was left of the sandwiches I had packed and a bottle of water. I glanced around fearfully, as if I were an intruder or a thief. Once the taxi driver turned from Eagles Square to Umm al-Tubul Square, the beating of my heart became louder than his voice. He asked me to show him which turn to take after we passed the barracks of the military police on our left. Were these the same houses? Some seemed to be ruins, where briars and weeds grew to the road. The bas-reliefs there at Eagles Square resembled the scary skeletons I imagine when I call the Tower of Babel to a mind muddled by Iraq's bloody history. The taxi reached the inter-section of the fast public highway that linked the districts of al-Harithiya and Qadisiya.

I gave the driver faulty directions and asked him to turn right, only to realize we were heading toward al-Harithiya. I became lost among its houses, which had not lost their lus-ter, although their walls showed their age. Mature trees and shrubs rose in front of garden gates, and the remaining high garden walls partitioned the area. I lost myself in their aes-thetics, and in the contrast between what we were seeing and memories of visits to a wealthy friend who once lived there. When I realized where we were, I cursed the devil and told the driver to head back toward Qadisiya. We entered the in-tersection where Abu Kamil's store was located—people said he had been wiped out, along with his whole family.

We passed the houses of my Christian and Sabian-Mandaean neighbors: the family of my friend Fakhry, who was a painter and sculptor; Umm Layla's daughters Jamila, Su'ad, and Layla, who were Nabiha's friends. Who lived there now? For some time, Abu Kamil's grandchildren had lived in the house. Then they sold it and moved to Britain and America. Umm Layla's daughters had joined their maternal uncles in Denmark.

Who said time and space are the same? No, my dear! Time is in your head, and space is located in this transitory world. It is born, dies, and propagates. This is my space that produced me, but its time is in my head—like my breathing and pulse. Time is spirit, while space is composed of bodies that pass out of existence—and of others that are born.

At that moment, the vehicle stopped in front of the Qadisiya house, which seemed well on its way to annihilation. To me, it looked like a tomb, with the pomegranate tree serving as the headstone. The vegetation looked like unkempt green and yellow hair. The house's flat roof was filthy. The lemon tree, which was losing its fragrance, was caked with dust.

I paid the driver—the rate had climbed into thousands of dinars. In the old days, I could reach this house from the airport and pay less than ten dinars. All those different eras were raging in my head—except for the current era, which I entered now like a director preparing the stage for the final act of his play, before ordering the curtain to close.

But what happened to me less than an hour after I arrived was the work of another director, whose voice I heard assail me from behind before I saw his face: "Hajji Karim's son? What brings you here, traitor?"

The iron rod struck my head violently, even before I could turn. I fell—astonished, frightened, and nauseous.

The Second Day

This wasn't my first trip back to Baghdad, but it was my first back to Qadisiya. Over the last five years I had come and gone several times, ever since there was a glimmer of hope of recovering the house in Qadisiya. All the same, discussions with cousins on my father's side and mother's side about counter-signing Nabiha's document, which surrendered all rights to me for the house, took place once in Mosul, several times in Kurdistan, and twice in Baghdad's Karadat Maryam District—where the first house my paternal grandfather owned stood.

It has been occupied since then by a succession of uncles and grandchildren. The grandson who owned it now was a civil servant in the government's supreme council. He promised me a happy ending—that I would reclaim the Qadisiya house, sell it, and pocket the money, or retain it for my children and grandchildren, as he put it. During all those visits, I never had the courage to set foot in Qadisiya. It always felt like some ghoul was stalking me. This nightmare tormented me day and night, as I fluctuated between bursts of desire and aversion—unable to ward them off or submit to them. I would get halfway there, approaching the house from al-Rashid Street, passing by Bab al-Sharqi Square, either in a taxi or a car belonging to a cousin. We would cross the al-Jisr al-Muallaq bridge heading to the al-Muhandiseen District, and from there to al-Harithiya. Then I would hop up as if stung by a scorpion and shout: "No! No, brother! Let's turn back, for God's sake!" This place jumped back and forth from my head to my heart, astonishing me.

My cousin, who drove me during these visits, would ask: "So, are you Amin or someone else?" He shepherded me through routine import-export procedures, which have never changed over time, although the faces and goons of the customs officials have. Then he would add: "You're Amin, the nice guy, an astute contractor who doesn't negotiate; a refined man, and a friend to members of the cultural and artistic elite. We call you the family sage; the trustworthy depository of the family's secrets. After Baath rule swept over the land at the end of the 1970s, you were the last to leave. You preserved the family's archives and the Qadisiya house, which symbolizes its continued existence. Everyone realizes that, in your own special way, you are a combatant who defends his convictions and who isn't swayed by a desire for wealth or influence. Does such a person fear the ghost of an old house now? Are you afraid of a family that has vanished into oblivion? Where are those folks, my dear? What do you fear? It's your house and it belongs to you. They occupied it and seized it, but weren't able to claim title to it."

My cousin continued and praised me in a profuse way that I won't deny enjoying. I was moved by his words, but my submission only lasted a few moments. Then my demons attacked once more. "No! No, my dear—I don't want the house in Qadisiya. Let's forget about it. That would be better."

Later, it became obvious to me that I would never forget the house, and that my desire to reclaim it was stronger than my desire to sell it. I knew that the money I received for it would delight my three children, who together with their own spouses and children would anticipate an undreamed-of fortune. They each lived with some amount of public assistance from whichever country was sheltering them: whether it was the UK, Sweden, or Germany. They were alienated from me and accused me of neglecting them. My daughter married and settled in the UK; her brother became a physician in Germany; and my other son shuttled between countries in North and South America, guiding tours and jibber-jabbering in many of the world's languages. Yet the only phrase he knew of his homeland's tongue was, *Hallo, ayni*, meaning, *Hello, darling.*

My children had no idea that their mother ruined our life. I informed all of them of my decision not to apply for asylum in any country, and instead began to travel with Arab contractors on jobs in various Asian and Gulf countries. I refused to relinquish my Iraqi passport and join them. Reem stayed with me for a time, but eventually her maternal instincts won out. So, she left me and joined them.

Never mind. Reem and I enjoyed a special time far from our children and any home base, even though she finally departed to be with them. When she said that at last we could reunite and revive our beautiful time at the conclusion of our lives, I summoned the inner strength to settle all the open questions about the Qadisiya house. We would either recover it and live there, or I would use the money from its sale to buy another house in some other area of Baghdad—one she loved, like the Arasat al-Hindiya District—or we could head off to Kurdistan and settle there. During our last long-distance call, when we were both on the road—she in the East and I in the West—I asked her: "Why can we live together . . . even though Qadisiya once seemed desolate? Why not die together now?" She caught my drift, and was currently on her way to Baghdad.

I found myself repeating all this, as if attempting to memorize a lesson that I had long struggled to master. I was still in the same place beneath the pomegranate tree, trying to regain consciousness. Is this a nightmare? The speaker, the man who called me a traitor, was dragging the iron bar behind him while circling me, after eavesdropping on my conversation with our house. He hadn't said anything for a long time. I hoped to shake off the nightmare completely. But then he started singing in a voice that sounded beautiful to me, even though I hated him furiously:

The pomegranate flew over me, drop by drop,
The lemon came and gave me a helping hand,
I don't want this nice guy,
Take me back to my folk . . .

My God! What's become of me? His voice resounded, re-peating that stanza and bringing tears to my eyes as it awak-ened my chagrined heart. I wanted him to continue singing, and to stop tramping circles around me. I wanted to see his face but couldn't look up. Apparently, I was afraid to unmask him and get clobbered. I still imagined him as one of the phantoms that swarmed my nightmares. What did he want? Why did I tell him all that? What connection did he have to Reem, our children, the Qadisiya house, and me? But I didn't dare ask. Did he have a revolver? Where was the iron bar he had dropped on my head? What else did he want to know?

He surprised me by responding in a husky, hoarse voice: "Nothing. All I want to know is your relationship to the Yar-mouk Hospital fire."

The Yarmouk Hospital fire? The hospital located behind the Qadisiya house? That happened last August—two months before I came back to Baghdad. How was I connected to that fire? Moreover, what relationship did the specter interrogating me have to it? I couldn't even see his face, though he wasn't veiled. He was wearing a kaffiyeh, jeans, and a cotton T-shirt. But I couldn't examine his face or his frame well enough to identify him. His footsteps and limberness suggested he was a young man. He was wearing dirty sneakers that betrayed his social milieu. At least that's what my wife said about foot-wear. So, he was a guy from a rural heritage—from a group that had developed among settled Bedouins. He didn't know that we were the original inhabitants who made Baghdad a highly cultured city. In any case—that didn't matter. He was clenching the iron bar firmly and putting me squarely on the defensive—thirty years after I left this city without ever being accused of belonging to a party, a movement, or an orientation. Every faction assumed I belonged to some other one, even though they all considered me a potential ally, should the need arise. They excused me on the grounds that I was an outsider, whenever they made deals to cooperate and support one another.

He wasn't listening for a response; he began to sing again. My God, how could my captor have such a touching voice?

Oh mother, don't watch over me,
Give up the guarding,
What I want will be,
There isn't another way out . . .

His voice, steps, and body language reminded me of my lifelong friend Fakhry, who was from this neighborhood. Was this his son? After he drained his third glass, Fakhry would always sing:

O you oppressed women,
Go all on foot to al-Kadhim Shrine,
By the head of the Prophet's sons,
Put an end to your grief,
The pomegranate flew over me, drop by drop.

He would repeat that and add: *There's no hope, none . . .*

There was no hope; you were right, my friend. I must wait to learn what ties you and I have to the Yarmouk Hospital disaster. Naturally I've heard about it. I wept like everyone else at the death of eleven infants—all newborns.

"What? Yes, yes, you wept! But didn't lose your child!" the man shouted. "He didn't die. He didn't disintegrate like strands of wool. I looked for his hand. A finger. An eyebrow.

Even for a single hair. Do you know what a hair would've meant? A fingernail? They said the fire consumed everything. It consumed him but spared me and that cheating bitch who awaits my judgment, while I'm in this crazed state that you see!"

He fell silent and I grew increasingly apprehensive. A dead infant; a faithless wife; a fire. What was my relationship to all this? Did I dare ask?

"Brother, may God have mercy on you. I would like to understand, just for my peace of mind," I pleaded.

"What do you want to understand? This is your house. That woman and I spent a year here. We paid more than half a million in rent because they said the place had an un-usual spirit in it that helped women get pregnant," the man explained. "We don't know why people in the neighborhood have passed down this story. They say this has been true for . . . for more than twenty years. They say a virtuous woman—a *hajjiya*—died here. The lease included a special clause if she was slow to conceive, but she became pregnant after only a few months in this house. The *hajjiya* died, and the neighbors handed down the story. I came to Qadisiya about two years ago. I lived with my in-laws in al-Dora. I made up my mind to round up the money to pay for the rental once I heard the story about the house in Qadisiya. The agent gave me a little room, which he said was the most expensive because the *hajjiya*'s spirit had risen from it. For your information, he locked all the other rooms and rented that one—occasionally by the day. My point is . . . he rented the room only to one person or family at a time; he did not use the house as a pen-sion. I was lucky, and my wife became pregnant after we spent a number of months there. Before that, I had been away for an entire year doing military service. When I returned, we sat like you—at night beneath this pomegranate tree, and sang, wept, and prayed. We also went to the shrine of saintly al-Kadhim, and made a vow to him."

He paused for moment, then continued: "What do you want me to tell you? I was overjoyed when I learned she was pregnant. She gave birth in Yarmouk Hospital. Then we returned to al-Dora, assuming the infant would spend three more days in the hospital—they said there had been some complications in the delivery. What's important is that there was a fire, and we lost the boy. But even more significant is that he should have been in the preemie ward, where all the babies survived the fire. After we heard this news, I was sure he was safe. I laughed, as I remembered her saying that the *hajjiya*'s spirit had blessed us, since she became pregnant the first time we had sex. I could not have touched her till after I returned from the army—exactly seven months before she delivered. How come the boy wasn't in the preemie room?"

He started to pace, emotion inciting his memories: "A mistake! She said they had made a mistake! She didn't say *she* had made a mistake. Later, I realized that must have meant she got pregnant while I was away, when she stayed with her family in al-Dora. I had heard talk about a man who came and met her beneath this pomegranate tree. That idea evolved in my mind when a guy told me that he thought I had returned from my trip because he had seen a car parked here—and she had been sitting in the garden with a man who looked like me. But I know no one who should have been visiting my wife. I know too that her family was thinking of marrying her to a relative after she said it was my fault that she hadn't gotten pregnant, even though the doctor confirmed that my sperm were fine but few in number, and that there was no consensus about me being sterile."

He paused once again, gathering the rest of his thoughts: "Fine . . . great! How was my son the only preemie in the room for healthy newborns? Why was there a cover-up? Was that boy my son or a bastard? I don't know. It's almost driven me crazy. Were you the guy who used to visit my wife while I was away? Doubt is killing me. I know you have gray hair. If you weren't the one, find that agent for me; he disappeared. Why did he vanish? Should I believe sperm are blessed in this house; that more than one baby has been conceived here through the years; that every child born here is protected by the *hajjiya*'s spirit, as people say? She still hovers here and appears at times in the garden—beneath this very tree. At times, she reveals herself as an attractive and extremely seductive girl in the garden of some house in Qadisiya, al-Harithiya, or al-Mansour—but only beneath a pomegranate tree."

He sighed, and continued as if to himself: "That would mean the *hajjiya* was responsible for the pregnancies of all those women. Are all those other kids safe, but not my son? My son, who I suspect to be a bastard? What can I do but weep for him?"

I was shocked. What had reduced this young man to this state? As my aversion to him increased, I whispered: "But how does this relate to *me*? You're telling me old wives' tales, brother—like the ones about the *hajjiya* who—"

Threatening me with the iron bar, he growled: "Don't pretend! Either you know the lover with whom she betrayed me, or you work for the realtor who disappeared when I demanded that he return the rent money I paid him in advance for the year, or you belong to the gang that set fire to the hospital and made off with a billion dinars. What was your cut? They say you're a small band. So fork over my rent money with some sugar on top or admit your role in the disaster that the Qadisiya house has caused me. You and the spirit of your wife, the *hajjiya*, have brought me to this sorry state of affairs."

The Third Day

"The *hajjiya*'s spirit, the *hajjiya*'s spirit, the *hajjiya*'s spirit," I muttered, deliriously grasping the key, heading with faltering steps to the rear walk—which led to the opening of the small secret path hidden behind the cactus. No one knew this entry was here. Residents of Qadisiya hated cactus plants, and disliked seeing them. It reminded them that the structures they've built, the American bluegrass plugs they've imported, the flowering dahlias and roses from Basra and Kurdistan they've planted, and the saplings of Baqubah orange trees have never suppressed the cactus. The cactus was self-propagating, either at the entrances to elegant houses or along the streets. This was true at the bus stop, and on dirt paths created by hands or feet pounding the earth—which formed a lane behind the houses in the neighborhood that allowed residents to move back and forth between their kitchen doors and the barrels storing kerosene or refuse, showing their harmony and solidarity with the community. This was especially true for homes like ours and those of Umm Layla, Abu Awf, and the house of the Sabian family—which were the final ring in the chain of houses in our small, quiet neighborhood before Qadisiya grew larger and expanded—before its geography changed and it became Qadisiya 1, Qadisiya 2, and Qadisiya 3. Now I no longer knew which Qadisiya our house was located in. All I knew and wished to know was that I was here in my original space, where I was devising a new time for myself. Would this be another rebirth like those Reem, the children, and I experienced over the last thirty years? Or another form of death, which would afflict me over the next five days?

The man with the iron rod departed. I learned that his name was Qasim, but did not dare ask if he was a son of my lifelong friend Fakhry. He threatened to return tomorrow with members of his gang. He explained that everyone here had a gang—big or small—to protect themselves. He didn't believe I'd come alone—a solitary soul separate from the mangled and bloody age. He said that what mattered was for me not to betray him. He expected me to cooperate; otherwise I should write my will. He didn't care about the punishment he might receive for killing me, because he had, as he pointed out, already lost his son and wife. He shocked me by asking: "Did she really cheat on me?" He spoke as if he were a child interrogating me. "Perhaps I'm being unfair to her. But . . . how could that be? How?"

If I allowed him to stay in the house, even if only for the next six months, would he ask her to return? Perhaps. Perhaps the *hajjiya*'s spirit would bless them, and his wife would become pregnant again. Nothing is too difficult for God the Mighty and Exalted to accomplish.

"Brother, since you submit to God's will, why do you need the *hajjiya*'s spirit?" I asked him.

Did I really ask him that? Did I confront him? Did I curse him? Did I throw him out? I don't actually know, because I still felt dazed. I opened the door and experienced a quick flashback—like in a film—of the man with the iron bar, but instead I was confronted by another surprise.

The Fourth Day

My respectable daughter said I was crazy. She accused me of being a victim of my genes. Since the previous night, since the moment I opened the secret door to the pantry off the Qadisiya house's kitchen, I had experienced a series of mishaps and surprises. I didn't know if these were manifestations of the insanity my daughter attributed to me, or whether my misadventures were responsible for my incredible discovery.

The Yarmouk Hospital man departed, leaving behind the iron bar as his calling card. *Yes.* I would tell Reem and my daughter that. I would keep it to show them that I wasn't demented or hanging out with my old friend Majid—that crazy artist who restored art's genuine dignity to Baghdad's squares, museums, and exhibitions. No one believed that a contractor like me could be a friend to an artist like him. *Yes, daughter, believe it.* In fact, I acted as his trusted agent in deals with companies that furnished materials he used for the monuments and statues that adorned our city. I smoothed the way for him with small contractors who pocketed modest sums surreptitiously from major contractors, heads of government agencies, and their goons who worked for the government's whales.

Never mind. These were all sordid tales, and the time for them had passed, although my daughter wanted to revive it. "Against your will and that of your cronies!" she screamed.

How could her scream reach me in this house in Qadisiya, when she was at the far edge of another continent? Sitting in Hyde Park in London, she clutched her marvelous smartphone and her face shook on my own phone, which she wanted me to upgrade. "You need to download Skype and Viber," she declared, insisting that I only cared about updating my wardrobe.

She didn't believe me when I told her about the iron-bar man. "By God, daughter, I'm not lying!"

She also denied that this happened: When I entered the house the day before, I had expected to find it empty of everything but our scents and memories. But then laughter began to ring out beneath the stairs leading to the upper floor. That happened the moment I left the guest bath to the right of the kitchen door to the garden. The Yarmouk Hospital man left me not a moment too soon. I almost wet my pants as I hurried there once he left, thanking God that I hadn't disgraced myself. All the same, I was totally unprepared for the surprise that distracted me from my most essential task: to call Reem and tell her how it felt to enter the Qadisiya house after all these years away. But what feeling should I discuss, given what happened next? The sound of laughter started softly and then grew louder. Footsteps approached and hands grasped me, as if wanting to strangle me. A light flashed on some moments later, but failed to reassure me. Yes, I was fine. It was Majid, Ahmad, and Fakhry—childhood friends from our neighborhood and companions of my glory days, days when we announced our mutual loyalty—cursing any separation, flight, or travel abroad.

"The jackal's got you! We've caught you, you traitor!" Fakhry squealed. "Once the taxi dropped you off here, we slipped in behind you. Majid contacted us when he learned you were coming. Then we saw you had an important meeting beneath the pomegranate tree. We remembered the secret entrance from when we were kids. So we crept through it and got inside. Come on! Don't waste your time or ours—let's go."

"Where are we going?" I asked as I tried to cling to whatever wits I had left.

"Open the new app and see."

"What app? Which one?"

"Here! Here on your phone," Fakhry said.

I couldn't believe this hick had a cell phone. He'd always been a bumpkin, from teenager to party leader to submissive secretary for some high-ranking bureaucrat in any regime—with a preference for floral shirts and pistachio-green trousers.

The only thing that had changed about him was the white shag rug on his head.

"What a loss you are!" Ahmad crowed next. "Even though you have white hair, you haven't repented, you bastard!"

Ahmad wouldn't leave me alone. His cousin, who was also from our neighborhood, had opened a restaurant in the al-Mansour District. From life as a pathetic English teacher in our Qadisiya during the 1970s to that of a prince, God's will be done. Now, he was in his seventies.

"He deserves a statue," I told Majid, who had remained silent throughout the ambush.

Majid understood how to communicate silently with me in a language that only the two of us recognized, due to our contracting partnership right before I left Baghdad. All the same . . . never mind. None of this related to Reem or my daughter. What happened after our tempestuous surprise gathering was no one's business but my own, apparently, because my daughter ignored my suggestion to try the app we opened and linked to, and Reem failed to reply to my attempts to contact her, even though she had promised to respond.

"What can I say, daughter? I swear by you and Nabiha. See for yourself. Open your app and look with me: Fakhry carries a bottle of arak, Majid holds a hand over his scalp to conceal his bald head, and Ahmad swings a plastic bag filled with cherries and grapes. We rush to Umm Layla's house, cross the lane by the Tel Kaif family house, reach the main road—no, not the main highway opposite the military police headquarters. It's the Road of Water Blockage. There's Majid's car, his beat-up car with the number ten, because over the past thirty years he has bought ten cars, insisting on this old model for half a lifetime, as you know. He says it looks good. What matters is that we climbed into it and immediately shot off to our lair on Abu Nuwas Street. What I'm telling you is that Baghdad is coming back. Yes! We've resumed the necessary insanity. Yes, yes, by God. We removed our suits and stripped to T-shirts and shorts—just like the old days. Exactly like the old days. But what used to be a two-hour dip in the waters of the Tigris lasted only two minutes. I twisted my leg but swallowed my pain for fear that they would make fun of me. But I discovered that Majid had peed on himself, Ahmad's shorts fell off, and Fakhry screeched like a woman. You won't believe what I'm saying, but Abu Nuwas Street is still solid, daughter. You see the poet's statue in the distance. Apparently, they only chopped off his head. The pedestal is still there, and the river is still beautiful. The riverbank is dirty, but the lush grass is growing. I watched it grow! Ajaj Café still has chairs scattered along the bank. Next to them is the fire pit for grilling *masgouf*. What am I saying? I'm sure Reem will agree to return. As for you—may God bless you! Are you punishing me or yourself for our estrangement?"

The Fifth Day

After I returned from the outing to Abu Nuwas Street, I was alone and abandoned. The three musketeers scattered after the last sip of arak and the last chickpea. I found myself inside the Qadisiya house—in the dark, because the power had been turned off. My daughter said that she knew the area, Baghdad, and our homeland better than I did. She contacted me this morning to check on me after our call was cut short yesterday. Her encouragement for me, though, was mainly criticism and reproof.

I could only huff at her: "Enough blame already! What do you know about this area? You were young then. Young! You still are. You didn't grow up here, unlike me and your aunts. You grew up in phony capital cities devoid of any spirit. They were civilized but lacked heart. Now you want to judge me for feeling homesick, weak, and full of yearning? Have I no right to recover my soul? Recover your mother? Recover our life together? What app were you talking about when I showed you the picture of us at the Tigris and Abu Nuwas? Do you remember the Zawra'a Garden, our loved ones, and the days of our prime? How about Uncle Majid and the way you slapped his cheek when he carried you around like a doll? Have you forgotten Uncle Ahmad, who taught you how to sing the birthday song in English with a proper accent, after all of us had been butchering the pronunciation? Have you forgotten Uncle Fakhry? You ask: *Who's Uncle Fakhry?*"

I reminded her of the dishes he made so well—like *pacha*, kebab, and dolma. "He's the person who helped your Uncle Ahmad open a restaurant in al-Mansour. Come see al-Mansour; its restaurants are a million times better than yours in Oxford. Have you forgotten him? Have you forgotten how we laughed at him?"

"Fakhry, the hick?" she asked.

She remembered me telling her that he would never be more than a follower or a gofer for important people. But she accused me of putting him down: "Papa, don't forget you all mocked him while asking him to help you get clearances and approvals from government offices. That's what you and your friends are like, Papa. You all see only what you care to see."

"How about you, Miss Daughter?" I inquired. "What do you see in your app that you want me to download?"

"Yes, Papa, I'm looking at Qadisiya, al-Mansour, and al-Ma'mun now!" she professed angrily, in a way that reminded me of Nabiha and her mother. "Have a look yourself. You can see all of these from afar via virtual reality. I want you to see my school, Papa—the al-Hussari School that I attended daily. Like you, I want to smell it, sense it, touch it. I want to see my grandmother take me there. She holds my hand and leads me from the lane of the Tel Kaif family to the lane of the Armenian family, and then to the Kurdish family from Salah al-Din. I play with girls in front of the gardens of those houses. We use chalk to draw squares and play hopscotch. Look, Papa. By God, where's the school? Where are the houses? Look at all the dirt. See all the trash. See all the cacti. See the dust. This is all very clear in my virtual reality app. I see skeletons, Papa. Where are the clean streets? Where's the fragrance of night musk and jasmine? Please focus your phone's camera on the sludge, the potholes in the streets, the aridity, and the reek of garbage that smells to high heavens and reaches us even here. Yes, Papa—here in Hyde Park, in London."

I opened my mouth to reply to my daughter, to prevent her from exaggerating, to restrain her. But she disappeared before I could clear my throat. She faded away like the light on my phone.

Another voice called me from the little room just then: "Amin! Amin! Where's the deed to the house? Where has it gone? Has it flown away?"

The Sixth Day

The color white doesn't stand for death, contrary to what Majid says—or for a good heart. Those are myths, my friend. White stands for your childhood memories: a soft, colorless gelatin. Black isn't for mourning or consolation. It doesn't represent a slap or an abaya. It's not night or the devil. Instead, it's muddled and impudent. White is a dot of light in a painting. Black is the frame protecting it. White is unrestrained history—self-existent, swimming in God's own realm. Black is a monument—a grim chunk of stone limited by measured edges and borders. Without those, it wouldn't be possible to discover the path to glorifying God and the divine realm.

Majid left me fluctuating between white and black, and disappeared with the other neighborhood boys—Ahmad and Fakhry. I was left alone in the Qadisiya house. White stands for me staying in Qadisiya and black stands for my leaving it. Soon, I would see white as a representation of my freedom far away, and black as my suffocation here.

The night of my arrival passed, and so did the night of the man with the iron bar, the night of Abu Nuwas, and my daughter's night. Now, it was the black-and-white night, and it pulled me to the little room. The deed. To the *hajjiya*. The *hajjiya*! What remained of her in my head, heart, or memory? By God, I wished I knew. I'd become entirely like the air, a void. My heart was not merely a weeping child's, it did nothing but weep. Where was my heart? What memory did I have left? Where was my spirit in time, and my steps through space? What space? The little room: the pallet was spread on the floor there. The walls were bare except for part of a saying attributed to the Prophet or Imam Ali.

"Ali," the *hajjiya* whispered, while drawing her last breaths.

As if to correct her, Reem repeated: "Lord! Lord!"

Nabiha was reciting the Throne Verse over Grandmother's head. On the telephone now, Reem's voice reminded me of all that. I sat in the little room—saw, heard, and sensed—conscious only of those moments, of the *hajjiya*'s heavy breathing, and of desire's frenzy raging inside me and infecting Reem.

I whispered to Reem over the phone: "I want you."

"We're grown up now," she pointed out. "Will you always say that, dear?"

"The heart never ages—longing is the only thing that grows more youthful as it matures," I answered.

She laughed, and the sound drowned out the *hajjiya*'s wheezing. "Your children don't want to return," she told me.

"How about you?" I asked.

As if she were one of our kids and not their mother, she replied: "Me? Me?"

Evidently my son had grabbed the phone, because I heard his voice: "When are you going to grow up, Papa? We never knew the house in Qadisiya, your grandmother, or anything like that. We've heard about the sweat and blood you put into building that house, and they must receive their due now. But you also know that even millions of Iraqi dinars won't buy a single room in the most insignificant neighborhood in Europe. You should also understand that we're entitled to the proceeds from the sale of the house—my sister, brother, mother, and me . . . as well as you, of course."

"I don't want anything. Sitting here in my grandmother's little room means more to me than all those millions," I admitted to him. "Ultimately, I'll make my decision without reference to any external factors. Yes, without reference to you, your mother, and your brother. None of you have any ties to the Qadisiya house—that's true—except for your mother and sister, who are older, of course. You and your brother, though, are the white and the black."

"What does that mean, Papa?"

"Nothing. You wouldn't understand because you grew up in vacuums: without colors, blocks of material, or frames," I replied.

"Don't be angry, Papa. I think you should see a psychiatrist," he said. "I'm afraid you're entering the early stages of dementia."

What could I say to that? At that very moment, a friendly hand reached out to pat my shoulder as I turned off the phone—a sweet but feeble smile reassured me. A voice said to me: "Amin, shame on you! Didn't we agree you'd meet me at the airport?"

Reem went upstairs after voicing her opinion about the house: "It's still beautiful, though dusty and empty."

I gathered from her slow steps that she was sleepy. I didn't stare at her features, which were winsome and refreshing; the affectionate gaze of her wide eyes; or the halo of her figure, which she believed had changed.

"I was afraid you wouldn't recognize me," she confessed.

She wanted to remind me of all the years we were separated, but I placed my finger on her mouth. She understood that words no longer served any purpose, and that what counted now was our remaining time together.

Reem went upstairs to let me weep with all the happiness of a loving heart. She left me in the little room. My grand-mother was stretched out there. Clean and calm. Her child-like face smiled radiantly at Nabiha, who whispered from the kitchen that she would bring some delicious soup momentarily. Then Nabiha emerged gracefully; her face, which was smiling—eyes, cheeks, and chin—reminded me of the Egyptian actress Shadia. Her dishdasha was flowing, and her hair, always care-fully groomed, gleamed immaculately, scented with musk. In a whisper, she asked me whether Reem and I had made up. She didn't want Grandmother to hear our conversation, for fear it would upset her. I told her, "We're not quarreling—just playacting."

"Too much playacting leads to arguments and tears," she advised me with a laugh.

I nodded my head reassuringly, and left her with Grand-mother while I slipped to the kitchen, and from there to the back hall to smoke a cigarette. "By God, relaxation!" I sighed.

Reem was asleep in our room upstairs. Nabiha was with Grandmother in the little room. This was how things were in the last years, after my mother died and my brothers left to marry or join the military service. Then came the exodus at the end of the 1970s, and the even more terrifying flight at the end of the 1980s. That was followed by the mass migra-tion of the 1990s. *Yes, yes, yes.* Thirty years elapsed before the circle was retraced and we returned to the essence—to my grandmother.

How beautiful she was, sleeping! Like a fairy tale. Majid should have painted her picture when she woke. He said he'd come back tomorrow to learn what I'd decided: to stay on here, move somewhere else in Baghdad, or leave the country. All the same, he was convinced the three options were equiv-alent. When Reem awoke, we'd join Nabiha and our daughter in the cottage next to the Qadisiya house. Nabiha was waiting for me now. *I'm coming . . . I'm coming . . .*

I dozed off beside my grandmother. I woke up when her cold hand thrust the title of the house into my hand. I saw my hand over her mouth and her hand with the deed over my chest. Then Reem came closer and held my hand. She whispered that she wanted to wipe the saliva from my grandmother's mouth; the gasps were coming faster and louder. She was suffering, suffocating on her own breath, which had not yet ceased. We should've been compassionate and helped her. We moved closer. Reem's hand was over her mouth, and mine was on Reem's. At that very moment, my grandmother released her final breath.

Reem and I were in our cool, comfortable bed on the roof terrace. The weather was cold. *Cold.* I told Reem we might as well be in October, not flaming August. Baghdad's dawn breezes stirred desires.

"You're being silly," she said.

We closed our eyes. The roof of the Qadisiya house was empty. The terrace was damp and clean. Our pallet was spread there—just like it had been when our family lived here. Bedspread, pillowcases, and blankets were freshly laundered and fragrant. I lay down like a child and clasped Reem's hand.

"Grandmother is fine," I whispered. "She's sleeping now, and Nabiha's in the cottage. No one needs us. Our sons are also asleep in their homes. What more could we ask for than this lovely night with the North Star and the rustling of trees, here in Qadisiya? Oh, what were you saying?"

I waited for Reem's reply, but she didn't speak.

"Oh, darling, are you sleeping?" I didn't want to open my eyes to see if she had dozed off. I didn't want her to fall asleep. I waited for her to lazily open her eyes, so the tears I love would flow. I awaited a teasing whisper: *I love you if only to spite you.*

I dozed off to the rhythm of my anticipation—of what I wanted to hear and see. All I wanted was to hear and see. Who said a person who sees differs from one who hears? That's nonsense! Not because it's wrong, but because whoever said it didn't know what we heard in the stillness.

The Seventh Day

I was awakened by heavy pounding on the doors, which reverberated throughout the house. "I'm coming!" I feared I'd trip on the steps and fall from the roof. But I found myself in my grandmother's room. Perhaps I came down during the night

to check on her. Feeling drowsy, I dozed off again. The pounding grew louder and more powerful, but even though my body
was light it didn't seem able to move any faster. I tried to make
my way to the main door, which was in the living room. Then
I realized that the pounding was growing more frantic and
louder at the back door. But that's the secret one. No one
knew about that door, except . . . except for . . . ?

Anyone who knew about it would know how to shove
the fake bolt aside and open the door. So what was all the
banging about? Why were people pounding? Then, I decided
the pounding was coming from elsewhere—perhaps from the
neighbor's house or the metal garden gate. Where was my loyal
dog Tushka? My German shepherd had become my guard and
companion; he drank with me and jumped up at Reem men-
acingly; he even jumped at our young kids if they pretended
to attack me. He was the only one who acknowledged me as
his master, lord, and commander. Why hadn't he started to
bark the way he always did when he sensed an approaching
stranger? The banging intensified. Reem didn't come down
from the roof terrace to fix us breakfast and tea, or coffee for
herself. Perhaps she had gone to Bahiya's cottage, where they
were exchanging complaints about their husbands—laughing
at us and our sorry conditions. Perhaps she was . . . but the
house had been spruced up. She had tidied it yesterday and
hung the paintings we loved and photos of our children. The
aromas from our celebratory dinner had dissipated. Where
was she? Why didn't she open the door? She was faster than
me when dealing with the house, our children, and guests.
Oh, praise God. The knocking finally ceased. Perhaps the
stranger was at the wrong house. Perhaps neighborhood boys
were teasing us. Perhaps Tushka was angry with me. I didn't
know. I felt tired.

My God! The morning of the final day had arrived with a mysterious drumming followed by a profound silence.

I went out to the garden; I was back at zero, nil. The pomegranate tree was the only living witness. The weeds that reared their heads and covered both gardens had overpowered the squares of American grass. A grape trellis shaded the smaller garden, which wrapped around the house's living room. The larger garden, which extended to the rear and bordered the entry walk leading to the stairs to the roof and the main front door, was carpeted in dust that reeked of rot and sad little lemon trees. The last mint stalks had dried out and stiffened, and the yellowing leaves were all that remained of the tomato and radish plants.

The hen coop had become a depot for castoffs from the old house, and for all the tools and games my siblings and children used—before escape and displacement had carried them away. It didn't matter. All this could be sorted out and fixed up. Reem and I would figure this out when she awoke and came down to prepare breakfast. She would finish cleaning the house and suggest a plan to save the garden. At each stage of our struggles she had done that. I knew she'd become a religious woman; she was the one who'd told me I wouldn't recognize her now. She wouldn't fix mezes for me anymore, because she'd convinced herself that alcohol, which was often served with mezes, was haram, forbidden. She had asked me to return to the Great God, as she had done. I'd told her that I was a firmer believer than anyone else—including all my siblings and children—with her at the head of the line. I'd told her that God was my friend, and that I sat with Him every night. We would converse and exchange thoughts and opinions. I didn't want to hear her reply. "I take refuge with God and ask your Lord's forgiveness," I would avow. Our differences on this point would remain a red line that neither of us should cross. As for my children—I was capable of convincing them to return to God or remain neutral.

I walked around the empty garden. I waited for Reem to come down from the roof terrace or to leave my grandmother's room. I paused by the alcove which held the bath's cistern. In that space, Tushka had passed—three days after a car struck him. He spent those three days in the veterinarian's clinic and in my arms; I was his constant companion. Then he withdrew to die. We spent a week searching for him in the neighborhood's streets and gardens. We observed no trace, scent, bark, or panting to lead us to him. Finally, we found him in this alcove: rigid, silent, and proud.

"Farewell to you, my sincere friend Tushka." I recited the Fatiha in his memory and returned inside. I wanted to reassure myself about my grandmother and see what Reem was doing. She was sleeping later than usual.

Once I was back inside and had closed the secret door, the banging grew loud again. Someone was pounding on the front door; and on the back door; and on the windows too. There was pounding on the roof. Pounding from Nabiha's cottage. Pounding from Grandmother's room. I felt paralyzed. I was incapable of responding to any knocking. I didn't even know which door to answer. Which pounding should I ignore and forget? Then another stimulus surprised me: my local phone with the Baghdad SIM card started ringing. My international cell phone, which I used yesterday to converse with Reem and our children, started ringing too. I answered the Baghdad one.

The Yarmouk Hospital man asked: "Have you decided?"

Will we hang on to the house or surrender it?

The lawyer asked me: "My dear, have you made up your

mind? Will you sell the property or register the deed in your own name?"

Abu Yasser cut in: "I would sacrifice my life for you, my friend. You've raised your children and settled abroad. But I have no alternative. I must stay here. The only shelter for me and my son and daughters is your Qadisiya house. You know that Daesh devastated my son, and the American shelling crippled my daughter, and my third child is undergoing chemotherapy for cancer caused by napalm. What can I say, my dear? Accept this price; the lawyer said you had agreed. I will consider this a favor I will never forget, and a boon I will carry with me to the end of days. You won't lack for dinars. Praise God! May your life and children rest secure in countries that respect human rights. This time is our fate, where we live like dogs off scraps from the regime's thieves, and have to deal with the religious militias and cartels. Thank you, Master. I kiss your hand and head, even your feet. You should always consider the Qadisiya house to be yours. Your house, by God! Whenever you want to visit or stay here. It will remain your house. It will bear your name and that of the kind *hajjiya*. Man, had it not been for her spirit, which continues to hover overhead, none of us would still be here today, and we would have no children or grandchildren. By the grace of God, thanks in advance."

The Eighth Day

This day had not arrived. The banging and pounding continued. My children expected to receive the proceeds from the sale of the Qadisiya house. The man with the iron bar was waiting for another chance to rent the house and live here so his cheating wife would conceive. Abu Atfa was waiting to buy the house and gather his family, which had been devastated by the exodus, expulsion, and the wars waged by sectarian factions, goons, and the regime.

The attorney was still awaiting my decision. I was searching for the deed, which Reem and I hid in the house—in a secret location. But I hadn't yet found it. I couldn't find it anywhere. By God, where was it? I shouted to Reem to come help me search for it. I feared if I waited any longer, I'd be too late. The deed and the opportunity would slip from my hands.

Then I remembered that the hiding place was in the *hajjiya*'s room—Grandmother's. I remembered that it was hidden behind the little door. I remembered the day we discovered the aperture and entered it, finding ourselves in a cellar. Yes, there was a tunnel that led to the garden. All the houses of the era were outfitted with tunnels to protect their residents. Sabians, Kurds, Shias, Sunnis, and the Christians all escaped through these tunnels, as did the Communists, key Arabs, and treasonous intelligence agents.

We hid the deed in a small crevice in the tunnel. But where was it? I couldn't find it. Again, I shouted for Reem to come help me. But I only heard the echo of my own voice. I was afraid of waiting and wasting time. I tried again and again. I feared I had forever lost the spot and thus the title. Stretching out my hand, I felt only the chill that flowed in from the tunnel. Had I slipped? I extended my hand ahead of me. The cold became more bitter and the darkness more intense. I dragged myself farther. I raced to the kitchen, to the garden, to the chicken coop with its useless old tools. I returned with the hammer. I slammed it down on the frame of the aperture. I widened it. I pushed my head and arm through and pounded and dug some more until the hole was widened further. Now it was big enough for me. I found myself inside the tunnel, where I was surrounded by darkness and the cold.

My heart was empty—a void. I proceeded cautiously. After a few steps, I bumped into a wooden panel that blocked the end of the tunnel. I lifted the panel out of the way and saw a hole. I pushed the dirt away with my head and hands. Then my fingers struck a root. I looked up to see the pomegranate tree shading me.

Translated from Arabic by William M. Hutchins

THE FEAR OF IRAQI INTELLIGENCE

BY HAYET RAIES

al-Waziriya

L ife in Baghdad in the late 1970s and early 1980s was massively politicized, and there was no neutrality, not even in romantic relationships or in the most intimate situations. During that time, I was a student in Baghdad at the Faculty of Arts, located in the neighborhood of al-Waziriya.

Everything functioned for the political benefit of the Baath Party. The atmosphere was laden with a kind of phobia known only under autocratic regimes, which I might call Iraqi-security-apparatus phobia. Everyone feared everyone; everyone informed on everyone; everyone suspected everyone; everyone mistrusted everyone; everyone spied on everyone else. Friends wrote reports on friends, and brothers betrayed brothers. Wives informed on husbands and accused them of terrible political crimes if they cheated with other women. We used to hear legendary stories about the Iraqi security apparatus and its penetration into people's lives.

One day, our friend Nuha entered our room at the main university dormitory in a state of panic. Room 51—I will never forget the many dramas we saw in that room. I lived with Syrian Sabah, Lebanese Nuha, and Palestinian Nawal. Nuha grabbed Sabah and me by the hands and took us out to the balcony, where she told us in whispers that some guys at the Faculty had warned her about our rooms being under surveillance. Our rooms contained listening equipment and wires—hidden with masterful secrecy, inside the walls, between the wood of the beds and our wardrobes. The surveillance was directly connected to the General Intelligence Center, and Russian engineers had designed the equipment when the dorm was built.

We were stricken with anxiety and started to reexamine what we had said, whether we had uttered words about the Baath Party, or criticized a position, or discussed the behavior of politicians and leaders, or spoken ill of the Saddam Hussein regime and his entourage, or wronged Hussein personally. We entered a state of hysterical madness, between laughter and fear, between seriousness and fun. Sabah in particular was the most sensitive of us on this subject. She belonged to a Syrian family that lived in Kuwait. Her family had fled from Syria because of a death sentence issued by the military court against her brother Jihad.

Sabah dragged her heavy bed to the spacious balcony to sleep there, attempting to escape the bugged room. I had tried to dissuade her, telling her calmly: "Maybe this story isn't true; it could be the result of the exaggerations and security phobia that have become a collective madness."

Nuha, who was known for her sharp tongue and inability to keep secrets, egged Sabah on, mocking her: "Maybe the bed itself is stuffed with listening wires? You must watch your words and not repeat more than once, *Saddam Hussein rules the country with iron and fire*, because here, the walls have ears, as they say."

The joke that the bed was bugged was enough for Sabah to lose her temper, and she screamed, hysterically: "Is it reasonable to expect our dreams to be monitored to this extent?!"

Most of our friends were sincere young people at the

Faculty—they all warned us more than once about talking politics in the dorms and elsewhere, because there were infiltrators among the girls living there. Baathists, Iraqi, and non-Iraqi spies were charged with recruiting women in the dorms, and were tasked with monitoring specific students. We even discovered some of the infiltrators, which caused huge quarrels between us.

I recalled the report written by Khuddouj—a female Lebanese Baathist responsible for recruiting newly arrived students, especially those from South Lebanon—against a girl from her own country—her name was Rawiya—a left-wing Beiruti who belittled, secretly and publicly, the Baath Party's principal slogan, *One Arab Nation with an Eternal Mission*. "If there is one Arab nation, why then are relations severed between the neighboring sister states Syria and Iraq? Both countries are ruled by the same party, the Baath!" Rawiya would exclaim.

Of course, this often led to arguments. And the charges were ready: betraying the nation and betraying the party—the party that sheltered us and provided us with free education and accommodation (even though several of us did not enter the Faculty via the Baath Party).

What really hurt me was how the Baath used the settling of personal scores between students (both male and female) for their own advantage. We were cautious in our romantic relationships with young Baathist men, fearing they would turn on us or harm us if the romance went sour, or if there was a change of heart.

Da'ad, a Palestinian Baathist and our neighbor in room 52, joined in these heated debates: "Girls! You shouldn't do that. You are giving the party a bad image and slandering its reputation. To the Baath high morals! Yes, the party teaches us to have principles and high morals!"

The phrase, *To the Baath high morals*, appealed to me. I would agree with Da'ad, joking: "Of course, of course, the Baath has high morals, as love has high morals—exactly."

I was trying to reduce the severity of the problem.

Sabah volunteered to prepare pots of tea, which had seemingly magical powers in reconciling us. We would drink the tea, and then Sabah would take a pack of Kents out of her handbag and invite us to smoke. As we smoked, the cigarettes would absorb all the tension from the room. And we would end all disputes with: "We can't fight like this. After all, here we are: students, Arab women, immigrants who have only each other. We came here to study, not to take sides." But such declarations did not much please Lebanese Khuddouj. We winked at one another with the recklessness of children, blaming "global imperialism" that worked to disunite and divide us, while Iraq strived to unify the Arab world. We had to be content with unity whether we belonged to the party or not.

On winter nights, we would often hear gunshots right before bedtime, and we would rush wildly to the balcony—but we would only find pitch darkness, the night concealing gloomy, damned Iraq. In the morning, we would hear Iraqis whispering about the disappearance of some people after their conversations were overheard.

Sabah persisted in sleeping on the balcony. Later, Nuha joined her.

"If I were in your place, I'd marry that Iraqi lieutenant Najim Abbas. He's in love with you," Nuha teased Sabah. "So that way, we'd be safe from suspicion. Especially since we're so far from our families and there's no one here to protect us." Then, sarcastically, she added: "Who refuses an offer of marriage from an Iraqi officer?"

"You go and marry him!" Sabah said, stretching out on her bed. "You want me to marry an officer to protect your life, while I'm tied to him for the rest of my life? What happens if we get in a fight and he goes and files secret reports against me, or maybe against my family? Who knows what he might do to me physically . . . I'd be a madwoman to trust a Baathist military officer!"

"If you don't like him, why did you go out with him before?" Nuha asked.

"Well, just be happy I haven't gone out with him since that day," Sabah replied, rolling her eyes. "You all know that I returned frightened to death the day he invited me out to the corniche by the Tigris, then surprised me by taking his pistol out of the car's glove box. I was trembling, imagining him pointing the gun at me. I had never seen a weapon before, except on TV. He told me that he wanted to take me on an *excursion!* How much I wished then that I was with an uncomplicated young man, walking along the riverbank safely, like the lovers enjoying themselves on Abu Nuwas Street."

We knew that Sabah was engaged to her cousin Mohammad—but that was before she came to Iraq, and she was still very uncertain about marrying him. She had told us that Mohammad had cut short his studies and had not passed beyond the elementary level. Instead he went to work with his father and became rich. He was madly in love with Sabah, and would go crazy if he saw her with another man. Yet Sabah often turned against him, usually when she came into contact with the young men at the Faculty, for they made the intellectual gulf between them ever clearer to her.

Sabah was pretty and flamboyant, with long black hair that flowed past her shoulders. She had a soft, likable nature and good humor, as well as a simple elegance. Sabah's personability especially aroused the jealousy of wealthy Nuha, who received expensive yet tasteless dresses from her family.

Mohammad lived with his family in Kuwait, and often traveled back and forth to Iraq in his black Mercedes. He would come laden with presents for all of us; he would show up at the dorm with crates of fruit, cans of soda, Kit Kat bars, and he never forgot his chain-smoking fiancée's Kents. Her affliction had spread to the rest of us. We all eagerly awaited the Kents and smoked them greedily, particularly when we gathered on the spacious balcony for soirées around the dinner table. We used to compare Mohammad and Najim; we gossiped about the couples on campus—who broke up, who got angry, who was reconciled. I persuaded Sabah to tell me the latest news about Faris—her relative and fellow countryman—specifically about the day he visited her at the Faculty of Science. It was all about the smallest details: Who did he sit with and who did he talk to? What was the reason for the visit? Why did he talk to her? Did they mention me? She knew my weak points and exactly where to strike. She pressed and did not let up . . . and I delighted in it . . . That was our favorite entertainment and perhaps the basis for our friendship. Sabah presented to me the idea of a relationship with her relative, and I fell more and more in love with him. Nawal would pick up on Sabah's theatrics and try to stop her, but she would ignore her. I did not care, because when you love someone, you will believe anything about them. As we say in Tunisia, the most important thing is to have a nice conversation, smoke incessantly, drink delicious tea, enjoy hanging out, chat on the balcony, and have promising dreams when we sleep. After all, is love not the most beautiful illusion we experience?

Sabah was not happy with Mohammad, except when he would show up for a few days, pampering us and taking us to the best restaurants. We stayed up until morning at clubs like Baghdad Nights and Scheherazade Nights, and Faris was invited to join us for my sake. Mohammad also invited Nawal and Nuha, because they too were residents of Kuwait, part of the Lebanese, Syrian, and Palestinian migration there.

Once Mohammad returned to Kuwait and Sabah went back to the environment of the Faculty and its students, she would call her mother and tell her that she was having difficulties with her prearranged engagement to Mohammad.

Sabah had recently told her mother the story of her and Lieutenant Najim Abbas—he wanted to marry her and was determined to visit her family in Kuwait—but her mother only reluctantly agreed to speak on the phone, after his great persistence. Her mother wanted to understand Najim's side of the story, without showing that she actually supported him instead of her nephew Mohammad. They spoke several times. Najim asked her to call if she wanted further reassurances or needed anything from Baghdad.

One night, for a change of scenery, I proposed that we go out and spend the evening at the Tigris corniche gardens on Abu Nuwas Street, to celebrate finishing our final exams. Sabah agreed, provided we did not stay out late. We all laughed and told her that we understood, that we would leave a message for him with the night supervisor; we all knew that Mohammad was about to arrive in Baghdad via Basra—so we would tell him to join us on the corniche.

We yearned for the Tigris; the river cleansed restless spirits simply by crossing it, breathing its air, sitting on its banks; it touched Abu Nuwas Street, the place that first embraced our exile when we arrived in Baghdad.

That night, when we reached the corniche, Sabah, Nuha,

Nawal, Khuddouj, Da'ad, and I began to search for other young people from our cohort, who usually gathered on the riverbank. Young Tunisians, Moroccans, Syrians, Lebanese, Egyptians, Palestinians, and Sudanese flooded the Tigris corniche every night in a mosaic found only in Iraq—attracting both students and Arab intellectuals. We fled our dorm for these gatherings, escaping from the severity of the June heat to the fresh breezes of the riverbank. For those who were still studying or who had not yet finished their exams, the corniche was furnished with tables, chairs, and lamps.

As for me, I was looking for Faris, even though I had not made plans with him. I had not seen him in four days, during which time he had been absent from the Faculty and his party activities. My longing to see him had intensified, but I relied on luck and my intuition, which told me I would meet him that night. I conjured visions of a date with him in the riverside gardens. Perhaps the heat would drive him at last from his house in al-Waziriya to our dorm, to the breezes of the banks of the Tigris, which might help him finish his master's thesis. He was studying English literature, with a focus on Shakespeare.

The Tigris gardens themselves were a theater, filled with stories, soirées, lovers, suffering, and desires. The Tigris nights were replete with love, intimacy, pleasure, joy, good fortune, fun, and fights . . . overflowing with waves of people. The true observer of the pulse and clamor of Baghdad's nights, during celebrations to mark festivals and holidays, was the statue of Abu Nuwas standing guard over it all. He gazed from afar with a contented eye at the crowds gushing with life, with his famous cup in hand, bursting with passion, drinking in all the pleasures of the earth in its great variety—an eternal, immortal poet. Turkish artist Ismael Fattah had designed the statue in 1972. It aroused your appetite for love, intimacy, and desire—as life assaulted you unexpectedly—and you hoped it would seize you and never let go.

The riverbank was also full of foreign tourists, who were particularly fond of such excursions. The boats bobbed on the surface of the water, pulsing with life under the light of the moon, staying up late with us. I dreamed of being swept away on a moonlit trip by Faris . . . I secretly cursed all his party meetings and political activities, which always took him away from me. As his comrades would joke: *Faris is married to the Baath Party.*

Large television screens were erected on the riverbank; Iraqi families gathered around on wooden benches or the sand to follow the episodes of Arab soap operas, as if they were watching in their own homes. We enjoyed them too; they relieved our homesickness and reminded us of our families.

We often encountered our professors here, as well as poets, journalists, politicians, and intellectuals. The conversations drew people into heated debates, converting the riverbank garden into a sort of literary salon. We were content to listen and learn, but afraid to participate—aware that it would not be free from the eyes and ears of the Baath Party.

The murmur of the waves reminded us that nights on Abu Nuwas Street were also nights of music, where voices sang with Iraqi sorrow. The songs of Nazem al-Ghazali, Zuhur Hussein, and Salima Murad blended with the Egyptian songs of Umm Kulthum and Mohammed Abdel Wahab. We were attracted to these Iraqi wedding songs and Sabah's songs, and we danced the *dabka* while children's laughter rang out around us from the playground. The glint in lovers' eyes embroidered love poems in the moonlight. Meanwhile, the boats swayed in the breeze, their lights like scattered pearls.

My heart leaped suddenly when I spotted Faris, just as my intuition had predicted. He was bent over one of the study tables—locks of his fair hair covering half his brow, glowing in the lamplight, which cast a long, semicircular arc in front of him—completely absorbed in his studies.

Sabah also noticed him. I wanted to walk over and take advantage of this beautiful coincidence, but Sabah grabbed me. "Behave yourself, let him come to you," she advised.

My strong and uncontrollable feelings toward him were mixed up. Sabah always enticed me away from such spontaneity with lessons of ancient Oriental love; she repeated to me endlessly that the man is the one who pursues the woman and it is she who rejects him.

"Let's go and talk to him together," I suggested. "We can ask whether our rooms are really bugged with listening wires!"

"Won't he just laugh at us and make light of the matter, like he always does?" Sabah replied. "He'll try to remove all suspicion about the Baath Party—they're above the rumors of *biased enemies*. And we might become included among the enemies in his eyes, according to the rule, *He who is not with me is against me*." She winked at the other girls.

"I want to get out of here before he starts reciting the latest studies and theories of the Arab Socialist Baath Party," Nawal said.

"Yesterday, Faris took me to the Faculty of Science and invited me for tea at the club on my break," Sabah added. "He made my brain ache with talk of politics. He left me some books by Michel Aflaq and Tariq Aziz on the party. I'm afraid he'll ask me now if I've read them."

"Let's stay here instead." Nuha said, agreeing with the other girls. "We can listen to Nazem al-Ghazali's songs instead." She began to sing in a loud voice: "*She appeared before him from her father's house, going to the neighbor's house . . . dressed in red and white, with the eyes of a gazelle*—"

Interrupting the song, Da'ad called out that she had found a group of young Palestinians she wanted us to join by our favorite spot near the statue of Shahriyar and Scheherazade. So we headed toward the group, passing a row of popular cafés and restaurants along the riverbank. The aroma of *masgouf*, the famous Iraqi delicacy of grilled fish, wafted through the air. Baghdad was famous for having the best river fish—carp and barbel, freshly caught by the fishermen of al-Karrada, close to Abu Nuwas Street. We could also smell kebab, served hot with fresh Baghdadi bread.

Our other friends joined us later at our usual spot. We jokingly called ourselves the Ali Baba Gang, because our "leader" Ahmed al-Salemi was always stealing things from us, and we had to look for him all night long. We spread out in a circle on the sand on the banks of the Tigris, right next to the water, and spent the evening in pleasant conversation—debating, arguing, singing, and dancing.

Jamal, from the Palestinian group, sat beside Nawal and had been flirting with her for a while, inching closer to her; Ahmed al-Salemi sat beside Nuha in order to pick a fight with her, the tension growing between them; I sat sideways, so as to keep one eye on the river and one eye on Faris; then I withdrew to the steps of the marble base of the statue, drawing from it the power of the word to protect the man I loved.

Suddenly, we heard the sound of heavy gunfire. We were frightened; we had not been able to get used to the shooting since we came to Iraq, although it had entered the general climate of the country and the Iraqis no longer paid it any attention. Next, we heard an Iraqi voice beside us saying: "Don't panic, dude! These are just firecrackers from a wedding in al-Karkh." But we did not see a trace of fireworks or anything else in the sky.

I turned to speak to Sabah, but she was no longer there. I looked around but could not find her.

"Leave Sabah in peace. She isn't your spoiled child," Jamal said, noticing my concern. He laughed, and everyone else began to laugh with him.

I waited a long time and busied myself talking to some younger people. After an hour had passed and Sabah had still not appeared, I began to feel anxious, but no one else seemed to notice. The corniche area gradually began to empty, the Iraqi families having gone home after the soap operas. As the crowd thinned out, the few remaining students noticed Sabah's absence.

At first, we figured that she had gone to walk by the river, as was her habit. Jamal took Nawal by the hand and they hurried along the riverbank, following Sabah's usual path, while Ahmed went to search elsewhere. We conducted a visual sweep of the whole garden but we did not see anything. By now, it was almost two in the morning.

"Sabah disappeared well before the shooting, but you didn't notice," said Da'ad.

We went into nearby restaurants, passing quickly between the tables, asking about her; perhaps she had gone to use the telephone or the bathroom. Some of our other friends soon joined the search. We looked everywhere, to no avail. When we gave up for the night, Nuha said that the matter must be related to what had happened today at the dorm.

Ahmed soon returned from the statue of Abu Nuwas, exhausted by crazy questioning from the Iraqi Intelligence Services about the wiretap story that had spread in the dorm earlier that day: *Who spread the story? Who was there at the time? How did everyone react? What did Sabah say about it?* This increased our own frenzy and we fell once again under the oppression of the state, just when we had thought we could go out to Abu Nuwas Street and rid ourselves of it. Khuddouj watched the scene coldly, scornfully, like she was not there with us at all—and she had been behaving that way since our arrival at the corniche.

Eventually, Jamal returned with Nawal, both out of breath and shaking their heads, indicating that the search had been in vain.

"Maybe Mohammad came and took her," Ahmed guessed.

We told him that it was impossible that Mohammad would come and not say hello to us, or join in the party. He was our friend too. Besides, we had a later appointment with him at the dorm; he did not know where we were, unless the dorm supervisor told him we had gone to the corniche. It seemed very unlikely that he had come and taken her secretly, like a thief, without seeing or telling us.

Nawal jumped up suddenly and asked: "Shouldn't we call the dorm supervisor before doing anything else, in case Mohammad did call for us?"

Jamal took her by the hand and they went to the nearest restaurant to contact the dorm and inquire about Mohammad.

The night supervisor, Um Sa'd, told them that she had not seen Sabah, that Mohammad had not arrived yet, and that she too was waiting for him. We all knew that Um Sa'd longed for Mohammad's arrival, since she loved the Rothman cigarettes that he usually brought her from Kuwait.

"In that case," Jamal said, "the lieutenant must have kidnapped her."

"That's not funny," I said tersely.

"I'm not joking," he said. "I never did feel comfortable about that officer since he started coming out with us. I think he's hiding something. And why did he start the relationship with Sabah, even though he knew she was engaged? Maybe he was carrying out some other mission . . ."

"And what mission might that be . . . huh, Mr. Imaginative?" I asked him.

Playing devil's advocate, Jamal described a possible scenario: "He took Sabah away from Mohammad to marry her in secret—before Mohammad arrived tonight—to prevent any possibility of Sabah returning to her fiancée. You know officers . . . they have no limits. And he had obtained official permission, or so he claimed."

"She wouldn't have told him about Mohammad's visit tonight," Nawal said.

"Even if she didn't tell him, the lieutenant knows everything about his future wife."

"Why couldn't Mohammad have kidnapped her after he found out about the lieutenant?" Da'ad interjected. "You know how possessive and madly jealous he is. When he drinks, doesn't he always say he would kill anyone one who might take Sabah away from him?"

"Enough!" cried Nuha. "Stop making up crazy stories, like we're talking about Georgina Rizk."

At that point I left the group and raced to Faris, since he would surely know how to help us with this calamity. I rushed across the sand, stopping when I reached the studying tables where I had first spotted him. But I could not find him, so I went back, dragging my feet, miserable and disappointed.

A few of us suggested that we inform the police, but the majority objected, fearful that we would be detained and subjected to another Q-and-A session, beginning with what happened today at the dorm—which might have been a trap in the first place. We were once again overcome with suspicion of one another. Why had Nuha egged on Sabah, warning her to hold her tongue and not repeat what she was always saying about Saddam Hussein ruling with iron and fire?

Meanwhile, Ahmed came running back to us, saying that about an hour earlier one of his Syrian friends had seen Sabah get into a taxi with Faris—they were going off somewhere together.

I became frantic and was seized by the fires of jealousy. How could she go with Faris when it was she who kept me away from him all the time? I remembered Nuha's claim that Sabah had secretly gone out with Faris, although I had not believed her at the time. I looked at Nawal and saw the same suspicion in her eyes.

I was overcome with anger, and a cold sweat trickled down my neck. I had been stabbed in the back and betrayed by my closest friend. I immediately hailed a taxi and grabbed Nawal by the hand, dragging her with me to bear witness. I called out to the others to join us at Faris's house. Jamal opened the front door and got in beside the driver, directing him to al-Maghrib Street in al-Waziriya, near the al-Ma'moun school.

In the taxi, I felt like I was sitting on hot coals. Nawal tried to get me to calm down until we knew all the facts. I leaned back into the comfortable backseat, trying to hold it together.

I had known Faris since I joined the Faculty of Arts. He had been at the service of new students; he was one of the most long-standing of the master's students, and he had helped me solve a lot of my problems. He asked about me every day. The truth is, he was obliging and charming. He won the respect of everyone and was sincere, decent, and noble. His personality was cheerful despite his seriousness. He bestowed lavish generosity on you, but if you wanted to get close and intimate with him, he was an impenetrable fortress.

Faris was tall, and he had a fair complexion; his wide, almost emerald-green eyes were unlike anything I had ever seen in my life. They were like spring pastures, or the reflection of a pine tree on the water's surface. So I fell in love with this good and handsome young man, who was well mannered and upright. One Friday, he had invited me to have lunch with him—just the two of us—at a Lebanese restaurant in the upscale al-Adhamiya neighborhood. I wore a dress the color of spring grass; I did my hair; I passed a crimson lipstick over my lips; I put on French perfume and then went out to meet him.

After we had eaten, he invited me to walk along the al-Adhamiya riverbank. We sat on a wooden bench and I watched the river flow by. A verse from Abu Qasim al-Shabbi was transformed on Faris's tongue, as the boats drifted across the water and carried me away: *"You are sweet, like childhood, like a melody, like a new dawn, like a beaming sky, or a moonlit night, like a rose, or the smile of a newborn."*

I recalled that when he had taken me back to the dorm by taxi, he had asked me to call Sabah—he even stayed to wait for her. I did not think anything of it at the time; I had fallen under his spell and the sweetness of our meeting had afflicted me.

When the taxi stopped at 68 al-Maghrib Street in the al-Mashtal District, we were immersed in darkness—there was nothing but a faint light, as if candles were burning in the living room. I got out, rushing toward the front door, and started knocking. My heart was pounding harder than my hand against the door. Nawal was behind me, trying to calm me down again. A curious silence reigned and no one answered. We knocked again. Jamal went to check the back garden, but a few moments later we glimpsed a shadowy figure behind the curtain at the window. Then we heard footsteps approaching cautiously from inside. Suddenly, the door opened.

We were all stunned when we saw the figure of Lieutenant Najim Abbas filling the doorway. Cold sweat broke out on my skin. I did not know whether to be pleased or perplexed.

The lieutenant reassured us that Sabah was safe inside, and that she was fine. Faris, behind him, closed the door after inviting us in.

We sat down in the semidark living room, where Sabah was holding the telephone receiver and weeping—we knew that she was speaking to her mother.

"I received an urgent call from Sabah's mother today, in the late evening," Najim explained, his voice tinged with concern. "She asked me on my honor to save her daughter tonight and protect her from Mohammad, who had left Kuwait in the blackest mood, with sparks flying from his eyes, promising to kill both me and Sabah—after he heard that we had married in secret. She was frightened for her poor daughter because of his wickedness, his crazy love, and his drunkenness— which blinded him. At the time, I was away on a mission in al-Fallujah. I thought about it and I contacted Faris, who Mohammad doesn't know, and asked him to get Sabah and take her to his house as quickly as possible . . . somewhere safe until I could join them, and to make sure she didn't go back to the dorm at all tonight."

* * *

In the morning, the news reached us that Mohammad had been found dead on the road between Basra and Baghdad. Police reports subsequently recorded the perpetrator as *Unknown*.

Translated from Arabic by Becki Maddock

ROOM 22

BY MOHAMMED ALWAN JABR
Bab al-Sharqi

From the moment he entered the hotel's courtyard he realized what a huge challenge he would face in coping with these new developments. The leather case he carried made him feel increasingly uncomfortable, and with every step he took toward the lobby his anxiety about the possibility of a confrontation increased. He would be meeting with them face-to-face now, after suffering and waiting for days, unable to communicate with them except by phone. For this reason, he knew he needed to pull himself together. He finally approached the doorway of the hotel, which was located beside the entrance to the Granada Cinema, across from Hadiqat al-Umma in Bab al-Sharqi.

I must be steadfast, he told himself several times, as he tried to calm his nerves and dispel the fear that threatened to overwhelm him. He wanted to appear strong to them.

He had insisted on meeting the officer, who had begun by asking him many questions—a lot of similar questions. He recalled the policeman's face and queries the previous day, when he asked about new developments in the case of the kidnapped child. He didn't know why the officer had seemed frightened yesterday.

"They've made contact," he had revealed to the officer, tersely.

"When?"

"This morning." In a low murmur, he had started to explain, and the officer didn't interrupt him. "They told me: *Memorize what we tell you, word for word. Bring the money. Head to Baghdad. Bab al-Sharqi—the area opposite the garden. You will find a small wooden placard. The hotel beside the Granada Cinema entrance—the al-Bataween Hotel.*"

He wrote these instructions on a piece of paper and gave it to the officer.

Then, with the same calm, commanding, and self-confident intonation as the caller, he repeated the threat: *"Don't tell the police. You know the rest."*

The officer had removed his dark glasses and held the paper close to his face.

"They want the meeting to take place at al-Bataween Hotel."

The officer studied the paper and then asked the question the man had been asked time and time again, since he had reported to the police that his sister's young son had been kidnapped: "Do you suspect anyone?"

"Certainly not," he had replied for the hundredth time.

But this time he really wondered: *Is there really no one I suspect? Is it ridiculous to suspect someone? Let me try to reconstruct what happened, step by step.*

He began with the moment he had answered the telephone. His sister's agitated husband, whose eyes never left her face, had handed him the receiver. He had heard a raspy voice that sounded like wind whistling through a small opening. It was a cold voice, but sharp as a knife. "Your child is with us," the voice said. It was the voice of a confident, domineering man.

He had not been able to achieve much in the negotiations, which ended after several calls to a number they had specified. All his subsequent attempts to contact them had failed. Whenever he rang the number, no one answered. When they renewed contact with him, they excoriated him: "Why did you try to call us?"

"She did it," he had answered, referring to his sister, who was wailing nearby. "She wants to hear her son's voice." He had become quite emotional and declared that he would not honor their demands if he did not hear the child's voice. His efforts succeeded.

When they next rang him, they said the child would come on the line. Upon handing the phone over, the boy cried out: "I want my mother!"

His sister grabbed the phone and sobbed loudly. Then she tossed the phone back to him and collapsed to the floor. The voice spoke to him again—specifying the sum he had to deliver in exchange for the child's safety. A threat followed: "Follow our instructions. Beware of disobeying them. Beware!"

He had recognized a dialect and accent that had been etched into his brain, but he couldn't quite place it. He should have been able to distinguish it from a thousand other voices and accents he knew. Was it a familiar voice? He needed to search his memory's recesses for the person the voice belonged to. At first, he suspected that his search was in vain. Later, he thought the voice resembled that of Mullah Hassan, the imam of the mosque near his house. But he then attributed this association to the fact that he heard that voice daily, especially at dawn, when everything was pristine and disrupted only by the mullah's voice. He began to pay more attention to the voice that sundered the dawn's stillness—to the mullah's voice as he recited the same prayer every day, right after the morning call to prayer, always the same words. The accent was definitely similar to the voice of the kidnapper.

Why his sister's son? They lived in a neighborhood where almost everyone knew each other. Relative to Baghdad as a whole, it was very small. He assumed they understood that his sister's husband was not an entrepreneur, nor did he possess a fortune. He was just a low-ranking civil servant with no political leanings or patronage. So why had his brother-in-law's son been taken? How could these people expect a large sum from him? The proposed amount had to be raised with great difficulty. Was it conceivable that Mullah Hassan had kidnapped the boy?

He kept a lid on his mounting suspicions about the mullah. He decided not to tell anyone about them, not even the police.

"Did they set a time and place?" the rugged officer had asked, removing his glasses and then putting them back on.

"Yes. Next Sunday. I should be in room 22."

"Why room 22? How?" The officer in charge of the investigation had started to repeat his own questions.

He now pondered this same question, as he made his way through the dark courtyard between the hotel's entrance and the steps that led to its lobby. There, at the center of the large room, he found a man with a big head and eyes that protruded as if they were ready to pop out of their sockets.

The big-headed man smiled in welcome. On learning that he wished to book a room, just for himself, the hotel's proprietor pointed to a chair nearby.

Before he sat down, he added in a shaky voice, while staring at the red sign with white letters that read, *al-Bataween Hotel*: "With only one bed, please."

Four men sat opposite him, near the proprietor's table, smoking quietly. The proprietor, meanwhile, examined his ID card and the money he had handed over before he sat down.

He started to wonder: *Why is this place called the al-Bataween Hotel? Especially since the area is named after al-Fanahira and the Shukr Café . . . not al-Bataween?* Since he left al-Saidiya, where he lived, even before he reached the outskirts of Baghdad, he had been thinking about the name of this hotel, where he needed to wrap the affair up all by himself.

He studied the four men. The first was portly and sat at the far right, next to the proprietor's table. He did not stare at him for long. The man's waxy face had no distinguishing features. He moved his gaze to the man sitting beside him. What drew his attention to this guy was his head, which kept moving in all directions, as if he were searching for something. Finding the man's jerky gestures annoying, he felt he could skip an inspection of the other two. He turned to face a wall, attempting to free himself of the sense that he had entered a machine that would squeeze him from all sides. He could already feel the first hint of pressure on his body. These premonitions of imminent torture increased, emerging from the darkness that dominated his mind. He slowly became more conscious of the weight of the leather case he had placed on his thighs.

The proprietor began to record his name in a large ledger with overt condescension, which swiftly swept over the other four men's faces, making them look arrogant as well. He felt totally isolated in the middle of the lobby; he wondered whether his name was responsible for this communal display of pomposity. He would have quickly set aside this notion, which he attributed to his mission here, if the proprietor's lugubrious voice had not asked: "How are the sheikhs of al-Saidiya?"

He jumped as if he had been stung and then froze like a statue; his features went immobile, even as he attempted to fake a smile—a smile that refused to materialize on his face. So he merely inclined his head in a nod.

"Good. Here," the proprietor said, handing him the room key with a smile.

He took the key, but before he could rise, the proprietor moved toward him, attempting to take the small briefcase: "Let me help you carry this."

He declined the offer vehemently, and then they walked along a hall that led to a short flight of stairs. The proprietor led him to a door with the number 22 on it. So it seemed the matter had been settled in advance. The proprietor opened the old wooden door, entered first, turned on the light, and then clapped a hand on his shoulder. "I want you to tell everyone in al-Saidiya that I gave you a warm welcome, was hospitable to you, and satisfied all your requests."

He thought he would be suffocated by the proprietor's foul breath. Yet he survived this assault and reflected that Mullah Hassan's link to the affair was now confirmed. "Certainly," he replied.

The proprietor laughed and added almost in a whisper: "I hope you enjoy your stay in this room. You may have a nap or spend some time strolling the streets till Mr. Tariq arrives."

He was bewildered by this reference to Tariq, Mullah Hassan's son. At the same time, he was surprised that he had not yet received a call from his brother-in-law, who he had asked to watch the mullah's house and the mosque next to it. He had wanted to know the mullah's movements and actions on the day specified for trading the money for the child. Would he come in person to receive the cash or send someone else? *So the mullah is sending Tariq,* he said to himself.

The proprietor withdrew quietly; the smile had not left his face since he handed over the key.

He wondered whether the proprietor and the four other men were tied to the crime. If not, why had he been led in such a ceremonial fashion to room 22? And though he was surprised that his brother-in-law hadn't telephoned him, he dismissed that concern.

He closed the door, hoping the crisis that began when the child was kidnapped would soon end and that his sister and her husband would stop their bawling; he had wept along with them, imagining the fear his nephew was experiencing in the hands of strangers. He hid the briefcase under the bed and studied the room, which resembled a torture room in a movie. A single bed was pushed against a window that overlooked the concrete walls of adjacent buildings. Near the metal bed was a stand that held many tin-framed mirrors. Light reflected off them, and a plethora of images appeared, overlapping and intertwining on the mirrors' surfaces. He gazed at the face in the silent silver sea of one mirror; the unity of its image set it apart from the others. He did a double take, though, as he stared at the face before him. *That's definitely not me!* His telephone rang and roused him from this nightmare. The same commanding voice scolded him, brutally this time: "Didn't we warn you not to contact the police? Do you want the child to die?"

He replied plaintively that he had not contacted the police. To prove it, he almost said he knew he was speaking to Mullah Hassan and had not mentioned that to the police. But he managed to set aside the inane musings that his lethal anxiety had provoked.

The voice asked him to remain in the hotel for two days. "Then you will be informed of the new plan. You and your damn officer are responsible for all this delay!"

They told him to search al-Saadoun Street for a small coffeehouse right next door to the Tajiran Restaurant. He should wait there or loiter nearby till their next call. He almost cursed the police officer, who made him wear disguises when they met at locations far from al-Saidiya or in congested areas of Baghdad, never addressing each other in public. They had chosen places that absolutely no one could discover. For example, the officer would contact him and he'd ask the officer to go to the home of one of his friends. When he arrived, he would find the officer seated there. They had absolutely never met in the police station. *So how do they know that I contacted the police, unless one of my friends is a member of the gang?*

In his mind, he pictured the houses where they had met. He knew most of the people and felt sure they could not be kidnappers. He tried to find a link between the voice, which was burned into his mind, and those of the men he was reviewing. None of them aroused his suspicions or doubts—except for a guy the officer had chosen. He remembered his name, which the policeman had mentioned—it was Said or possibly Saad. The man had seemed troubled and angry with the officer. At the time, he had attributed the man's ill temper to some misunderstanding between the two men. He was compelled now to assume the gang knew everything about him and the actions he took.

But as he wandered the streets near the hotel, his stress increased in response to the dark vapors their call had fomented. He realized that his situation was worsening, and he felt increasingly isolated. He understood, moreover, that his circumstances were perilous. At first, the rhythm of developments had seemed slow to him, but now they had begun to speed up in a way he could no longer control.

Mean streets, he said to himself. He returned to his room, taking a different route than the one by which he had come.

He tried to continue his deliberations, beginning with the hotel proprietor's questions and the appearance of the intolerable strangers in the lobby. He thought he might try to strike up a relationship with one of them, though that seemed almost impossible—even just chatting, given the emotional storm in his chest, which was beginning to billow out like a windblown sail.

His feelings about the plot seemed naive and meaningless now. He headed down streets that looked alien to him, even though he had wandered them frequently. He walked along al-Saadoun Street from its start near Abd al-Muhsin al-Saadoun Square, all the way to the Sheraton Hotel. This current version of the street did not correspond to the hoard of images crammed into his memory. He sensed that his situation's new realities were filling him with a mixture of bitterness and fear.

He was sinking beneath the pressure of his own existence when he traversed the hotel's lobby, carrying the briefcase, attracting everyone's attention. He realized that he was construing every movement, gesture, and word as directed at him, personally. He couldn't bear spending any more time in the lobby, so he hastened to the small coffeehouse near the Tajiran Restaurant overlooking the end of al-Saadoun Street. Through its dusty window, he frantically watched the passersby.

When I entered this place, the atmosphere felt familiar, but I don't have a clue when I was last here. The coffeehouse's small room only had six benches, which were arranged in opposing pairs; some chairs were propped in the corners. He found himself drawn to the glass, which provided him a glimpse of the world outside—a world far removed from the nightmare of the hotel lobby. Although the window was filthy, through it he could see facades glinting in the sunlight on the far side of the street. Bookstores and shops were scattered along it, drawing larger crowds than his side of the street. In front of a small restaurant on the far side, he saw clouds of smoke rising. Even though his view offered him a luminous expanse, he felt like a prisoner of the room, the walls of which were decorated with dark images that contained murky splotches of red, blue, and yellow. They depicted cavalrymen thrusting spears at one another. On the wall opposite him hung the portrait of a solitary woman; her era was far from clear. He did not know why, but he believed she was just as alien as he was in this rowdy coffeehouse. He tried to avoid reading too much into her expression when he examined her face, although it exuded femininity.

As he returned to the hotel, the portrait of the solitary woman mounted on the wall never left his mind. The hotel's large lobby was decorated with pictures and many Koranic verses, and he found the same four men by the proprietor's table. Before greeting them, he noticed their distrustful glances; they appeared to be threatening him rather overtly now. He had a strong desire to bolt from the hotel and its terrifying lobby, but the ringtone of his phone prevented him.

"We will contact you when you get to your room." It was the same voice.

He took the key and went to his room. He was not surprised to find that his mattress had been thrown on the floor. He might have been caught off guard if he had not just seen those pompous faces in the lobby.

This is intolerable!

His phone rang . . . a voice, again. But not the voice he had heard before.

"We will free the child. Your sister will contact you. She

will tell you she has the child. You will set the briefcase down in the room and depart quickly, leaving the door open. Do not look back or loiter in the hotel. Continue speaking to your sister on your phone. She will tell you when the business is concluded. Then you will return quickly to al-Saidiya."

He stood there motionless while waiting for his sister's call. But this new voice puzzled him; he almost recognized it, just as he had recognized Mullah Hassan's voice. His ringtone sounded once more and then his sister's voice captured his attention. "I have him!" she cried.

She was quite emotional, and he did not understand much of what she said. He grasped that she had heard a knock on the door, opened it, and found her son there—the boy seemed sleepy and stood there with his eyes closed.

He wept for joy with his sister, then placed the briefcase on the bed. The key was still in the door. He opened it and rushed out.

Something, however, prompted him to lurk by the huge concrete column that rose from a corner of the hotel's court-yard. He froze there. From this vantage he could see his room's doorway, even though it was dark. He waited, his senses on full alert, for Mullah Hassan's son or someone else to enter the room.

The strapping body that shot past his eyes into the room looked really familiar—and when the officer passed through the open door again, he saw him put the briefcase into a large sack. It truly was the officer—although not in uniform—with large dark glasses covering half his face. He wanted to call out to the officer, but instead—and he didn't know why—he remained frozen by the column. At the same speed with which he'd arrived, the rugged body dashed out of the hotel.

He peered at the room, saw that its door was now closed,

and then found his way to al-Nahdha Garage. He called the officer and told him what had happened . . . *Did he know?* Suddenly, in the background, he heard the familiar new voice that had told him precisely how to leave the hotel room. This voice informed the policeman that the case was now closed and that the child had been returned to his family.

The officer brought his attention back to the call, breathlessly asking: "What did you do? Did you see or recognize anyone?"

"I suspected Mullah Hassan from the beginning," he told the officer. "But today I saw a stocky man who reminded me of someone I know. He took the money and then vanished."

He heard more heavy breathing and some panting. Then he turned off his phone and just stared in the direction the stocky man had disappeared.

Translated from Arabic by William M. Hutchins

PART III

WAKE ME UP

PART III

THE APARTMENT

BY SALIMA SALIH

al-Ghadeer District

That Saturday didn't begin the way Anissa al-Mukhtar had hoped. The first thing she noticed when she opened her eyes in the morning was an overcast sky that augured a rainy day. No sooner had she sat up than she became aware of a headache, which she recognized as the harbinger of a bad cold, turning her plans for that day on their head. She slumped back into bed and didn't get up for another hour. By that time, the commotion in the house had died down; three of her sons had left for work, while the fourth was still having breakfast in the kitchen. The moment he heard her enter the bathroom, he got up, placed the teapot on the stove, brought out a clean plate, and sat down to wait for her. When she came into the kitchen and took her place across the breakfast table, she said: "I won't be needing you today. I have a terrible headache."

They had made plans the previous day: he would drive her to the al-Ghadeer District to see her aunt, the last surviving member of the older generation; but before that, she would have to prepare some food for her aunt, who lived alone in her apartment even though she was well past eighty. Anissa had suggested to her in the past that she come live with her family, or that she rent a place for her nearby so she could visit whenever she wished, but her aunt had refused all these of-fers. The only option for Anissa was to visit her once or twice a week, bringing her whatever food she was able to prepare. During those visits she would clean the house and collect the dirty towels, bedsheets, and clothes in a plastic bag to wash at home and bring back on her next visit.

Despite her advanced years, Anissa's aunt would visit her niece from time to time. All she had to do was make her way down the street and flag a cab to drive her over. Occasionally, she would stop by for two or three days at a time, and then take another cab back to her place in al-Ghadeer. When the long summer days got to her, she would take a cab to the Blue Sky restaurant and have a light lunch while making chitchat with one of the waiters, or with the person seated at the neighboring table. The sole hardship in her life was climbing the three flights of stairs up to her apartment, but she endured this obstacle with heroic fortitude, as if she wished to prove to everyone that she was still at the peak of health. At times, she wouldn't refuse the offer of Huda, a neighbor in her midforties, to pick up some supplies for her on one of her shopping trips; or the offer of Red Adel, the young man living with his mother in one of the ground-floor apartments, to replace her gas cylinder when it ran out. Red Adel drove a small truck and worked for a company that made oil heaters, and he would sometimes run into her as she was carrying up her shopping bags and offer to help. A certain familiarity developed between them as a result, and she would invite him to have tea with her whenever her niece had brought around a bit of cake.

Two days later, Anissa got in touch with Huda, to ask after the old lady and apologize for the late visit. She told the neighbor about her cold and asked her to inform her aunt that she'd be coming around as soon as she got better; she also expressed her frustration about the inconveniences of travel-

ing between her aunt's place and her own house in Baghdad's
al-Jadida District.

On Tuesday morning, Anissa rang up Red Adel's house,
and his mother informed her that he was out of town and that
her aunt was fine. She said she had seen her two days before
and that there was nothing to worry about.

As her sons sat down for breakfast that day, Anissa packed
up the food she had prepared for her aunt, and she asked one
of her sons to drive her to al-Ghadeer. Less than an hour later,
they were on their way.

When they reached the al-Samarra'i mosque, there was a
crowd of people blocking part of the street and slowing down
the traffic. One of the bystanders noticed her inquisitive look
and volunteered: "A minor car accident. Everything will be
back to normal in a few minutes."

The reassuring words failed to stop her from muttering:
"Tuesday is never a lucky day for me. I would have preferred
to visit on Wednesday, but I can't put this off any longer."

When she reached the apartment and rang the doorbell,
she got no response. She began to feel sick in the pit of her
stomach, and a terrible fear came over her. Had what she had
always dreaded finally taken place? She rang the doorbell a
second time, and then knocked on the door. She waited. She
glued her ear to the door, but not a single sound reached her
from within. Overhearing the knocking, Huda came out of
her house to find Anissa standing at the old lady's door. Both
women realized that something was awry. Huda asked Anissa
whether she had a spare key, and when Anissa replied in the
negative, she offered to call the police.

Less than half an hour later, two police officers arrived
and broke down the door. Entering the apartment apprehen-
sively, they were met with an overpowering stench of rot. The

officers backtracked and instructed the two women to remain outside; one of them hurried back to their vehicle and returned promptly with protective masks. Each of the officers placed a mask over his face, and after quizzing the two women about their relationship to the apartment's occupant, they handed Anissa a third mask and gave her permission to follow them inside. A sense of disorder reigned in the living room, something that was in itself no cause for surprise. Crossing the threshold to the kitchen, however, they spotted a pair of naked legs and immediately rushed over. They found the old woman sprawled on the ground with her head lying in a pool of coagulated blood. Her body was so swollen that it was hard to make out her features. Anissa closed her eyes, and one of the officers took her by the shoulder and led her to the far end of the living room.

Shortly after, two more police officers arrived. One photographed the body and the lesion on the old lady's head, as well as the broken dishes on the floor, the sink, and the cupboard. The other officer, who introduced himself as the criminal investigator Naji Nassar, started jotting something down in a notebook he was carrying.

Naji turned to Anissa and began to outline his assessment of the facts while the others were transporting the body out of the apartment: "It seems that your aunt stumbled, fell, and hit her head . . . She lost a lot of blood. Everything looks pretty straightforward, but it will still be necessary to send her body to the coroner for an autopsy and a forensic report about the cause of death." He explained that he had to verify certain facts, and asked her about the age of the deceased, whether she had lived alone, and whether anyone else possessed a key to the apartment, even though these questions had been mostly answered when the officers broke down the door.

"She didn't trust anyone . . . She could have given us a key, or left one with her neighbor," Anissa said plaintively, before bursting into tears. "If only I had come to visit on Saturday . . . she might still be alive."

It was time for everyone to leave the apartment. The investigator was the last to emerge, but upon reaching the door, he had the sudden sense that he had forgotten something, so he went back into the kitchen to take another look. The body was gone, but everything else appeared just the way it had when he'd first walked in—yet he just couldn't shake the sensation that he'd forgotten something. He took two steps out of the kitchen and then turned around again, and this time he saw more clearly what it was that he had overlooked. A small mound of cigarette ash sat just outside the pool of blood in which the head had lain. The mound still held together, as if it had only just fallen. This discovery unsettled his earlier hypothesis that an eighty-year-old woman living alone had struck her head against the edge of the cupboard because of a simple stumble.

When Naji got to work the following day, the autopsy report was waiting for him on his desk. The cause of death was extensive hemorrhaging due to a head injury produced by impact with a hard, sharp object. The time of death was placed at four days earlier.

Even though this was in keeping with Naji's initial evaluation of the incident and he could have declared the case closed, he realized that he would not be at peace until he was truly sure the death was as it appeared. He needed to visit Anissa's house to ask her some questions.

Upon arriving there, he first informed her about the re-sults of the autopsy. It added to her distress to learn that her aunt had died on Saturday—the very day she had not turned up for her usual visit—which then released a tide of self-reproach for her failure to go see her on that day. After he had managed to calm her down, the investigator began with his questions.

"Did your aunt receive many guests at home?"

"No," Anissa answered. "Her neighbor used to give her a helping hand here and there, as often happens among neighbors."

"Did your aunt smoke?"

"Whatever put it into your head that she smoked?" Anissa asked a bit defensively.

"I need a clear answer: yes or no?"

"Certainly not," Anissa proclaimed. "She never picked up a cigarette in her life."

"And her neighbor? Did she smoke?"

"I don't think so."

"Does the neighbor live on her own?"

"No, she lives with her daughter and granddaughter. Her daughter's husband died in a car accident a couple of years ago. The daughter works as a teacher. They are good people."

"Were there any other neighbors who helped her out?"

"The young man living with his family on the ground floor—he'd help her carry up the gas cylinder to the third floor."

"Would he go into the apartment to change the cylinder?"

"No, he'd bring it up and leave it at the front door. When I would go see her, I would carry it into the kitchen."

"When was the gas container last changed?"

"Maybe three months ago. My aunt didn't use a lot of gas."

"When did you last visit your aunt?"

"Last Wednesday. I'd planned to visit her on Saturday as well, but I felt ill."

"Did you clean the house on Wednesday?"

"Yes."

"Which rooms did you clean?"

"The bedroom didn't need any cleaning, so I started with the living room, I cleaned the kitchen next, and then I did the bathroom."

"What did you clean in the kitchen?"

"There were a few dirty dishes, so I washed those first, then I dusted the top of the fridge and the cupboard, and I mopped the floor."

"Do you always do that when you clean the kitchen?"

"Do what?"

"Mop the floor."

"Always—the floor gets wet and dirty and I find that annoying."

"What do you know about the neighbor who lives on the ground floor?"

Anissa paused for a second, taking the time to think through what she knew about Red Adel. "He's a young man of about thirty . . . He lives with his mother, his brother, and his brother's wife . . . I don't know much about the family, but I'd bump into him from time to time when visiting my aunt. And I'd have a chat with his mother whenever I bumped into her outside her house."

"What kinds of things did you talk about?"

"Oh, about the weather, the traffic, my aunt's health—nothing important."

It crossed Naji's mind to ask Anissa if she ever smoked, but at the last moment he checked himself and pretended to be fumbling for something in the pockets of his jacket. "I must have forgotten my cigarettes in the office," he said.

"I can't offer you one, unfortunately," Anissa replied, "since nobody smokes in this house."

The investigator was happy that he had obtained the answer he had wished for without having to pose a question that might have sounded intrusive. He was also interested in knowing whether the young man living on the ground floor smoked, but he decided to defer his question for the moment, since this woman might not be the best person to answer it.

When he returned to his office, he pulled out the pictures that had been taken of the scene. The deceased was lying facedown, more than half a meter away from the cupboard, and her head was positioned at least twenty centimeters from the corner of the cupboard that had caused the injury. There were several more questions he would have to answer to confirm his suspicion that a murder had taken place, despite all the evidence that suggested otherwise.

It was possible she had stumbled, fallen down, and struck her head on the corner of the cupboard, but he couldn't see anything that might have caused her to trip. Very well then, perhaps she had simply felt dizzy or weak all of a sudden, and this had caused her to fall. This kind of thing could easily happen to someone her age. What he needed to do next was get in touch with the doctor who had examined the body, in the hope that he might pick up on something that went beyond what he had mentioned in the autopsy report.

Naji received confirmation from the doctor that the old woman's death was most likely from a fall. "If she fell down quickly, she would have tried to clutch at the cupboard and slid down near it," the doctor had told him. "But we don't know whether she lost consciousness immediately, as a result of the concussion. She could have moved away from the cupboard before stumbling to the floor."

Given the doctor's opinion, the only thing still left to raise doubts in his mind was the small mound of ash; if he could find a way to account for that, he would declare the case closed.

He returned to the scene of the incident in the company of the photographer, who was tasked this time with taking close-up shots of the cigarette ash. When he was done, the investigator carefully transferred the ash to a small sheet of paper and placed it in a small transparent bag. Now his job was to establish where it had come from.

When Naji arrived at the building in al-Ghadeer the next morning, he found a group of young children clustered around a pickup truck parked outside. As he approached, one of the kids offered an unsolicited explanation: "Red Adel bought new sofas!" The new sofas held no interest to him, but he did want to meet Red Adel. He waited for a moment and saw two young men emerge from the building, open the back door of the vehicle, and lift a cover that revealed a set of brown sofas underneath. The reddish hair immediately identified one of them as Red Adel. Naji offered to help them carry the sofas into the house, and after that, the two young men made for the front of the truck. Red Adel paused for a moment, lit a cigarette, and then climbed into the driver's seat. Hearing the engine start up, Naji realized it wasn't the right time to try to talk to him, but he had at least gotten an answer to one of the questions that had been preoccupying him. Perhaps the young man had visited the old lady before she died; perhaps his remaining inquiries were about to be brought to an end.

As soon as the truck had driven off, the kids thronged around him. At that instant, it occurred to him that they might be able to offer him something valuable—after all, they had helped him identify Red Adel without his even having to go to the trouble of asking—so he didn't rush to leave.

"Are you a relative of the old lady?" one child asked.

"Did you know her?"

"Everyone knew her around here," the kid said.

"Why's that?"

"She used to tell us off when we tried to help her. She was cranky. My mom would say she's at the vilest age."

"What's the vilest age?" another kid asked.

"It's when a person has grown so old they can't live without other people's help," Naji volunteered. And becoming skeptical that he could turn the conversation in the direction he wanted, he decided to leave. The children followed him with their eyes and then dispersed.

When he returned to his office, he called Anissa and told her he would like to have another look around the apartment—they agreed to meet there at five o'clock.

When she arrived, he was waiting by the door, as the lock the police had broken had been replaced with a new one. She was wearing a black dress with long sleeves, and her face was very pale. He apologized for having to put her through the trouble of coming over.

"I had to come here anyway to look for some papers," Anissa replied.

She opened the door and walked in ahead of him; he was astonished to find that the place had been entirely stripped down, with nothing remaining but piles of leftover odds and ends and scattered papers.

"The neighbors divided the furniture and everything else among themselves," Anissa said, before he could ask a question. "They left me all the junk. And now they're asking me to clean up, even though I offered them the furniture in return for taking care of that."

There was nothing in her explanation that intrigued Naji, so he turned toward the kitchen. The shards of a freshly broken glass were scattered around the sink, and the shelves were empty. The bloodstain had turned brown and the spot from the ash had faded into the tile floor, so there wasn't any remaining evidence to further his investigation.

"I'll bring someone in to clean up tomorrow," Anissa said. "They're putting pressure on me because of the smell." They went down the stairs together and Anissa left the building, while the investigator headed for Red Adel's place on the ground floor.

Naji rang the bell and a moment later a woman who looked to be in her fifties opened the door. He introduced himself and explained that he needed to ask a few questions regarding the old woman on the third floor. He told her it was simply a matter of routine. When someone in their eighties dies in their bed, matters are clear. But when they die in an accident, there has to be a formal report, and testimonies must be gathered. She invited him to come in, then called for her son Red Adel, who was in the kitchen. Naji noticed that the sofas from the morning were now sitting at the far end of the living room, a set of clean white sheets draped over them; an older sofa and a couple of large armchairs stood alongside the window.

Naji sat down on one of the armchairs, while Red Adel took a seat at the end of the sofa. The investigator repeated his earlier remarks about routine procedure and needing to file a formal report before closing the case.

"I've been told you used to help the old lady with some day-to-day things," Naji said.

"Yes, I did. When these buildings were constructed, it didn't occur to anyone that the people living in them would grow old one day and no longer be able to carry their gas cylinders up to their homes, so they built them without elevators. I used to bring the old lady's gas cylinder up the stairs for her, and I'd sometimes find her trying to lug stuff, shopping bags and other things, and offer to help."

"When was the last time you brought up a gas cylinder for her?"

A faint look of irritation appeared on Red Adel's face, but he responded without hesitation: "I'm not sure exactly. It must have been two months ago, maybe a little longer."

"And did you happen to carry up her shopping bags during this past week?"

"No, I haven't had to do that for quite some time now—ever since her niece started coming in and bringing her whatever she needed."

"Did she ever invite you inside after you carried up her gas cylinder for her?"

"She'd sometimes invite me to have a cup of tea with her."

"Did you accept these invitations?"

"I'd usually tell her I was busy. Her place felt grubby and I didn't like that. Maybe that's not quite right . . . Her niece cleaned the apartment whenever she visited. Maybe it was the smell of old age. I would just stand at the door while she chatted away. She needed people to talk to. She'd sometimes wait at the entrance of the building to exchange a few words with passing neighbors."

"Did you see her on the day of the accident?"

"No, I wasn't home on Saturday. I had to head out early in the morning to transport a batch of oil heaters across the region. I only came back this morning."

Naji hadn't made any reference to Saturday, so how did Red Adel know that the accident had taken place that day? The medical report hadn't mentioned that either; it had only said that the death must have taken place four days earlier, judging from the body's state of decomposition and the distension it had suffered as a result of the hot weather.

The investigator left Red Adel's home with his mind in a whirl; one moment he felt sure he was about to piece together clues that revealed the presence of a crime, and the next he doubted what had struck him as clear evidence of wrongdoing.

Back at the office, he ran through the details of the accident once again, as if vocalizing his suspicions gave them a new solidity and power to convince: 1) a woman in her eighties had been found dead in her kitchen; 2) the door of the apartment was closed and there were no signs of forced entry; 3) there were no other means of gaining entry to the apartment—but that didn't mean somebody hadn't entered the place that day; 4) someone she knew and trusted may have knocked on the door to offer their help or to simply make sure she was all right; she invited this person to come in; they followed her to the kitchen, grabbed her from behind, hit her head against the side of the cupboard, and threw her on the floor; then closed the apartment door and left.

But the most important question remained unanswered: why would anyone want to do such a thing? There were no signs of anything having been stolen, and Red Adel knew the old lady had very little money. So how did the cigarette ash find its way to the kitchen? No one else who smoked had entered the old lady's place.

"You're agonizing over this case far more than it's worth," said Naji's colleague, after Naji had voiced all his concerns and suspicions. "A woman in her eighties with no enemies and no money has no reason to be murdered. If she hadn't died now, she would have died in a year or two. There are people meeting far more brutal ends in this city every day—people in the prime of their life. If I were you, I would close this case immediately."

"Maybe you're right," Naji muttered.

Yet the investigator decided to undertake one last visit to the scene of the incident the following day. When he arrived at the building in al-Ghadeer, he met Huda coming down the stairs. "They've cleaned and disinfected the apartment," she told him. "The old lady was a good neighbor. We'll have to see who the blushing bride is that'll take her place now."

"Bride?" Naji asked without thinking.

"I believe Red Adel's mother has spoken to Anissa about the apartment?" Naji shook his head, and could only stare at her as she went on: "Red Adel's brother got married a few months ago, and he's renting a place over in the next district. Their mother decided to buy the old lady's apartment because she doesn't want her sons to live too far away from her . . ."

The inspector sighed. Just another day in Baghdad.

Translated from Arabic by Sophia Vasalou

EMPTY BOTTLES

BY HUSSAIN AL-MOZANY

al-Thawra City

The crime occurred at dawn, in a small, dusty alleyway branching off from 60th Street, which was part of Sector 55 in al-Thawra City, today known as Sadr City—about seven kilometers from the center of Baghdad. At the time, I was either twelve or thirteen years old, and I was lying in the cement courtyard next to my three younger siblings. Our house had two low-ceilinged rooms and was right next to the site of the incident—not too different from the house in which our neighbor was killed. I almost woke up at dawn, after the call to prayer hissed from a defective speaker that hung from the wall of a small mosque nearby. The muezzin would usually begin by awakening his sleeping friends as if he were playing the role of an alarm clock. In that age, when most residents of al-Thawra did not even know of alarm clocks, they relied upon the timings of the call to prayer, and the sunrise and sunset.

Suddenly, I heard the iron door open and then shut with force, making a noise that truly jolted me from my slumber. The light was seeping languidly from the cloudy, distant sky, and the air was delicate. I could see my mother; she hadn't yet finished her prayers, since the muezzin had stopped speaking just a few moments before. I saw her rush directly toward me, and in a low, choked voice, as if she wanted to let me in on a dangerous secret, she whispered: "Her brother killed her and escaped."

I shuddered as I grasped what my agitated mother was saying, without knowing exactly who this killer was or who it was that had fallen victim to him that early morning. I rubbed my eyes and went to the tap in the courtyard for a little drink of water, then I looked again at my mother, who began to circle around my siblings, examining them.

"I saw him carrying a dagger in one hand and the dead woman's hand in the other," my mother muttered under her breath as she left the house.

I was aware that my mother possessed a reasonable degree of courage, but I feared for her, because she could encounter the dagger-carrying murderer while he was still high on the ecstasy of having killed. I imagined that the man who had flashed the victory sign would not hesitate to stab whoever stood in his way. Since I did not dare to stop my mother, who occupied my father's position after his passing, I followed her with shaky footsteps and a violently beating heart. I stood there watching her from the stool at the door, and saw her wave her hands in the direction of a man smiling and pacing around in circles in a way I had not seen before.

The man took a few footsteps closer to my mother, until his features became visible beneath the light of the sole lamp on the wide, dusty street. Then he brandished his dagger threateningly, as he bellowed with laughter. He was short and thin, with a bushy mustache and narrow eyes; I couldn't make out his other features because he had wrapped a large red kaffiyeh around his head in a conical shape. He also had on a faded robe that he had secured in the middle with a broad sash. I could see the severed hand, which looked plump and pale yellow and was covered in dried blood. I saw it clearly, and I realized that it had to be the hand of a woman who was still young. But I did not hear the voice of the man—the killer—who retreated gradually, farther and farther away, after having made sure that he'd scared my mother and deterred her sufficiently.

It seemed he had successfully carried out his mission, and that he didn't need to speak anymore; there would be those who would talk about him later and he would be celebrated in his clan's accounts when they entertained their guests. Until now, I have not been able to determine the exact distance that separated him from me at the time, but I still remember the short, sudden flash of his eyes and the ring of his laughter on that cold, gloomy morning. For an instant, he seemed cheerful to me. He reminded me of my maternal uncle—the witty man who lived in the adjacent house. Where was he? Was he still fast asleep after staggering home drunk? Where had the other men gone? Did they also prefer to stay warm in the arms of their wives, or had they gone to work early? Perhaps they had heard of the incident from their wives and had taken recourse to silence, instead of confronting this strange, evil man. But at that moment, I saw no trace of the women in the neighborhood. So why had my mother risked her life? Was she more courageous than the other women, or even the men?

Later on, my mother told me that the victim's husband was a worker in a state-run leather tannery; he was on the night shift during the day of the incident, and returned home only after he learned of his wife's murder; he took her things and left for some unknown destination. Since then, no one had seen the bereaved husband—he remained without a name or face until he completely disappeared from people's memories. My mother knew that the killer was named Sarheed—he was a vegetable seller who came from a small village on the outskirts of Baghdad. It was an unusual name, and it never left my mind. *Sarheed.*

I was greatly surprised that I was the only one among my siblings to take an interest in the affair. I felt relieved, because the murder did not have any noticeable impact on them, as opposed to my mother and me; her face would often be overcome with anxiety, and she would then sit in dreary silence.

I tried more than once to recall the features of that murdered woman who used to be our neighbor once, but I would never succeed in picturing her. There only remained in my mind the vision of the severed hand and the imagined cry of the victim when her brother pounced upon her, after she opened the door to him and before her husband returned from his night shift. How lonely and isolated she must have been in that dusty, deserted, impoverished alleyway! The killer doubtless took advantage of the increasingly shrill voice of the call to prayer to attack his sister; she had possibly arisen from her bed at that moment to say the dawn prayer or to greet her husband returning from work.

I remembered a story that my mother had once told me about a female relative who was attacked and devoured by wolves when she was alone in the desert. Her son and brother had gone to look for a horse of theirs that had run off in a far-flung wadi and left her alone near a palm tree. A pack of wolves discovered the woman clad in black, waiting for her son and brother to return—and just like that, they feasted on her. And when the two men returned, they found nothing of the woman except her bones lying in the sand.

That night, I dreamed that two masked thieves, armed with sticks, had made an opening in the room of the house where we slept, and began to empty out the clothes from the wardrobe into a burlap bag. I noticed that they had just grabbed my new checkered dishdasha; I had it made for Eid. I could see myself hearing their roars of laughter, which resembled Sarheed's, then I saw my mother wake up in panic and attack the two thieves with the lid of a cooking pot, trying to wrest the bag back from them. But one of them took her by surprise with a blow from his stick and a round iron piece became fixed in her head—we called it the *sakhriya*—so my mother teetered and fell unconscious to the concrete floor, with her blood spurting out profusely like water from a fountain. The thieves got away with our clothes, nonchalantly laughing at that late hour of the night.

I leaped up awake and out of bed, trembling and looking around my room, terrified. I glimpsed my mother standing by my head, watching me with exhausted, drooping eyes. Then she started to wet my face with cold water, wiping my hair with her hands. But I didn't tell her about the nightmare, Sarheed, or the blow of the *sakhriya*. Still, I asked myself, *If Sarheed had been rich and well-off, would he have gone and killed his sister? Why do the rich not kill their sisters to wash away their dishonor? Do all of them lack honor and shame, or are honor and killing reserved for the poor alone?*

The thought seemed to be much larger than my capacity to absorb it at the time, not to mention that a fever was about to split my head in two, and I began to see frightening visions that seemed as if they were coming from the Day of Judgment. A feeling struck me like a thunderbolt that *honor* was the only wealth the poor had that could not be squandered or frittered away. At that moment, the word *honor* became absolutely strange and mysterious to me. For, in truth, who was honorable? I felt an instinctive sympathy for that woman who had lost her life because she had rebelled against her community and dared to fall in love with a man who did not belong to her tribe, choosing to elope with him to that derelict corner of Baghdad. And had this not suddenly occurred to me, I never would've remembered the demise of the woman in love who had once lived next door to us.

After that night, I decided to pursue the trail of the killer, whatever the cost of this adventure may be; I began to search for the location of his village, his tribal origins. These people and their way of life kept me occupied for many long years—out of curiosity, and not with the sole aim of investigation alone, because the more details of their life I discovered, the stranger and more mysterious they became to me. In reality, they were poor Iraqis like me, but their temperament seemed to be extremely rough and completely different from that of other farmers.

One day, I decided to actually go along with my brother to the village; perhaps I would see Sarheed's face at least, or the secret behind the crime would be revealed to me. Had the country's situation not been stable at the time, I wouldn't have dared to take the step of foolishly searching in the killer's village. So, many long years after the crime, I would actually go to the mud village of al-Wawiya, or "The Foxes," located on the outskirts of Baghdad, where the killer was said to have come from.

I searched an entire day for his home and any sign of him. I saw many men around his age. Some of them bore his features, yet everyone I asked denied any knowledge of him.

One person mentioned to me that his name itself would guarantee identifying him as soon as anyone spoke it, like magic. Saying this was tantamount to conclusive evidence that he was not in that village, to the point that one of the men threatened me with an ax, yelling: "You are not wanted here!" He regarded me closely and accused me of having gone there to cover up some crime of my own.

I stared at his face and saw that it closely resembled Sarheed's. Stunned, I could only utter: "Sarheed?"

He held the ax up and said that if I did not leave the village immediately, he would strike my head with it. He started brandishing the ax just like Sarheed had done.

I returned home frustrated, but my determination to carry out my mission actually increased, so I reviewed all the old facts about the incident that were available to me. I became aware that the crime had never been repeated, as there had been no other honor killings of women in all of al-Thawra City, as if the community had abruptly forgotten this custom. How did Sarheed have the audacity to commit his crime with such boldness? And did he do it simply because the victim was a defenseless woman?

Every time I tried to penetrate the killer's psyche, hidden aspects of Sarheed's mentality and his way of thinking were unveiled to me. While I would often catch myself red-handed having thoughts of revenge—like a killer—I began to realize from another angle that murder was an absolute crime, one which could not be reversed. Perhaps at the time, Sarheed wanted to divide his own guilt among the members of his tribe, to share the responsibility for his offense and make them all participants in a crime that made up a part of their traditions and customs; maybe he wanted to unburden himself of the sense of guilt, since he had killed his own sister, whom he perhaps had felt some affection for, or even loved once. And maybe he was a person of sound mind, a man with a family; what he did was trivial, like picking ripe vegetables from the fields of the al-Wawiya village. In this sense, he did not commit the alleged crime on his own but in fact made the members of his tribe complicit. Therefore the victim's murder went unavenged.

From the gossip of the neighbors, it became clear that the lover had eloped with Saleema—just like that, people made up a name for the victim—and taken her to al-Thawra City, where he rented a small two-room house. No one at the time could say with certainty whether the man had married Saleema or had remained her lover until her demise. In those days, I could sense that the neighbors were steering clear of talking openly about the affair, before lowering a heavy veil of forgetfulness over it as time passed. Yet to this day, I shudder every time the image of the slaughtered woman and her severed hand appears before my eyes. Sometimes I would wake up in the middle of the night and stare at the door, frightened, and listen closely to the street—silent except for the wind, which would start blowing lightly, then howl every now and then. I would tremble with fear whenever the door moved or there was a commotion in the street or I heard the voice of a man talking or laughing loudly late at night. And sometimes when my uncle would visit us at night and I'd hear the creaking of the iron door, my heartbeat would quicken and I would feel as if the blood had frozen in my veins, so much so that I was afraid to shake his hand lest he detect my fear and the quivering of my limbs.

The front doors of houses in al-Thawra City did not lock either from the inside or the outside, since we all had a great sense of safety in the sprawling, poor neighborhood—as if we were part of a single family. One night, it so happened that I was returning from my job as a lottery-ticket seller in central Baghdad. I reached al-Thawra City somewhat late, so the streets were deserted. I began to look at the high facades of the houses, and I listened closely in the hope of hearing within them a human voice that would make me feel at ease in the stillness and desolation of the night—and when no voice calmed me, I remembered Saleema on the morning of her death.

All of a sudden there appeared a mature, svelte woman with a shapely figure; her face seemed to be white; she had supple limbs, making it easier for the killer to sever her hand without difficulty. I also remembered that her corpse had not been taken to its final resting place, nor was a wake held for her. No one had asked about her afterward. Perhaps the Baghdad municipality had buried her somewhere set aside for "impure" souls, without any gravestone. What would they write on her gravestone anyway? *Here lies the remains of Saleema, the Baghdadi who was butchered at dawn to protect her tribe's honor?*

Our street seemed long to me at that late hour, and was devoid of lighting, other than a few iron pillars upon which uncovered lamps had been hung; those sickly yellow lights made the street even more depressing and deserted. I heard a faint voice whispering behind me, a strange voice that was near one moment then distant the next. So I quickened my pace, without looking back, but the voice came closer and closer; I began to hear the fall of footsteps behind me that hurried one moment and then slowed down the next. Stones were being tossed at me from behind, landing between my feet; I tried to gather my strength in order to walk straight, and I looked over at the facade of a house. I found it serene and asleep, with its lights extinguished—on its outer wall was an iron hand hanging by a scrap of cloth: the Hand of Fatima. Residents would usually put this up to drive away the envious and the evil eye. But this time, it was the hand of Saleema

herself—the murdered woman—her youthful severed hand.
I envisioned the blood trickling and dripping from it, with a
strange serenity, onto the yellow dust of the street.

The voice of someone calling out arose behind me again
as the stones were being thrown more frequently. I thought
that even if I fell on my face in the dust, no one would come
to my aid in this neighborhood of the dead, and maybe no one
would hear my voice calling out for help in the first place. A
cold sweat ran down from my neck and seeped onto my chest
before it turned into a cold gust of air that blew from under my
thin shirt. Then I pictured that folklore creature who abducted children before they could reach their mother's bosom,
and would take them to the river to bathe them, before spir-
iting them to the remote marshlands; that djinn who took on
different shapes and sizes depending on the nature of his task,
which usually ended with killing the abducted. Our community used to call it *tantal*; when they described it to us children
on long winter nights, they would say it had a form that was
at once devilish and cartoonish, filling our little hearts and
minds with horror and alarm. This mythical creature, as they
told us, would come, sometimes with great agility, and knock
on closed doors, pretending to be humble, good-hearted, and
innocent; it would ask for water or a loaf of bread. When it
saw a child alone in the house, it would deviously entice him
little by little to walk a few steps, before lifting him on its back
and flying far away, or running with him to the river, while
making itself impossible to be seen or touched.

I was on the verge of collapsing in the middle of the street
in terror. I found myself unconsciously taking off my sandals,
and the stone-throwing from behind abruptly came to a halt.

The moment I reached home, I began to hyperventilate
and walk around the house restlessly, before flinging myself

into bed. I wrapped myself in the covers and my body began
to shake. My mother was sitting with my uncle, quietly talking
about some matter. When she heard me drop into bed, she
immediately came to me. She lit a lamp, then sat beside me
and began to dry my sweaty hair with her thin, warm fingers.
Then my uncle entered, overcome with anxiety, and asked me
to tell him what had happened. So I told him, stammering,
that I had seen the *tantal,* who pelted stones at me from behind and hissed loudly in my ears. This made my uncle laugh,
and he said that all I had seen was Sarheed, whose image had
haunted me for years. He told me that there was no such thing
as a *tantal* or any other mythical creature. He said it was nothing but the image of a killer that had invaded my mind and did
not want to let me go.

My uncle professed that he was capable of ousting this
demon from deep inside of me once and for all. He then took
out a revolver from under his long white robe and pointed it
directly at my head, saying that my mother had ruined me by
spoiling me rotten; he said that I was very different from my
clever and courageous siblings even though they were younger than me. He went on, saying that their older brother had
started to fear even his own shadow, imagining that his slipper
was a slingshot in a nighttime battle. But my mother rebuked
him and ordered him to leave the room, along with his revolver.
He fired a shot that boomed loudly, leaving me paralyzed at
first; then I instinctively grabbed my head to make sure it was
still intact.

"You're going to kill him! What exactly do you want from
him?" I heard my mother scream. "Would you act like this
with him if his father was still alive? Where were you when
your neighbor Saleema was killed right in front of you? Were
you afraid of your own shadow? Where was your revolver

then, huh? Get out of my house, I don't want to see your face again!"

As he was on his way out in the middle of the night, he told her that the killer's name was not Sarheed and that her son had been stricken by a bout of madness. He walked out with his revolver in his hand, and fired another shot as he roared with laughter in the dead of night.

But seriously, where was my uncle on the day the crime had happened? And why did he not talk about it? Did he know the killer from before? Or was he possibly an accomplice to the crime? Every time, I would reach the same conclusion, both simple and profound: the powerful only ever punish the weak.

At that moment, Sarheed the killer was roaming through the eighty residential sectors of al-Thawra City, alley by alley, in search of any trace of his runaway sister. He carried a large sack on his back, in which he collected empty bottles that he bought from residents, camouflaging his identity by this vocation that was widespread at the time, thereby not attracting any suspicion to himself. This simple occupation, in which he selected bottles and dishes that were fit to be recycled, made it possible for him to enter homes. I thought that maybe I too had once sold him empty bottles, as I would do that every now and then. I started to scrutinize the faces of the men who would call out, "Bottles for sale!" What were the faces like of the men more needy than us? Was Sarheed's face any different than those of the other bottle-buyers? Or did they all resemble each other in that era, just like today? Perhaps he was able to find the victim's address on his own, or someone led him to her house out of the goodness of their heart, or maybe out of wickedness. He may have described her features to this or that person and repeated her name hundreds of times, along with the name of her husband who had forcibly snatched her from her family in the harmonious village of The Foxes and brought her to this godforsaken place. At the time, she had not then changed her first name or family name or reincarnated herself under a different identity; she kept everything as it had been and lived as a stranger without any family or tribe or neighbors. Had they not heard her screams and cries for help when she was stabbed by her brother's dagger? When I look back now at the details of the incident, I ask myself whether the murderer had been held at all liable under the law in the first place, let alone taken into custody! I knew that these murders could be judged as a crime committed against the people, but Sarheed had dodged even serving those six months against "the public interest," and had gone back to his original vocation, selling vegetables in Bab al-Moatham Square.

I had seen Sarheed several times, standing in front of his cart with his red kaffiyeh, his thin mustache and narrow eyes, scorched red by the sun. I would hear him cry out in his weak and rasping voice: "Red! Red tomatoes! The best you can find!"

He sold small cucumbers as well—so I would envision the blood dripping from him while he held his sister's plump hand. Was this short, skinny, poor man really capable of committing such a carefully plotted, clandestine crime that any traces of it completely vanished?

I started to gaze at his features every time I saw him, until I began to arouse his suspicions and annoyance, since I wasn't buying anything from him. Maybe he figured I was a police informant, so he grudgingly put up with my glances. But was there anyone who had examined the hand closely and thus recognized whose it was? And who could say unequivocally that the murdered woman was actually his sister? He may have gone into a state of desperation after the long years spent searching the streets and dusty alleyways of al-Thawra City for his next victim—so he decided to pounce on a woman who wanted to sell him empty bottles!

I finally summoned up my courage and decided to confront Sarheed the killer face-to-face. I prepared myself well for this mission, taking into account any movement he might make, and told myself that I had to arrive at some solution before I left Baghdad and Iraq forever. This time, I really tried to adopt the personality of an investigator in charge of a criminal inquiry. I headed to Bab al-Mu'azzam Square, where Sarheed stood with his wooden cart, calling out in a feeble voice, worn out by dust and the scorching sun: "Red! Red tomatoes!"

I approached him but maintained a short distance, extremely wary of the sudden stab of a dagger; I saw the long knife that he had put on top of a pile of tomatoes and cucumbers. Yet in spite of my moving near him, he did not seem to pay any heed and continued calling out, as if he were addressing someone other than me. Right away I asked him: "Are you Sarheed the used-bottle seller?" I wanted to cut off any possible paths of escape.

He ceased his shouting, grabbed his knife mechanically, and glared at me with a look in his eyes that simultaneously carried anxiety and curiosity. "Who? Sar—? I've never heard this name before." He narrowed his small eyes, feigning surprise, and added: "My name is Hameed al-Shaalan, and I am a vegetable seller, as you see."

Before he could say anything else, I asked: "Didn't you used to buy empty bottles in al-Thawra City?"

Instead of replying, he tried to laugh, but it evaporated between the lines on his sharply furrowed face, which had been browned by the noonday sun, becoming a yellowish gray. "What do you want from me?" he asked. "Do I have something that you've lost?"

"I saw you some years ago roaming through the streets of al-Thawra City, looking for a missing woman. Did you ever find her?"

The man fell silent, his eyes darted away from me, and he started to shake his head in bewilderment. Then a customer in military fatigues approached, possibly having just come out of the Ministry of Defense building; he bought a few tomatoes and cucumbers, so I found myself compelled to do the same, and now thought that I might have accused the man wrongly and unjustly, just as my uncle had predicted. Perhaps I was suffering from some sort of psychosis! For more than ten years had passed since the incident took place, and all I had seen of the killer at the time was his red kaffiyeh, the glitter in his eyes, his dagger, and the severed hand.

The man calling himself Hameed silently put the tomatoes into a paper bag, then glared again—I could sense a kind of challenge. I thought maybe he himself had become a secret informant. For who was this man who dared to station his cart in front of the Ministry of Defense in Baghdad during the years of the Iran-Iraq War, when even pedestrians were not allowed to walk next to it? This Sarheed—or Hameed al-Shaalan—must have instinctively realized that working as an informant not only cleared him of suspicion but acquitted him of the murder charge.

Hameed lifted the bag and tossed it to the side of the cart. "Take your bag and go—I don't want to see your face again!" he growled. He waved his knife, the blade glinting in the sunlight. I moved to leave, but then turned around and saw him following me with his fiery gaze; I glimpsed the sudden brightness in his strained eyes. I nearly threw the bag of tomatoes into the street when I imagined that it was smeared with blood.

Before leaving al-Thawra City and Iraq completely, I headed to Bab al-Moatham Square several more times. I looked at the vegetable carts and their owners, but I saw no trace of Sarheed the seller of empty bottles. And every time I now recall Saleema's death, I have the impression that people were all colluding together back then, or were even accomplices to a crime that had become a mundane family matter—a crime that didn't arouse anyone's interest.

That incident happened more than fifty years ago, and I was a witness to it, perhaps even an indirect victim of its savagery—yet still, at this moment I do not want to believe that the murder actually took place.

Translated from Arabic by Suneela Mubayi

GETTING TO ABU NUWAS STREET

BY DHEYA AL-KHALIDI

Bab al-Moatham

I come to in the morning, and see that I'm in an abandoned metal shop. Tied up. My head is pounding as an oppressive calm tightens its grip on everything in this place: dusty tables with hammers, screwdrivers, and other tools; grubby men's clothes on a nail in the wall by a broken window; and paper bags and old newspapers begrimed with veggies and other leftovers litter the floor. Mulberry branches rustle behind the window nearest me, when out of nowhere, the barking of neighborhood dogs breaks the silence. Perhaps I'm in the countryside, far enough away that I can't get help.

Light floods in from the dilapidated windows. The shop door opens with a commotion that doesn't match the pint-size bodies coming into sight. Children between ten and fourteen years old, looks of glee on their faces. Eating potato chips and chocolate, they're dressed in colorful clothing, like they're on a holiday outing or a school trip. The spectacle escalates when one kid goes over to the metal lockers propped in the corner and opens several latches. The kids throw their food aside then look at me with a weird kind of enthusiasm.

A tall kid hands out an array of revolvers to his friends, and then they spread themselves throughout the shop—near the windows, the big door, behind the huge aluminum-cutting machine. Then another kid comes up to me, his eyes full of rage. I don't really know what's behind his gaze. He's wearing a T-shirt with Mickey Mouse on the front, pants with suspenders, and sneakers. Grinning, he stands there pointing his six-shooter at my face. "Do you want to die?" he asks.

"No."

"You want to live?"

"Of course. Who are you?"

"We're armed!"

I remember. Just before midnight yesterday, I decided once and for all to leave the hotel, no matter the consequences. I wanted to smash the clock; I thought I could ignore the curfew and get over to Abu Nuwas Street. I also remember the bottle of J&B whiskey that came along for the ride. A hotel employee had tried and failed to keep me from going out. Didn't make much difference to me when he told me to take care in one breath, and then threaten to throw me out in the next.

Baghdad's streets are desolate after midnight. The dark gathers in front of shops and alleyways. Wooden stalls for selling produce are set up and intertwined, as though they are broken-down trains at a station. I always watch the cats chase each other, hiss, and fight by the butcher's shop. But odd that there weren't any stray dogs around, since I used to hear them bark in the capital every day. Maybe they sensed something grave that night, so they were hiding, putting off the hunt for another time.

I kept on, walked out of the alley of a popular market. The booze wore off. One bottle clearly didn't do the trick for a lifelong drinker.

My nostalgia took me back two or three decades to those nights in Baghdad: the lovely Abu Nuwas Park, *masgouf* roasting over dancing flames, friends singing. Dreams would soar with clinking glasses of whiskey and local arak. At that time, anything seemed possible. At least that's what we believed. Those were the years. We had to be strong, daring, and rash. So now I had to get back what had been laid to waste, if only a small part of it—a scrap of an old dream. For most of what we did have was lost, forever. Like my beloved Sama—lost to a marriage she didn't choose. But today she has four loves—her teenage sons.

I kept to the sidewalk along al-Jumhuriyah Street, as I got farther away from my hotel, the popular market, and Bab al-Moatham. Could I have gone on to Bab al-Sharqi to get to Abu Nuwas Street, humming that old seventies song like I used to? Blackness shrouded Maidan Square and the near-by alleyways. The square had a glorious history. It used to be a lair for red metal creatures—the double-decker buses that were the backdrop for many of our memories. In the eight-ies, I got drunk in one. The 77 bus ran between Maidan and Nafaq al-Shorta. I fell asleep in the upper deck of one back then. I felt nothing, only heard the driver yelling at me as he slapped my cheek. He might have done that a few times, until I jumped out of my skin at the sight of a thick mustache on a pissed-off face.

I was worried that a soldier on guard duty would see me, so I stuck beside the walls of tall buildings. With each step I was closer to bliss—back to those bygone nights. Now I really wanted to smash the door bolted shut by life's losses. Night in Baghdad, night that set me apart; it didn't make me feel like some apparition gliding along, but rather a person seeking the utmost heights of a delayed ecstasy.

Would the guard know I wasn't a monster with its sights set on dearest Baghdad's face?

The sky flashed, and the smell of the rain washed the stench out of my capital. The droplets played an amazing melody as they fell. Far off, images upon images. Moments that flowed away like water on a sidewalk. I stopped at a squalid wall and scanned through the dark—when I heard the loudspeaker of a police car.

I'm trying to piece together what went down between last night's booze and these thoughtless children. It's like clay tablets with certain places scratched up and unreadable—I can't for the life of me fill in those gaps right now to figure out what's behind my blinding headache. It seems like there was a point in which I came upon the capital in the subtlest moments of its vulnerability.

American soldiers used to command Baghdad's nights— their Humvees roaring, keeping us awake and afraid. Then the night's custody switched over to our Iraqi brownness— bullets flying freely—even for a riled cat or a hungry dog.

My new buddy leaves me after a few minutes and goes over to another kid by the window. I need to know what they're talking about, so I eavesdrop and what I hear surprises me. They're busy discussing the latest episode of some cartoon on TV, how a dastardly wizard transformed the trees into hunks of concrete, the river into ice, and the animals into garbage. They couldn't wait for the brave prince to hurry up and come rescue everyone.

Their chatter isn't even beginning to broach my confinement. But it's odd as well. How can they long for the prince to come slay the wizard while they carry real-life six-shooters, just like the rest of their pals in the shop? I think about last night, whether I did something I should be ashamed of. Am I guilty like the evil sorcerer? Did I wreak havoc on the capital?

I call them over to ask them why I'm tied up and kept here. The other kids hear the question too and come over. They stare at me and smile.

An older one steps forward and plays with my hair. "You're nice and pretty," he says.

Then another kid with cotton skin, who looks like he attends one of those rich-boy boarding schools, tells me: "We won't kill you. We're nice, like you."

"Fine . . . then let me go?" I suggest.

I don't get an answer, and after a few minutes of their indifference, I bang my skull against the wall. That freaks them out and they get visibly upset.

"Untie me!" I yell. So shameful! I can't move at all because of these children; they didn't even exist during the eighties, when I was running under bombs and missiles in the war.

The knot is so tight—the kids couldn't have tied it. I realize this when a boy with a brown, slender face says, "The rope is tied too tight."

"Then who tied me up?" I ask.

"I don't know."

We hear shots nearby. The kids hide under the tables and machines, telling each other to get away from the windows. I can't know what's going on outside when there are gaps still left on the tablet in my mind. Specific areas are worn down but hold a secret. Maybe the children's minds went blank as well and that's why they're frightened, as if they've moved beyond the rules of the game.

A quarter-hour and then silence—the kids come out from hiding and set their guns on the tables. They haven't even fired a single bullet. They're calm, as though they are used to hearing the sounds of gunfire. So calm, in fact, that the skinny kid takes out chocolate from a black bag and begins handing it around. One of them comes up to me and tries to shove a piece in my mouth. I turn away. Bondage and sweets don't go together. I've long left childhood to a faraway place of empty booze bottles, gray hair, shabby clothes, and oblivion. Those things riddle every memory of mine.

I remember. At ease, I hid like a rat in the post office rubble, under the rain, stronger now. A storm was brewing. Moments went by and wind swept through the capital—sounds of slamming doors and windows, falling metal utensils. Bags and paper scraps flew through the streets and over the shops and buildings, while I was gaining a sort of unique warmth, wrapped in my coat and old tales.

Security barriers, rumors, and truths behind the dreadful curfew fell away, and my life flashed before my eyes: a small child among the streams and barley and cornfields; a young boy who longed to get away from his parents to see the capital; an audacious young man who made it out of his sleepy village; cheap hotels, wars, hookers, booze; and settling down as a street vendor in the Maidan market in the nineties. I unearthed precious items from piles of junk—old audio cassettes, tacky shoes, schoolbooks, switchblades, and other things nobody cared about except for poor people—happiness and intoxication, like the morning of a big sale. I even bought Bab al-Moatham PO boxes from two drunks who stole them during the events of April 2003. I wanted to own the mailboxes because of my obsession with keeping them from the drunk and needy. I'll never forget their wonder, as the boxes stood in front of me at the second-floor post office in the eighties. I'll never forget where my little box 754 was; it carried my family's pleas to go back home to the village. I'll never forget meeting my dear Sama in front of the mailboxes that winter day—that moment was a breath of fresh air in the isolating suffocation of the war. I loved Sama. I sent her rose-colored letters from over there—from a war whose secrets we haven't unearthed until now.

We have to hold on to the things we cherish even if we're poor. I needed money, but I wouldn't sell the memory boxes. So many letters passed through them to me and to Baghdad's people; sorrows, tears, and heartache; the elation that comes from secret love letters. Then there were the messages bringing good news.

Unfortunately, an American rocket blew the post office apart. So, to keep it in my head, I had to throw a guy out—he was ratty-clothed and looked like he could have been Indian. *Get out of here! I'm not selling you the boxes!* At the time, he said he'd break them apart and sell them individually, or sell the metal to an aluminum shop. Anything can be sold in my country, for cheap too—our memories, our streets, even the green leaves in our trees. Everything.

My box number 754 was back at the hotel. I tried to convince myself that some future morning I'd get a letter from Sama, or Mom or Dad, both now in heaven. Of course, they'll be different from past letters. Will Dad invite me once again to join them in a much quieter village? Or will Sama?

Hey, boy. I know you came by the alley after all these years, and saw me, Sama the mother . . . Sama the mother of four grown boys . . . my hair gray from constantly worrying about them in the streets of Baghdad. It won't ever be enough, even when my husband dies, for you to get close to me. My sons have grown up. Hey, boy from the post office building! We're old now!

Meaning: there were no more letters to wait for. We were alone now, withered by the moisture and mold. We could hardly remember the beauties, which had gone gray. The miniskirts strolling around the corniches of the capital were now just fragmented details. Tales of blissful lust at its peak— now a crushed Sumerian clay tablet.

The rain stopped, so I left my hiding place with hopes of getting to Bab al-Sharqi and Abu Nuwas that night. My right foot sank into a puddle. There was this kind of darkness that made you expect everything to go wrong. I had to get out of the post office rubble, cut through Maidan Square, so I could get to the wall of the Islamic Bank. But that'd be as dicey as it gets. I wished Bab al-Moatham were connected to al-Sharqi by a tall, never-ending wall. If that were the case, I'd have clung to it like a lizard and passed through to my final destination.

I left the demolished post office in a rush. A mysterious agility carried me along the wet asphalt to another wall. I felt secure in my drunken state, so I didn't falter. I got there and hid behind a concrete bus stop. I sat on the soaked ground and tried to warm myself up.

The war of the eighties—a memory that refused to be forgotten, a stretch I'd never get across. A hidden rope tied those days to today. Every once in a while, we'd get permission to take a few hours downtown, which brimmed with life and women.

I fled the Battle of East Basra, for death was a real presence among us. I didn't see him hiding like we were in the trenches. He wasn't wearing a helmet in fear of the hot shrapnel; he didn't worry about losing his loved ones who were waiting for his letter. He was harsh—stuck out his tongue at us soldiers, and then left us to go play the same game with the Iranians. He didn't care about sides or insignias. He went back and forth between us.

After that, I came back and was held prisoner in the brigade. I repented and pledged to be brave in the face of death;

I swore that next time I'd bore a hole into his skull and drive him from our lands, and from our heads, crammed with tons of questions . . . questions upon questions . . . until there was no room left for answers.

When I joined the army, I left at midnight from the musty Allawi al-Hillah Hotel to the al-Nahdha Garage. The whole time I was overcome with an intense, childish envy. Everything was better than me. I even resented the utility poles for being part of the city; they didn't care about bullets, whether from a pistol or an AK-47. No one wanted anything from them. They just stood there, lifeless. Not packed full of lofty or vulgar ideas, or anthems to mobilize.

I stayed there for a few minutes, then got up and hurried over to the wall, like a military patrol. Where the wall ended, the row of closed shops began. There, I'd pick a place to hide away from those eyes. All I wanted was to be on Abu Nuwas Street at night, where I could experience the capital's suspended carnival alone.

The children put aside their guns and start talking about this weird game with a funny name—it's called *Shabteet*. The kids split into two teams, each team on opposite sides of a chalk line drawn on the cement. I follow their conversation and their smiles, which have nothing to do with violence.

The chalk line stretches into my imagination, as a battlefront between two armies: the joys, giggles, panting, and anticipation in the kids' game are the bullets, rockets, missiles, coffins, and losses in the adult one.

Things get tense when the first kid from Team A crosses the white line into Team B's area. If he can touch somebody from the B side and then get back to his own side, then the kid he touched is out, thereby killing part of the army. Like this, the kids on offense take turns, armed with silent deter-mination. As for Team B, they defend by catching the kid who comes over and getting him out, either by making him laugh or forcing him to surrender. Then the armies switch places between offense and defense.

What a lovely contest—no smoke or explosions. Whoever stays quiet wins. Whoever laughs loses.

The sun curves away from its zenith, and light bursts in through the shop's western-facing windows. The passing time has not helped fill the last gaps in remembering that rainy night. Answers are still missing, questions are bouncing around like the rats here in the shop. It's always like this, lost answers to so many questions.

A bit of last night is coming back to me: the hotel boy's ear-nest way of trying to talk me out of leaving at night—*You can't go out during the curfew, you'll get killed.* That's what he said. I remember his fingers clutching my forearm. But I pushed him away and went down the dark staircase. I thought the door would be locked. I smiled. Instead of begging me, the boy could have just locked the door.

A wind blew through the capital. Streets without foot-steps, booze numbing fear, driving me forward. I wouldn't de-lay in following this to its logical conclusion. Or to the end I had chosen for myself.

The post office was leveled by an American missile in the last war, which left us with a bunch of dark holes for hiding in. Over there was Maidan Square and the Islamic Bank, and after them, dealers of Persian rugs, blankets, and other house-hold items. It was too dark to see, but my memory read the signs and showed me the way. I wasn't worried now about the shots ringing out, the bullets riddling my city's body and sky.

If a soldier or cop wanted to empty his cartridge into me, go ahead.

I heard voices in the dark at al-Wathba Square. What was going on? Bullets whizzed, sparks and RPG-7 missiles thrashed the security building. But why fret? I knew beforehand the risks of going out—explosions, bullets, and screams. *God is the greatest.* Smoke mingled with the dark of night, and bits of light shone from intermittent streetlights. Then the scene changed color.

The Department of Security was on fire. Ghosts flew toward me with bullets after them, zooming in all directions, striking the asphalt and storefronts. I remember jumping without thinking, as I ran with the others. Yes, I turned on my heels and went back the same way I'd come. The bullets were hunting us all.

The children leave the shop, as if their shift is over. Then there's silence for about half an hour, before gunmen come in and take off their face masks. They greet me like we know each other.

They tell me I'd been out cold since last night, that I slammed into some concrete ledge when the police and army were chasing them through al-Wathba Square. They start to ask me questions, but with kindness.

"You were running with us," says one of the gunmen. "Who do you work for?"

"Who's your boss?" another asks. "Were you on a mission to blow up the building last night too?"

"Don't be afraid, we're all in the same boat," they tell me.

These new questions inform me that my memory is more sketchy than I thought. The more blanks I try to fill in the tale of the broken Baghdad curfew, the further I get from remembering it. It may have been eventful, with all sorts of horrors and outlandish details. But I'll leave it to these guys with the masks to figure it out. I'm so tired that I can't find my true memory. I don't care if I have to borrow a memory from one of the fellows stuffing his face with dates, bread, and yogurt.

I'm still tied up, and my headache gets worse with each question. I can't answer any of them. My brain stops processing their words. I just follow their faces; their lips are angry now, their mouths hurling insults. Then they're slugging me in the face. I just want one answer: "Where are the kids?"

They smile and glance at one another, until a man with a shaved face says: "He's still reeling from yesterday's blow!"

"What kids? This is an abandoned metal shop," another gunman adds, sounding very annoyed.

I realize I have a head injury from the concrete ledge on some wall, and that the tablet of my memory is incomplete, and that the children's *Shabteet* game goes on—but with other rules; instead of silence and laughter, there's noise, corpses, and machinations.

Did I get to Abu Nuwas Street after midnight? Yes. I believe I did.

Translated from Arabic by Robert James Farley

PART IV

BLOOD ON MY HANDS

HOMECOMING

BY ROY SCRANTON

Shorja

A tumult of hands, pain, and a mouth filled with sand—then he was being carried back behind a Humvee. The medic checked his ABCs, dragged a nearby rucksack to one side of his head, and dug a helmet in under the other. He was slipping in and out of consciousness, but his pupils were fine, and the ugly cut on his scalp seemed shallow—the skull appeared to be intact. The medic bandaged his head, stuck him with an IV, and told another wounded soldier, a corporal sitting up against the Humvee, to keep him awake. Then the medic moved off to another casualty.

"You lucked out, Haider," the corporal said as he lit a cigarette. "That IED killed your buddies, but that's a victory wound you got there. You go home, everybody thinks you're Ali Hussein. Some real Rambo shit."

Haider just grunted.

The man patted his arm. "I know, I know. Things seem pretty shitty right now. But take heart: the good news is your little scrape doesn't even hurt yet."

Three days, two army trucks, and one taxi ride later, Haider was cursing Corporal Hamza's good news. He paid the driver, his hands clumsy and his whole body stiff, and grabbed his gym bag out of the backseat. Squinting at the clogged traffic, he listened to the car horns vibrating through the roundabout on al-Jumhuriya Street. He wove around old Datsuns, new Chinese pickups, and the occasional BMW; he cut his way across and into the swift human currents of Rashid Street, his head pounding in the bright June light.

He dodged a cart piled high with boxes, feet slipping on orange peels tossed in the street by the juice man, and ducked around a tray of river carp, slipping into the shade between the old buildings and the vendors' umbrellas. Market life flashed around him, glowing with the strangeness of a dream: sacks of spice like pigments on a palette, dusky red-pepper powders, luminous ocher turmeric, and the muddy green of za'atar; plastic Chinese housewares in rows of lurid pink and neon green; a rainbow mosaic of tea boxes, multicolored powdered drink mixes, and purple-brown jars of date syrup; frilly dresses in electric blue, hazard yellow, and bloody violet, covered in dancing mermaids and Disney princesses; innumerable squat bottles like great chunks of jade, amber, and garnet; hand soaps, dish soaps, shampoos. It was always a change coming in from the field, but this was something else. The smells made him queasy, the colors knifed into his eyes, and the swirl of bodies gave him a feeling of vertigo—part euphoria and part fear. His head throbbed.

He was relieved to turn off Rashid Street into al-Safafeer Market, practically empty these days, and leave the tumult behind him. It was quiet here. The street of the coppersmiths led off toward the river—the long, cool arcade gleaming within from the copper lamps, plates, pots, vases, and candelabra spilling into the otherwise vacant, brick-lined walk. The shining display always seemed enchanting at first, when you stepped into the souk, but nowadays it was mostly imported crap from India and China. Baghdad's legendary smiths had become just that: legendary. Nobody wanted to pay for handmade work, so the old men sold what people would buy, while their sons left the souk's backroom smithies in search of better prospects—like joining the army.

"Haider!" a voice shouted from one of the stalls. "Peace be upon you."

"Upon you be peace, Uncle," Haider responded, recognizing long-faced Sayid, one of his father's old friends.

"Are you home from the fight?" Sayid asked, stepping out into the arcade.

It took Haider a second to understand the question, which echoed oddly in his ears. When he caught the gist he smiled. "Daesh gave me a birthday present," he said, tapping his head. "Now I have a week of leave."

A complex look of concern flashed across Sayid's face. "I'm glad you're safe. Have you seen your father yet?"

"I'm on my way there now."

"Listen, Haider," Sayid said, glancing around the souk. "It's none of my business, but Abu Bakr ran into some trouble. He's not well. Up here, you know?" Sayid patted his forehead.

"What happened?"

"You should hear it from him, but there's no need to get involved, okay? Sometimes it's best to let sleeping dogs lie."

"What do you mean?"

Sayid put his hand on Haider's shoulder. "Just trust me, nephew, okay? Remember how your father gets sometimes. You don't need to fix things. What's done is done."

Haider looked at the old man with a measure of understanding. "God's will," he said.

Abu Bakr anxiously greeted his last living son from a wheelchair, as if hiding something. Haider's mother stood behind the old coppersmith, her mouth rigid and compressed but her eyes full of emotion. They were surprised to see him home and wanted to hear about his wound, but Haider waved it off and asked them what had happened.

"I'm not feeling so well," Abu told him, laughing.

"What's wrong?" Haider asked.

"It's just arthritis," Abu muttered.

"A cursed man," Haider's mother added.

"Nadia, please," Abu said, grinning again. "It's nothing."

"Father, would you let me see your legs?" Haider asked.

"There is no reason for that, they're fine," Abu assured.

"That's because they're gone!" Nadia snapped. "Gone! The old fool!" She slammed her tea glass down on the table and stormed out of the kitchen.

Haider could see it now, under the blanket, how Abu's legs ended at the knees. He'd thought that there was something wrong with the way they looked, but he hadn't understood what. It took Haider all afternoon to get the story. This was the tale his father told him:

Business had been going even worse than usual, so he went to his old friend Abu Lulu'ah to see if he had any work. Abu Lulu'ah told him that he had a job he could do, and he'd pay well for it, but it was dangerous. He needed a shipment driven to Rutbah, which was practically on the Syrian border, then another shipment brought back. It would be possible—if you took Route 9 south and looped around Habbaniyah to avoid the fighting around Fallujah, then took Route 1—eight or nine hours each way. Abu Bakr would need to use his own truck, since Lulu'ah couldn't afford to lose a truck to Daesh, but he promised him a wad of US dollars.

What would he be carrying? *Let's say it's canned food.*

Who would he be delivering it to? *Let's call him al-Maeiz.*

Where would he meet the man? *A pacha restaurant in Rutbah.*

So Abu Bakr drove out to Rutbah before dawn, heading south through the towns and farms along Route 8, the sky fading blue on his left as the sun broke like a soft-boiled egg over the horizon, milky white then golden yellow. Just north of Karbala, he turned his back on the sun and drove southwest over the Euphrates. The City of Martyrs shone like a holy vision in the clear, slanting light. Then he left the green farmlands of the river valley behind, heading northwest into the Sunni desert, nothing but sand, dirt, and dust for kilometers; past Lake Habbaniyah, a greasy gray patch floating on the brown earth; everything flat for kilometers, seemingly forever, desolate save for the occasional truck passing him going the other way; until, as the long hours wore on, the hills surrounding Wadi Houran rose in the west, rocky and austere, and the highway seemed to sink down, down, down toward Rutbah and the borderlands.

He'd made great time and rolled into town around noon. Everything was quiet, no traffic and few people. He passed a tall man in a pink shirt smoking a cigarette on a street corner; the man's beard was just long enough that he could've been a *salafi*, but just short enough that maybe he wasn't—he was so studiously *not* watching the truck pass that Abu felt a rising fear. He relaxed when he found the *pacha* restaurant, but it was closed, and when he knocked no one answered. *What now?* Well, Abu Bakr figured, they'll open soon enough, and in the meantime, thinking of the drive ahead, he might as well take a nap. He parked behind the restaurant, hung a towel in his window to give himself some shade, and curled up on the bench seat. The truck engine ticked as it cooled from the long drive, soothing the old man to sleep.

He woke with a crash, the driver's-side window shattered. When he jerked and tried to twist his body up, a rifle butt came through and slammed into his forehead. Everything went black-and-white, and the next thing he knew, he was grabbing at the steering wheel and looking down the barrel of an AK while someone tried to haul him out of the truck by his feet. He watched the barrel swing up past the face behind the gun—hard eyes and a long beard. Then the butt came down on his forehead again. This time when he came to, he was lying on the ground, bleeding in the sand, looking up at three men unloading the stuff from his truck into the *pacha* restaurant, while a fourth stood over him with the AK.

Abu's world spun with pain, but he lifted his hand. "Wait," he pleaded. "Wait . . . al-Maeiz."

"Who told you that name, fat man?" the one standing over him asked.

"Abu Lulu'ah sent me."

"Well, when you get home to Baghdad, you little Shi'ite bitch," the gunman growled, "you tell your boyfriend that al-Maeiz says hello."

"But . . . the other one . . ."

"The other one *what*, fat man?"

"I'm supposed to bring something back," Abu whispered, confused.

"Is that what Abu Lulu'ah told you, fat man?"

"Yes."

The gunman ratcheted the charging handle on his AK back and forth, chambering a round. "You want me to give you something to take back?"

Abu Bakr looked away and eyed his truck. Both doors to the cab were open, both windows smashed in. They were almost done unloading.

"God grant my life," Abu said. "I have a wife and a son, only one son left. Please."

"You tell Abu Lulu'ah that al-Maeiz got his shipment and not to worry about anything else, okay?"

The drive back seemed endless; Abu Bakr imagined a thousand different ways Lulu'ah would punish him. It was late when he finally returned, but he went to see Lulu'ah right away at his stall in the Shorja Market. The big man was there waiting, and listened to Abu Bakr's story patiently. When he finished, Lulu'ah picked up a handful of pistachios and let them run through his fingers like prayer beads falling off a broken string. "What do you think . . . I should do with this thief?" he asked meditatively, watching the pistachios drop.

Abu Bakr wasn't quite sure what he meant, or whom he was talking to. His head ached and he'd been on the road for almost twenty hours. The young toughs sitting around the stall didn't seem to hear Lulu'ah; neither did the kid whose job it was to watch the sweets; nor did the hatchet-nosed man who stood behind him—the one everybody called The Hawk. Abu hazarded a reply: "I don't know, Uncle. I'm not even sure I saw al-Maeiz . . . I mean, those men might have done something to him."

Lulu'ah looked up in confusion, which quickly hardened into disgust. "You think I meant al-Maeiz—my oldest friend, my brother, who has stood with me through everything? You think I'd call my own brother a thief?" He closed his fist around the pistachios. "You're stupider than you look, you fat fuck!"

The Hawk turned his head and stared at him. Abu Bakr was not an especially brave man, and he was no great warrior. No, he was just a coppersmith—but he was a Baghdadi all the same, and an Iraqi, and he'd had plenty of tough moments; he'd faced down his share of terrors. Yet the fear that trembled in his belly when The Hawk looked into his soul was something he never wanted to feel again.

"I d-don't kn-know what you m-mean, Uncle," Abu stammered.

"I mean, al-Maeiz called me a couple hours ago and asked me where his shipment was. He said he waited all day at the restaurant for this idiot truck driver and the guy never showed. So I was thinking you must have been dumb enough to get blown up or something, but then you show up here feeding me this donkey shit about how the restaurant was closed and al-Maeiz's own guys robbed you at gunpoint."

"It's the truth, I s-swear," Abu said.

"So I'm supposed to trust you, little coppersmith, over my oldest, dearest friend?"

"No, of course not, Abu Lulu'ah, it's just—"

"Shut up!" Lulu'ah flung pistachios into Abu Bakr's face. "Let me tell you what happened: You headed off toward Karbala, just like you were supposed to, but then you went and met your cousin who fucks your wife on Tuesdays, and you two unloaded my shipment and put it in his garage. Then you sat around all day fucking each other in the ass, and when you were both good and tired, you had some tea, and then he roughed you up a little so it'd look convincing."

Abu Bakr glanced around the market, almost empty at that late hour, hoping to find a friendly face. But everywhere he looked, people avoided his gaze. Nobody would witness Lulu'ah's judgment, though everyone would hear about it, as word would spread quickly through the Shorja Market.

Abu couldn't remember exactly what he'd said then, only that he'd started begging Lulu'ah to *believe him*, to *be merciful*, to *please listen, go look at the truck, go see*, but then the toughs grabbed him by the arms and hit him until he passed out. He woke up later strapped to a table, with The Hawk standing over him, smoking a cigarette. Abu started to plead again, but instead of responding, the thin, hatchet-nosed man picked up a power saw. He pulled the trigger once, twice, and the jagged blade buzzed into a silver blur.

Next time he awoke was in a hospital. He'd been in shock, the doctor said, when the men dumped him outside the ER, but someone had put tourniquets on his stumps to keep him from bleeding out. He was lucky to be alive, the doctor told him. Later, a policeman came by to take a statement, and Abu Bakr made up a story about his truck falling on him while he was working underneath it. The officer didn't believe him—it was clear—but he didn't ask any more questions.

Haider leaned back, took a drag on his cigarette, and peered at his crippled father. It had gotten dark and their tea had gotten cold, but neither of them moved to turn on a light. He could hear his mother watching TV in the other room.

"I didn't want to tell you," his father said. "I wasn't going to tell you."

"What would that solve?" Haider asked.

"I can still work," his father claimed, holding up his hands. "Your mother can find a job. We'll survive. And you—you have your career in the army. I didn't want to give you anything to worry about."

Haider's head throbbed all along the wound, which was slowly healing, across his scalp, and into his eyeballs. Patience was a struggle, as was controlling the anger he felt seeping out into his limbs, an icy, oily burn, languid and murderous.

"What about the tribe? What'd you tell them?" Haider asked.

"I told them what I told the police."

"And where's the truck?"

His father shook his head. "Lulu'ah kept it. Your mother

went back to get it after . . . but they said it was payment for what I'd stolen. Promise me you won't do anything, my son. Promise me, for your mother's sake."

Abu Lulu'ah was dangerous, it was true, and The Hawk was no joke. *Father should have never gone to them . . . and fucking up the delivery . . . why'd he have to take a nap, the old fool?* Haider thought to himself. He could imagine explaining the whole thing away as an old man's stupidity. You play *dambala* with a gangster like Abu Lulu'ah, what do you expect? He was lucky to be alive.

Still, the injustice rankled. And what was more galling, even more than the dishonor to his tribe, was that he was a soldier. Sure, he wasn't some Golden Division commando, but he was a veteran in a real fighting company, not one of those paper units that broke and ran like dogs. When Abu Lulu'ah touched his father, he touched him. It didn't matter who was right or wrong, who was a fool or who was a big shot. What mattered was that you let that motherfucker hurt you, or you make him stop. That's all this was—not honor, not justice, not prudence, but a fight. And Haider knew how to fight.

He stood and put his hand on his father's shoulder. "You should rest, Father."

The first thing Haider did in the morning was buy a pistol. It took a couple of hours, but in the end he found a nice American M9, cheap. Then he went to see Abu Lulu'ah.

At that hour of the morning, before the heat rose, the Shorja Market was a riot of bodies: bargain-hunters and deliverymen, vendors and beggars, and those like Haider, who came on other kinds of business. He wove through the crowded lanes, reliving the assault on his senses from yesterday, pushing past piles of clothes, toys, knives, copperware, and household electronics, all made in China, India, and Vietnam.

It was just like the markets in Souk al-Safafeer. Before the Collapse, they'd had nothing but what they could make or scavenge, plus the trickle of imports—mostly medical supplies allowed through the sanctions and the "Oil-for-Food Programme." The embargo cats ran a thriving black market in goods smuggled over from Syria, Turkey, and Iran—but the supplies were unpredictable and outrageously expensive. Somehow they got through, surviving the malnutrition, diarrhea, and starvation, on the strength of Iraq's farms and date orchards.

Now they imported their dates from Egypt and Saudi Arabia. The orchards still produced, but the foreign corporations that rushed in and bought up the country during the Collapse exported the Iraqi dates. The Americans had opened the country to globalization: after standing idly by while looters stripped the country for parts, the Coalition Provisional Authority invited the Egyptians, Chinese, Russians, Kuwaitis, Saudis, and South Koreans to come feast on what was left—at bargain-basement prices. And so, through eight years of occupation and eleven years of war—through the Collapse, and the Americans, and al-Qaeda, and Iran, and now Daesh—the country was flooded with cheap imports. These imports included staples like dates and eggs, rice and cheese, DVDs and cars, PVC pipes and cell phones, satellite dishes and knock-off designer shoes, flash-frozen chicken fingers, soccer jerseys, and copper pots. It was a miracle. The only problem was nobody had the money to buy anything. Unless a person worked for the government, the army, or an oil company, they were probably struggling just to feed their family—while every day new malls sprang up alongside new shops and new Saddams— Saddams like Abu Lulu'ah.

Haider could see Lulu'ah down the lane, sitting in his

stall, broad-chested and smiling, talking cheerfully to somebody's grandma. The Hawk was there too, reading a newspaper, and the usual gangbangers, and the kid. For all the world, it looked like a normal stand: largish, maybe, for a place that sold sweets and nuts, but nothing out of the ordinary. As Haider watched the big man, a bead of sweat slid along his spine, kissing the handle of his pistol where it was jammed in the back of his pants. His head still hurt, but he'd ignore that for now. He saw Abu Lulu'ah notice him. Then The Hawk, turning the pages of his paper, looked over to follow his boss's eye. Now they were both watching him, and their gazes were a force transforming the market lane into a cataract of energy. Haider could sense it in his wounded scalp, in his fingers, and all the way down the line of tables. It was the way you felt before an attack, locking into a pattern of violence that had its own force, its own will, its own rhythms. *Inshallah*, he thought, walking into his fate.

He didn't go two steps before a guy with a giant mustache blocked his path. "Hey, soldier, what's up?"

"Nothing, cousin," Haider answered, holding up his hands. "I'd like to speak with Abu Lulu'ah. I'm the son of Abu Bakr and I want to pay my father's debt."

"You think you're funny?" the mustache man said, shoving Haider in the chest. "How about you fuck off?"

"I'm serious," Haider said, looking down and away, keeping his hands up, not meeting the aggression but not giving in to it either. "I just want to talk to Abu Lulu'ah. I want a chance to earn back our truck."

The mustache told him to wait there, then walked slowly back to the sweets stand, where he talked with Lulu'ah for a minute. When he came back, he told Haider to spread his arms and turn around.

"I've got a nine mil," Haider pointed out. "For protection."

"Shut the fuck up!" the mustache barked. He took Haider's pistol and patted him down. Then he shoved him toward Abu Lulu'ah. Haider walked down the lane, feeling the giddy peace between life and death—that place where nothing mattered. When they got to the stand, the mustache laid the M9 on the table in front of Lulu'ah.

"Peace be upon you," Lulu'ah greeted.

"And upon you be peace," Haider returned, keeping his hands up.

"You can relax, *jundi*," Lulu'ah said. "What happened to your head?"

"We were ambushed on the road outside Taji," Haider explained. "We stopped and dismounted, returned fire, began to counterattack. I was advancing with my squad to one of the ambush positions when they blew an IED."

"Daesh?"

"Daesh."

"Fuck Daesh!" Lulu'ah hissed, spitting on the ground and stomping his foot.

"They killed my friends," Haider murmured. "Men who were like brothers to me."

"Praise God you survived, *jundi*."

"God is great."

"And what do you want from an old seller of baklava, brave warrior?" Lulu'ah asked.

"I come respectfully, as the son of Abu Bakr. I know he failed you and owes you a debt."

Lulu'ah picked up a handful of pistachios. He cracked one and slid the seed into his mouth. "That debt is paid, *jundi*."

"Some debts can never be repaid," Haider said, bowing his

head. "We are an honorable family, and my father's mistake has cost us dearly. I come today about our truck."

"What truck?"

"We kept the old man's truck," the mustache told Abu Lulu'ah. "You told us to keep it as payment for what he stole."

"So what?" Lulu'ah said. "There you have it, *jundi*. The debt's paid."

"We're a poor family," Haider said. "The weakest of our tribe. And it was a shitty truck, I know—always breaking down, nothing but trouble. But it was all we had, since my brothers died. I would ask you to give me the chance to earn it back."

"How did your brothers die?"

"My oldest brother worked for the Americans, so al-Qaeda killed him. My other brother joined the Mahdi Army and died fighting the Badr Brigade. My younger brother was caught in a firefight in Zayouna—killed by the Americans, by accident. They gave us two thousand dollars. My father used some of that money to buy his truck."

"So?" Lulu'ah said, cracking a pistachio.

"I'm a good soldier. I'm not easily frightened or foolish like my father. Let me be of service to you in some way, and all the payment I would ask is that you give us our truck back."

Abu Lulu'ah looked around the souk, cracked another pistachio, and ate the seed. "And what do I get for taking you on like this? Huh? Why should I bother? Why shouldn't I tell you to fuck off?"

"Like I said . . ." Haider replied, reaching for the M9 and laying his hand flat upon it. The Hawk's own pistol was drawn now, and one of the toughs was pulling out an AK from under the table. Haider froze, leaning on the M9, his other hand in the air. He spoke calmly: "I'm a good soldier, not easily frightened." He slowly lifted his right hand up, empty, leaving the

M9 on the counter. "Maybe you have something special I can do for you."

Lulu'ah laughed. "You're a fool, just like your father. But maybe I got something I can use you for. Come back tomorrow morning, and leave your popgun at home, okay, *jundi*? You make my boys nervous."

Later that night, Haider had dinner with his parents and told them how things were going in the army. Everyone expected more fighting, which was dangerous, of course, but good for promotions. Soon he'd be a corporal and get his own squad. After dinner they watched a movie, but his head hurt so much he got up halfway through and went to bed. He couldn't sleep, so he lay in bed staring at the ceiling, thinking back to the ambush, remembering the moment the IED went off, picturing the nut in Abu Lulu'ah's teeth when he laughed, imagining the M9 jammed down the man's throat.

In the morning, he put the M9 in an old backpack, along with extra rounds and magazines, then headed for the market. He stopped to greet his cousin, who sold hand tools at a small stand near the south entrance, and asked him to hang on to the backpack while he did his shopping. He picked it up about ten minutes later, after getting a set of terse instructions from The Hawk, along with the keys to a Chinese pickup. Abu Lulu'ah hadn't even been there.

He drove the pickup over to the Karrada, following The Hawk's instructions, off Jami'a Street and behind the Coral Boutique Hotel. Police had the side streets blocked off with checkpoints; he explained he was picking up a reporter at the International House. At the address The Hawk had given him, he buzzed the door. A private guard answered, and Haider gave him the name of the American.

Haider heard him before he saw him, saying goodbyes in that loud, hearty voice Americans had, aggressive and falsely cheerful. Then he appeared in the doorway with a backpack and a gym bag; he had gleaming black hair, movie-star stubble, Oakleys, khakis, hiking boots, and a crisp blue shirt under an armored vest. He looked like an extra from a movie about the Green Zone, circa 2004.

"Do you speak any English?" the man asked in passable Iraqi Arabic.

"No," Haider replied.

"Okay," the man said. "Where's the vehicle?"

"Right here," Haider told him, pointing at the truck.

"Motherfucker couldn't even get me a SUV," the man mumbled. "Wonderful. Tell me it has a CD player, at least."

"Just a radio," Haider said.

"Well then, we might as well go," the man said, heading for the truck. "I'll give you directions on the way."

Soon they were heading north out of Baghdad. The man had a high-level diplomatic pass that got them through checkpoints, and as Haider handed it over again and again, he wondered: *What kind of journalist has a pass like that?* The name written on the pass was *Steve Ricks*. The agency read: *Wall Street Journal*. And it was signed by Saadoun al-Dulaimi, the minister of defense.

Steve Ricks didn't say much at first, just gave directions, but once they were out of the city, he opened his backpack and took out an M9, just like Haider's. He also took out a holster, which he clipped to his belt, before sliding the M9 inside. Then, looking out through his silver Oakleys, he said: "Your boss tell you where we're going?"

"Mosul," Haider answered.

"Anything else?"

"He said I wasn't supposed to ask you questions. Drive you up, do what you say, drive you back. He said you'd have a message for me to deliver. That you're a journalist."

"That's all right. He said you're Iraqi Army."

"Yes sir," Haider confirmed, watching the road. "Here."

"Here, what?"

"Here's where my convoy was ambushed. Four . . . five days ago." Haider pointed at an empty spot on the road, a flash in his memory.

"No shit. Daesh?"

Haider nodded. "It's what happened to my head. They sent me home for a week. That's why I have time to work for Abu Lulu'ah."

"Shouldn't you be resting up?" Ricks asked.

"My family owes a debt to Lulu'ah," Haider explained.

"I see. And what's your name, *jundi?*"

"Haider."

"Pleased to meet you, Haider. Call me Steve."

They shook hands, and Haider was pleased to see the man knew enough to shake hands lightly and touch his chest, in the Iraqi way.

"You should know that what we're doing is very dangerous," Ricks warned. "I'm going to meet with a very dangerous man, to interview him for the *Wall Street Journal*. You won't like him, or his friends, but I need you to be cool the whole time. Just sit in the truck and wait for me and be cool. Then, after the interview, we drive back, no problem, and you forget you ever met me. Cool. You know *cool?*"

"*Cool,*" Haider said back in English. "*Fucking cool, bitches.*"

Ricks laughed. "That's right, Haider. *Fucking cool.*" Then he turned on the radio and settled back into himself, listening to Rihanna sing "Complicated."

* * *

Route 1 follows the Dijla Valley north past Samarra and Tikrit, then breaks west, turning at the vast Baiji complex—storage tanks and towers, pipes and flare stacks burning off against a low ridge—Iraq's largest refinery. As they drove by, Steve Ricks took pictures.

"Careful," Haider said.

"How good's security here?"

"So-so. They might shoot at us if they see you taking pictures. I think they're regional police, not army, which usually means they're worse, but sometimes it means they actually give a shit. Why? You writing a story about Baiji?"

"They will be," Ricks told him, putting his camera away. "Can't you drive any faster? I want to get back to my *shisha* tonight."

"Sure, boss."

Traffic was light, the first few checkpoints hassle-free. The story Steve Ricks told the soldiers on the road was that he was interviewing Lieutenant General Mahdi Gharawi, and with his special pass that seemed to work.

"You really interviewing General Gharawi?" Haider asked as they rolled through the desert.

"You really asking me a question?" Ricks shot back.

"No sir."

"You know about Gharawi?"

"Just rumors. They say he was Republican Guard under Saddam, and the Americans put him in charge of a police division after the Collapse," Haider recited. "He ran a torture prison for Maliki, then spent a few years in the Green Zone, I think. Now he's in charge of Nineveh."

"You're pretty informed for a *jundi*."

"Soldiers gossip about their daddies—especially now, with

the fight against Daesh. People say Gharawi will lose Nineveh. His divisions are mostly paper, and the army has pulled its tanks and artillery to Anbar. If Daesh hits Mosul . . . let's just say I'm glad we're not staying."

It was then that Haider saw the checkpoint up ahead and began to slow the truck. Something felt wrong. It looked like a normal improvised checkpoint: three Humvees and a few soldiers, but . . . what was it? If only his head didn't hurt so much.

"Why are you slowing down this far away?" Ricks asked.

Even the soldiers had noticed, and had begun waving him forward.

Then it hit him: those weren't soldiers.

"They're Daesh," Haider said.

"How can you tell?"

"The beards. Everything else looks okay, but their beards are too long. And see the Humvees: those markings are from two different units, both from Anbar. Fuck!"

"Okay, Haider," Ricks said, "just be cool, all right? I got this."

"I don't think these guys read the *Wall Street Journal*, Steve Ricks."

"Don't worry about it. You're not getting paid to worry. Just be cool and drive. Slow."

This didn't feel like moving into an assault. This felt like an ambush. *This is bad: if they make us get out, we're fucked, and if we try to drive through, we're fucked. We might survive the small-arms fire, but those machine guns on the Humvees will tear this little pickup to pieces.*

Haider breathed deliberately, slowly, holding his hand light on the wheel. His pistol was in his backpack on the seat next to him—the top was unzipped, like he'd left it, but it would still take too long to draw out. Their only chance would be to blast through and hope they make it. He slowed the truck, not looking at the soldier with the thick, bushy beard waving him on.

Then the beard was at the window, and they were caught between rifles. "ID," the beard said.

Haider pulled out his ID card and Ricks's pass, but before he handed them over, the American said: "How far is it from here to Raqqa?"

The beard's eyes narrowed. "To get to Raqqa you have to go through Dabiq."

"They say that to get to Dabiq you have to go through Rome," Ricks countered.

"Indeed," the beard said. "The road is long, but striving in the way of God will be rewarded."

"*Inshallah*," said Ricks, nodding.

Haider understood now, and began to see how things would go. He'd need to get in touch with a friend of his brother, who'd gone from the Jaish al-Mahdi to Asaib ahl al-Haq. But that shouldn't be too hard.

"Are you the American?" the beard asked.

"Call me Steve."

"Ali will ride with you."

"There's room in the back," Ricks said.

The beard nodded, and called for Ali. One of the other fake soldiers ran up with his AK; he was just a kid, his chin dusted with scraggly hairs. "You'll ride with them to Dair Mar Elia," the beard instructed. "Give them directions. Then you stay with Abu Abdulrahman, okay?"

Ali nodded and climbed in the back. With his boyish face, they wouldn't have any trouble with actual checkpoints, and they could say they'd picked him up hitchhiking. Haider felt a sense of relief, knowing they'd be safe now, no matter what came up—at least for a while, which helped to ease his disgust and anger.

As the afternoon wore on, they climbed the mountains south of Mosul. Then they came over the crest and the city opened before them: a metropolis of almost two million people spread across the lush Dijla Valley, verdant with grass and trees, a sudden, almost obscene shock of green after the desert. Beyond the river stood the ancient Assyrian ruins of Nineveh, and venerated mosques jutted up all around the city: the Great Mosque of al-Nuri, the Mosque of Prophet Yunus, the Mosque of Jerjis, and the Shrine of Mashad Yahya Abul Kassem. Haider had never seen Mosul before, and he had never thought much of Moslawis—Sunnis, mainly, and northerners, practically Kurds in his mind, hillfolk compared to Baghdadis like himself—but he couldn't deny the great beauty before him. It cleansed his heart, if only for a moment, even from the taint of what he was doing.

Just below the crest, Ali had them pull off on a side road, then guided them along the heights past a junkyard full of wrecked cars to a rambling stone ruin—or ancient squat—some kind of battered fortress.

"That's the Monastery of Saint Elijah," Ricks said to Haider. "It was founded in the sixth century AD by the Chaldean Catholic Church. It was a center for Christians in Iraq, and hundreds of people made pilgrimages there every year. Then, in 1743, the Shah of Iran laid siege to Mosul, took the monastery, and killed all the monks because they wouldn't convert to Islam. The siege of Mosul lasted forty days, but the city held." Ricks pointed at a giant hole in the fortress wall. "You see that? That's from a TOW missile in 2003. There was a T-72 just there," he noted, pointing beyond the wall, "and we were so close."

"You were here?" Haider asked.

"It was crazy. There was fighting all night, and I remember watching the sun come up over the hill—"

Suddenly, three men came out of the monastery and Ali told them to stop the truck.

Ricks woke from his reverie and got out. "You stay here," he told Haider, grabbing his gym bag. "Be cool."

Steve walked up with Ali and talked to the three men, two obviously Daesh and the third, the leader, with a much shorter beard. They didn't shake hands, they talked for about ten minutes, and then Ricks gave them the gym bag. The leader passed it to one of his men, who unzipped it and rifled around inside. A few short words were exchanged—then the American turned and walked back to the truck. The meeting was over.

"Okay," Ricks said, "let's go."

On the way back, Ricks turned garrulous, talking about what it was like to be in Iraq in 2003 and 2004 compared to 2007 and 2008, vague about the specifics but speaking with a heartfelt nostalgia. "It was a different time then," he recalled. "Before Obama pulled the troops out. We were winning, you know. We were holding things together."

Haider nodded and agreed, sometimes asking a friendly question, nothing too probing, just keeping the conversation going. The sun sank slowly into the west as they rolled back toward the city. After a couple hours, still well north of Baiji, they pulled off at a rest stop. Ricks got out and urinated against the rear tire of the truck. Haider watched his face in the rearview mirror, talking, talking.

"The problem was," Ricks continued, "we could never get everybody on the same side. It was always one group against another—Sunnis and Shia, this tribe and that tribe, this militia against that one. I mean, what can you do?"

Haider listened for another few seconds, then swiftly stepped out of the vehicle, aimed the M9, and shot Steve Ricks in the face. The American went down instantly, and Haider walked around the truck to find him sprawled in the urine-soaked dust. Haider had hit him in the cheek, shattering the whole side of his skull. Steve Ricks's remaining eye rolled wildly, looking up at him, his mangled mouth trying to form words.

"Tell me, my friend," Haider snapped, "tell me what it was like."

The dying man made a sick, gurgling noise. Haider reached down and took the man's M9 off his hip, then shot him twice in the crotch with it. The dying man moaned and curled in on himself, squealing quietly. Haider searched his pockets, taking his wallet, watch, and wedding band—and a chunky, gaudy ring with a bloodred stone that read, West Point 2002, USMA, Pride in All We Do. Haider didn't know what any of that meant, but it seemed important.

Haider got back in the truck and headed for Baghdad. Later, he stopped and looked in the backpack, which had a cell phone, some magazines for the M9, a GPS, a notebook, a couple of Tom Petty CDs, and some pens. He kept the magazines and threw the satchel out the window.

It was late when he got back to the market. The stalls were mostly closed, the empty aisles with their fluorescent lights haunted by the absence of crowds. Abu Lulu'ah was sitting down, smoking shisha with The Hawk and a few of his men.

Lulu'ah watched Haider walk up to the stand. "Well, my son?"

"We had a nice visit to Mosul, Uncle," Haider reported. "The American had me drop him off in the Karrada. But he said he needed to talk to you tomorrow morning, in person. Just you and The Hawk."

Lulu'ah furrowed his brows. "What's this about?"

"Abu Abdulrahman," Haider said, taking a gamble. "He said the situation has changed. Eleven o'clock, he said, at the Baghdadi Museum."

Lulu'ah and The Hawk looked at each other, then Abu Lulu'ah nodded and turned back to Haider. "Thank you for passing on this message, my son, and for doing this favor for me today." He touched Haider's chest. "Jamail, the keys."

Haider exchanged keys with Jamail. "Thank you for your generosity, Uncle," he said, bowing his head.

"You are brave, *jundi*," Lulu'ah told him. "Maybe you can do me another favor sometime."

"I would be honored, Uncle," Haider said, bowing his head again.

"Go in peace," Lulu'ah dismissed, waving him away.

It took some effort to walk calmly and slowly down the empty market aisle. There was still much to do, and he felt he was running out of time.

The next afternoon, Haider sat in the Shabandar Café on Mutanabbi Street, drinking tea and nursing his aching head. It hurt as badly as ever—probably now that the pressure was off, he was letting himself feel it more, and the explosion and gunfire no doubt made it worse. But still here, now, sitting among his fellow Baghdadis, on a chatty, easy afternoon in the best café in the city, everything seemed at peace. He almost felt like he could finally relax. A few blocks away, of course, the museum was still smoldering and probably crawling with police, but for Haider, it might as well have been on the other side of the world.

Everything had turned out better than he could have

hoped. One wrong step and it would have all fallen apart. He'd never been in great danger, moment by moment, but it was like hooking a fish: the sense of reeling them in, bit by bit, nice and easy. And if the fish got away, well . . . this fish would come with his own hooks.

Abu Lulu'ah and The Hawk had arrived at eleven on the dot. He'd paid a kid to wait for them and take them up-stairs into the museum, through the wax-figure exhibits of the Sumerians, Assyrians, and Babylonians; past the wax-figure reed weavers; past the wax-figure butcher, wax-figure musi-cians, and even a replica of the Shabandar Café, portraying the place in the 1950s—the golden age of the republic. He'd always loved the variety of the headwear in that exhibit: the businessmen in their *sidaras*, the old men in their *tarboosh-es*, the desert tribes in their *ghutrahs* and *shemaghs*, and the others in the simple taqiya. No American baseball caps . . . no Saddam fedoras . . . only Baghdadis being Baghdadis . . . enjoying themselves and each other.

The kid led Abu Lulu'ah on, through a barrier that read, *DO NOT ENTER: CONSTRUCTION.* Haider had paid his cousin, who worked for the museum, to put up the sign for him. He'd told his cousin that Abu Lulu'ah had asked him to arrange a meeting there, which was true in a way. Beyond the barrier, the kid led them to the coppersmith exhibit, where wax smiths stood forging lamps, pitchers, and vases, then asked them to wait there.

"What the fuck is this?" The Hawk had asked, but by then it was too late. Once the kid had turned down the stairs, Haider called the cell phone connected to the IED planted in the exhibit. There was a split-second when Allah might have sent a hundred thousand angels, but He didn't—and the whole end of the hall came apart in a roar.

Haider was up and moving as soon as the shockwave passed, stepping carefully out of the madrassa exhibit where he'd waited, kneeling in a borrowed robe and *shemagh*, watching the whole thing unfold. The hall smelled of cordite and blood, and through the smoke he could see that the damage was substantial. He focused not on the broken, melted, scattered wax figures around him, but on the two figures on the floor.

Abu Lulu'ah was a pile of blood and flesh, his broad body torn to pieces by the ball bearings and shrapnel in the IED, but The Hawk was still stirring. The stringy old man was mangled but alive—he must have been standing behind Lulu'ah, protected in part by his boss's girth. The Hawk held on to his pistol as he tried to pull himself up on a broken elbow. Haider kicked the pistol away, stepped on the old man's elbow, and ground his heel down into the joint. The Hawk collapsed, gritting his teeth but not screaming, and stared up in fury. Haider put one bullet in each of the old man's kneecaps, another in his stomach, and then flung the pistol into the smoke. Then he quickly turned and fled the upper hall, down the stairs, out into the street, where he bent over coughing and stumbling, putting on a show until he was around the corner in an alley— where he tore off his robe and *shemagh*, and walked away.

He'd made a circuit down Rashid Street and back around to Mutanabbi, letting the adrenaline course through his body, letting the shakes come and work themselves out; then he made his way to the Shahbandar Café, where he now sat, his head killing him, drinking tea while sweat cooled on his skin. He lit a cigarette, thinking back over the past thirty-six hours, recalling the strange beauty of the Dair Mar Elia monastery overlooking Mosul, the graceful turn of the Tigris through the beautiful city, the many minarets of the many grand mosques.

As the burden of the past few days began to slide from his shoulders, he embraced this powerful, expansive sense of release—almost an evacuation—a feeling so profound it brought tears to his eyes.

He blinked, ran his hand across his face, and took another drag from his cigarette. He would eat soon, alone, in a chicken place up the street, then return to his father's house and tell him about the truck. After that, he would lie down and watch some TV, maybe take a nap. He would need his rest. In a few days, he'd be back in the war.

This story was originally written in English

BAGHDAD HOUSE

BY ALI BADER

al-Rashid Street

During the summer of 1950, what happened to George Haddad, an accountant for Agha-Porter Automotive, would have been extraordinary—even for a supposedly optimistic person who expected his life to spiral downhill.

That July, the firm's Basra office notified George Haddad about his immediate transfer to their Baghdad office, where he would replace an accountant named Shukri Jamil for two months. Shukri had requested a leave of absence for undisclosed reasons, and abruptly vanished from the office. He was the second accountant to disappear under mysterious circumstances. Ted Lancaster, a British accountant, had also disappeared, and no trace had been found of him yet.

George Haddad boarded the train for Baghdad that very evening at Basra's al-Maqal Station. Even though the trip took all night, he had difficulty sleeping. The loud noises of the train in motion disturbed him, and a number of strange events upset him. First, he sensed that the door to his compartment had opened. Then he heard footsteps approaching. When he jerked awake, he found nothing. So he dozed off again.

Later, he sensed that something weird was happening in the compartment and became agitated. He wasn't sure where he was—lying in his bed at home or somewhere else. Then he remembered he was on a train. Lifting his head, he noticed an elegantly dressed stranger standing before him. The man's face, however, looked like dough that had been left to rise for too long. George was about to greet the stranger, but the other man spoke before he could, asking for a lighter. George thrust a hand into the pocket of his jacket, which he had hung up, and pulled one out. The man lit his cigarette as he swayed in motion with the train. He looked intensely at George—straight in the eye—and returned the lighter, nodded, and left the compartment.

George Haddad arrived the next morning at the crowded Baghdad Central Station. Sharply dressed travelers—trailed by porters carrying their suitcases—were heading to the main exit. Vendors hawked newspapers, foreigners with brimmed hats and umbrellas waited for their trains, and university students lingered in front of the snack bar. George navigated through this frenzied crowd to the main thoroughfare. The station clock flashed 10:05, but the weather was extremely hot, and the sky was a bright blue. He immediately took off his beige jacket because of the heat, and unfurled his brown umbrella, which he used to shield himself from the wicked sun. He looked around for an inexpensive way to reach Baghdad House, whether that meant a bus or a shared taxi—the wad of bills he had in his pocket was only meant to last a week, till the firm had sorted out his salary.

He found nothing but taxis lined up in front of a newsstand. So he climbed into the cab of an elderly driver who looked like he hadn't shaved for days.

After the taxi crossed Baghdad's agricultural zone, it entered the heart of the city and headed down to al-Rashid Street—a long thoroughfare lined by modern buildings on both sides. At this late-morning hour, it was crowded with vehicles—mostly American-made—wagons drawn by horses with black tassels and drivers dressed in traditional clothing, and red double-decker Leyland buses. Since the buildings cast a shadow over the street, George opened the car window to allow the cool, humid breeze to waft in.

About a quarter of an hour later, the vehicle slowly turned onto a narrow alley, the palm-shaded facade of the hotel appearing a few meters in front of them. The taxi stopped at the main entrance—a low gate, painted black.

The inn was a lovely brick building, and its high upper story had large balconies shaded by Chinese-style wooden roofs. The facade of the lower floor was made of glass and elegant ceramic tiles. A large cluster of palms in dense rows shielded the building from the sun and were filled with the nests of birds, chirping at this hour.

George learned later that Colonel Arnold Wilson had built the inn during the days of British rule—the colonel had been posted in Asia for a long time. Then the Agha family had purchased it and turned it into a hotel.

George left his luggage in the taxi and entered the lobby, escorted by a valet who sported a white suit and a gray necktie. The cool air inside caressed George's face.

The lobby was spacious, and two large mirrors hung on its towering walls. It was sparsely furnished with only some red armchairs and black marble tables. He looked toward the back of the room at the hotel proprietor, Madame Reem, who was exhaling smoke from her cigarette and chatting with an elegant man who sat in a chair upholstered with pomegranate-colored velvet. In front of them, on a table, sat two glasses of orange juice, a pack of cigarettes, and a lighter.

George walked up to Madame Reem and quickly explained his situation: "I am George Haddad—an accountant with Agha-Porter Automotive. I have come to take Mr. Shukri Jamil's place . . ."

"Oh!" she said, surprised. "Another one . . . Aren't you afraid? The two accountants before you vanished from the same room."

The man beside her laughed, but George was too stunned to reply. Finally, he felt obliged to justify himself: "I'm no hero and don't aspire to become one, but these are my instructions. I assume Mr. Shukri Jamil has left on holiday?"

"Oh . . . perhaps?" Madame Reem replied.

"Actually, I'll just pay for one week now—till the firm puts me on salary here." He showed her the transfer letter and his identification card.

Madame Reem smiled conspiratorially at him. Then she rose and crossed the room, swinging her hips.

Madame Reem led him to his room on the ground floor. They both stopped at the door; the room was elegantly furnished and had a balcony overlooking the garden, where stalks of flowering okra with faded red blossoms sought the shade of the wall, and lilies of the valley bloomed near beautiful rows of myrtle. Waving the cigarette in her fingers, Madame Reem gestured toward a little desk that held Arabic and English books, as well as a small record player with a modest collection of records. A diminutive refrigerator contained soft drinks and beer.

"We provide three meals a day," Madame Reem said, "according to the menu posted in the kitchen—but eating in the rooms is strictly forbidden."

George paid close attention to this lady—she appeared to be in her thirties and wore high heels. Her eyes were intensely black.

"There are only five residents here," Madame Reem told

him. "In the room across from yours is an engineer named Waheed. He's a graduate of Cambridge University and has been working for the Anglo-Iraqi Transport Company for two years. Meyer, who owns a nightclub on the banks of the Tigris, sleeps till noon and works all night. An Iranian woman named Rahima lives upstairs with her maid. They have maintained a residence here for a long time. She visits from time to time. There is a Kurdish physician named Barwis in the room across from Rahima's. She came from Sulaimaniya to open a pediatric clinic here. Barwis is on vacation at the moment."

He nodded at everything she said, sweat beading up on his forehead. He was so thirsty that the moment Madame Reem left the room—before even placing his clothes in the wardrobe—he rushed to the fridge. He grabbed a cold bottle of beer and drained it. Afterward he felt slightly tipsy and refreshed. He decided to stretch out on the bed.

Before he fell asleep, he heard a loud cry from the upper floor of the inn. The sound was muffled and came from deep inside the building. Yet it was followed by total calm. Then, however, he heard a shrill, quavering voice cry out. He went to the door, opened it, and looked across to the lobby—though he saw no one in the corridor. He went back inside his room, but before he fell asleep, he heard some voices on the stairs, and then someone yelling. George rushed out of his room and headed straight to the stairway. There was no one in the lobby, but after a couple of steps he saw the proprietor emerge from the restroom next to the lobby.

Madame Reem was agitated, and her face was very pale. "What's this noise?" she asked him.

"I don't know. I think it came from upstairs." He rushed up and found the door to the suite occupied by the two Iranian women wide open.

From inside the room, Sargon shouted, "There's been a murder! Call the police!"

George did not enter the room. Instead, he immediately sped back down the steps to the lobby, hearing a door close upstairs. He asked Madame Reem to contact the police.

"The police? Why the police?"

"Someone's been murdered," he said breathlessly.

"Who's been murdered?"

"I don't know exactly, but the crime occurred in the Iranian women's room."

He returned to the crime scene, which was truly alarming. Sargon was nowhere to be seen. When George entered the room, he found Madame Rahima dead, and her maid too. A vase of flowers had shattered on the floor, and a blood-smeared switchblade rested on the table. There was a bloodstain on the floor in front of the window, and a gold chain near it had broken. The maid's body was by the door, and the expression on her face was glowering. Rahima's body was spread out on the bed. Blood from her neck pooled on the sheets.

George returned to his room and waited till the police arrived—approximately half an hour later. They took fingerprints to send off to the lab; a crime photographer went upstairs to take some pictures; then an officer interrogated everyone who had been in the hotel. Since George knew nothing about the two victims, he wasn't questioned long. He had never even seen them before. The interrogator, though, revealed some information that disturbed him.

"Did you know the other two accountants?" the officer asked.

"I met Ted Lancaster only once. I may have met Shukri Jamil a few times, but didn't know him well."

"Fine," the officer said, nodding. "Would their disappearance cause you to suspect anything?"

"Like what?"

"I don't know. I just wonder whether you have some professional hunch," the officer replied.

"I know absolutely nothing about the matter."

"Personally, I think it's suspicious," the officer told him. "There is nothing that links them, but all the same, each of them disappearing under identical circumstances is fishy."

"What do you mean?" George asked.

"I mean that you should be careful. If you suspect anything, don't hesitate to contact us."

"But Shukri Jamil is on holiday," George responded.

"Yes, but where? A person taking a holiday should be somewhere," the officer said. "But no one knows where he is. Plus, he didn't even present his own request for leave."

"I don't follow."

"My meaning is clear: his request for a leave of absence may have been submitted under duress."

George Haddad was very perturbed when the police left—the evidence was clear and the threat obvious. All the same, he knew nothing about the circumstances and ramifications of the situation in which he now found himself. This crime had also made the matter murkier and more mysterious. Even if the events were unrelated, they were linked in many ways. But he did not know where this puzzle started or ended. The pressing question that engrossed him at the moment and kept him awake was whether there was any real connection between the disappearance of the two accountants and the murders of the Iranian women.

By the next morning, most of what he knew about the murders came from details he found in a local English-language newspaper, the *Baghdad Times*, which published the following story:

Residents of Baghdad House were frightened by screams
of terror that seemed to come from the second floor of
the hotel, which is located on al-Rashid Street. Madame
Rahima, an Iranian woman, and her maid, Kameel, had
resided in a room there for several months. Upon hearing
screams, the hotel valet knocked loudly on the suite's door.
He is a brave young man in his thirties named Sargon.
When no one answered his knock, he forced the door open
and found himself confronted by a gruesome scene. A vase
lay broken on the ground, and a knife smeared with blood
was found on a nearby table. There was a bloodstain in
front of the window, and a gold chain was found on the
floor. The maid's body, which was by the door, was still
warm. Her face was stained with blood, and a blue mark
around her neck had been caused by strangulation from a
strong hand. Madame Rahima's body was stretched out
on the bed, and her neck had been savagely slashed. When
the valet tried to lift her, the head separated from the body.
Gena, a laundress who was personally acquainted with
the two victims, said their only visitor had been a merchant
from Shiraz. His name is Hassan, and he was a distant
relative of the Madame Rahima.

Saleem, a grocer, said that Madame Rahima regularly
purchased food from his store and that she was a quiet
woman. Her maid told him once that she had some relationship with another resident in Baghdad House and that
she went to meet him from time to time. This person, however, had vanished awhile ago. Sargon, the valet, thinks he
heard a woman's voice before the murder. But he isn't sure
what language she was speaking. The police say it is unlikely that the killer was a woman, because the lethal hand

*was that of a powerful man. The question is how the crim-
inal fled without anyone noticing him, given that the doors
and windows were locked. Even the window of the bathroom
was firmly closed, and its glass had not been broken.*

*All clues pointed toward the Iranian merchant, who
had disappeared. While the police were searching for him,
he surrendered himself voluntarily.*

The newspaper also mentioned some details about the
merchant. Hassan was a wealthy businessman from Shiraz
who had been previously married. He had divorced his wife
after she failed to conceive, and was planning to remarry.

The merchant claimed that he had visited the two women
less than a month earlier, when Madame Rahima had invited
him to a dinner party for Shukri Jamil, who lived in the same
inn. She had brought him to a fancy restaurant on al-Maghrib
Street, but Shukri Jamil never showed up. The merchant
thought this was odd. Jamil's absence had also surprised Madame Rahima and her maid. The accountant had vanished
without a trace.

Although this information seemed straightforward,
George pondered a number of key issues as he read the newspaper: first, he wondered where the murderer had entered
and exited; secondly, when he was descending the stairs, he
had heard a door slam behind him somewhere, though Sargon
had forced open the door to the victims' room, meaning some
other door had closed—that must have been the door of Barwis, the Kurdish physician.

George's suspicion was strengthened by Sargon's report of
hearing a woman speaking a foreign language with the victims
before their murder. George asked himself: *A woman's voice—
speaking a foreign language—could that have been Barwis?*

George put his head between his hands as he rode the bus to work. He couldn't help but think about what might have happened the night of the murders: *The killer must have entered and exited through Barwis's room. That much is certain, because the killer could not have left anywhere else. Time will tell! But Barwis had not aroused the interrogator's suspicions—because she had been on holiday* . . . Then he asked himself: *Which of the two missing accountants had an affair with Madame Rahima? And what was the true nature of her relationship with Shukri Jamil?*

By the time George Haddad reached his bus stop, he had read the story several times and turned over every possibility in his mind. After exiting the bus, he placed the paper in his briefcase and headed down the street to the office.

A British woman named Edith ran this office, which was located on the top story of the Najib Building. She was in her fifties and had married an Iraqi. Her two assistants were Khayriya, a youthful middle-aged woman, and Jamila, an older woman. The office had more than ten employees—some Indian, some British, some Iraqi.

"Oh, you've finally arrived! We've been waiting for you. But I'm concerned . . ." Edith said.

"Why?" George asked.

"Oh—aren't you staying at Baghdad House? And didn't a crime occur there?"

"Yes, I was actually there at the time," he said.

"God preserve you! What's going on here? I'll ask the director to find different lodgings for you," Edith said. "We have lost two accountants in a single year. Now you witness a crime the very day you arrive!"

"Do you believe there's a link between Baghdad House and these crimes?"

"God only knows! Ask the police," she said.

"I don't think there is," I said. "This detestable event could have happened anywhere. I would prefer to stay there—it seems safer to remain somewhere familiar, despite the unfortunate circumstances."

George Haddad worked till noon. Then he headed downtown, ate lunch, and returned to review more files.

Something in the budget ledger drew his attention. For June 20, Shukri Jamil had recorded the number *12753* in the creditor column, but the 18th had been the last day he had worked, and the 19th was blank. Yet the 20th contained this strange number to which no value had been assigned, and no details of receipts had been recorded to justify it.

He rushed to show his findings to Edith. He told her he didn't understand this entry at all. She was also startled and nodded: "This number is strange. I don't understand why it's there either."

"They say he sent his letter on June 18. How could he have entered this figure on the 20th?"

"He kept the ledger with him," Edith recalled. "Two days after he disappeared, we sent someone to fetch it from Baghdad House. It's conceivable that he wrote an entry for the 18th on the page for the 20th. In that case, the entry wouldn't be significant. But do you think he meant to send a message with this number? If so, what's the message?"

George loosened his gray tie as he stood and faced her at her desk. "I don't know, but I wonder if he specified in his letter when he would return."

The setting sun had painted the massive columns along al-Rashid Street violet. The long street ran from Bab al-Moatham to al-Bab al-Sharqi. The English had named it Rodenburg Street in 1917. This section between al-Sabah Hotel and the Roxy Cinema was the most modern and elegant. The small alley on which Baghdad House stood was known popularly as the Street of the English, and it twisted its way to the river. Another lengthy street stretched along the riverbank. Its clean sidewalks and modern buildings extended to the King Faisal Bridge.

George looked at the tall buildings topped by signs of the many foreign firms that had offices on the upper floors. Down below were numerous coffeehouses, bars, and nightclubs with flashy facades. At the end of the street, there were upscale hotels, international clothing stores, and two cinemas—the Roxy and the Rex.

A hunch motivated George to cross the street when he noticed another neighborhood situated behind this trendy front. The low-rent area exuded a distinctive fragrance— inexpensive restaurants offered cheap meals, and the inexpensive hotels and hostels often had very steep and dilapidated stairways out front, housing all types of mysterious women.

When he walked past the Shahrazad Hotel, he noticed a lovely girl wearing tight-fitting clothes and holding a cigarette in her hand. Her dark eyes aroused him.

Before returning to the hotel, he visited the McKenzie Bookstore, which was run by a British fellow named John McKenzie. It imported Penguin books, newspapers, and current magazines. On entering, George caught sight of his neighbor, Waheed the engineer, standing at the back of the store. Their meeting was quite fortuitous, and they approached each other and left the bookstore together. At the bus stop, George asked the engineer if he would care to join him for a drink, and the other man agreed. So they headed to a dive on the cheaper side of the street.

The bar, which was dark and reeked of alcohol, was packed with a diverse cast of characters, but most were prostitutes of every age and variety. The male faces there were alert, predatory, and scouting for prospects.

George chose a booth near the front window. When the two men were seated, the server quickly brought them a pitcher of beer and two glasses.

Waheed was in his thirties. His complexion was a tawny brown, his eyes were small and intelligent, and his mustache was carefully groomed. He wasn't elegant, but he dressed conservatively in a distinctive way that was simple and practical—more American than European, perhaps due to living in New York City for five years after completing an engineering degree at Cambridge. He was the sort of person who spoke in a terse, composed way. George listened with great interest to what Waheed told him about the place and was astonished by the scope of his knowledge. After downing a couple of drinks together, George decided to ask Waheed—cautiously—about the disappearances of the two accountants. To start with, he inquired about Ted Lancaster. Initially, Waheed was slow to provide any details. He merely said that some matters relating to Baghdad House were complicated. The crimes were strange, and many vested interests were involved. Then George wanted to know whether the hotel itself was a factor.

"The matter does seem connected to Baghdad House itself, its proprietors, or its residents. I don't understand this and am genuinely at a loss," George said, his voice growing soft. "All the same, given the links between Baghdad House and foreign companies, the government, and influential people in Baghdad, this hotel truly warrants suspicion, and all these matters seem interrelated." He thought things were becoming even murkier and decided to speak more directly: "Is Madame Reem linked to the situation?"

"I don't know—but who is her husband?" Waheed replied judiciously.

"I have no idea," George answered, his voice tense, as he lowered the glass from his mouth.

"Answer that question and you'll understand a lot, I wager. I have no proof, though," Waheed said, backtracking.

George, however, was determined to learn more. "How do you think Ted Lancaster's disappearance is related to that of Shukri Jamil? And do you believe there is any connection between those two men and the murder of the Iranian woman? Are all these events related or merely separate strands?"

"When similar events occur in the same location, they must be connected in some manner," Waheed surmised. "There could be a single perpetrator, or two from the same organization. As I said, I don't have any evidence. I simply analyze matters from a distance."

"But I was startled to learn of a relationship between Shukri Jamil and Rahima . . ."

"The real affair was between Ted Lancaster and Rahima," Waheed said. "They were lovers for a long time. I don't think Shukri Jamil's relationship was comparable, but I have no idea why he vanished—perhaps to conceal Ted Lancaster's disappearance . . ."

"Oh! You're making my head spin."

"Naturally . . . I told you the matter is extremely complicated."

"But why didn't he disclose all this?"

"Because important families are involved and their dirty linen isn't easily revealed," Waheed said. "Rahima's husband is a well-known figure."

"She has a husband who lives here? No one has mentioned that."

"Her husband is an Iraqi who had ties to political groups that once ruled here," the engineer shared. "He belonged to groups linked to the former royalist government. He is, moreover, an eccentric individual."

"You're making me nervous. Do you believe the matter is political?" George asked. "They say Shukri Jamil was a Communist."

"He has Communist leanings, and the Communists think his disappearance is politically motivated. They don't believe that he sent the letter requesting leave. It's possible, but I doubt that he had an affair with Rahima. His name has merely been plugged in there—that's what I think."

The quantity of information that Waheed provided him—however mysterious and unverified it was—drove George to reflect further upon the character of the individuals around him. He wanted to search for more information, but he had to be very circumspect. Ted Lancaster, the Englishman, although he came from a solid middle-class background in Manchester, was somewhat dissolute. From colleagues in his office, George learned that Ted was a connoisseur of the seedy side of Baghdad. His infatuation with escorts had destroyed his marriage, but no one had mentioned his affair with Rahima. Even so, everyone seemed to have heard licentious rumors about him. They all agreed that he was addicted to pornography, and that he corresponded with a friend in the UK about sadomasochistic sex. Ted had mentioned to an acquaintance at the office that he had memorized a long poem about such practices. He had also assembled a collection of books that catered to his deviant tastes. He was terribly disappointed as well to have spent an entire year in Africa without witnessing anyone be-ing killed or tortured. He was also reputed to be a collector of torture devices, and had once corralled some whores into having sex with him while he watched a convict's public execution.

Rahima's husband, to whom Ted was also linked, was Ab-dul Rahim al-Agha—he was rumored to be insane and truly scary. His behavior exemplified the corruption of an aristo-cratic class—of men who mixed brutality with love and expe-rienced sexual gratification only when abusing a woman.

All those who spoke to George about Abdul Rahim said he was a complex and shady figure—the youngest son of an Iraqi family of Turkish or Dagestani heritage. He had been ar-rested in 1946 after the military coup, on suspicion of having financed Nazi groups in Iraq. He was also intimately linked with the Agha-Porter Automotive firm that George worked for. Al-Agha was not only his surname but also that of Ma-dame Reem. George was bewildered by all the complexities of this intricate triangle.

George had not realized that he had carried his inquiry too far until a few strange, inexplicable things happened. When he returned to the hotel in the evening, he found the door to his room open and discovered his belongings had been moved, even though he was certain he had locked the door before departing.

These were not merely hunches—they were actual facts. Many weird things were happening, so it was clear some indi-vidual was behind them. He asked Madame Reem about this, but she denied any knowledge. Then he questioned Sargon, who—instead of replying—said that someone had come and asked for George.

This answer hit George like a bolt of lightning. "What did he look like?" he asked the valet.

"He was middle-aged, had a thick mustache, and wore a black suit," Sargon answered.

"Did he say anything?"

"He didn't leave a message in writing, but he said, *Tell him I'll keep our appointment.*"

"Appointment?" George repeated. A wave of fear surged through him.

He returned to his room, where he sat on his bed and began to reflect: *Who is the mastermind of this operation? Is Sargon a member of this conspiracy? He was the first to enter the victims' room. If so, whose pawn is he? Reem al-Agha's? Was she the killer? What did her husband stand to gain from the death of the two accountants? Would the CEO of Agha-Porter Automotive benefit? Is the entire operation run by the authorities? Are these actually political crimes disguised as random acts of violence?* Though the main question he asked himself was what his own relationship to all this might be. Why did he feel threatened? What had he done to deserve all this attention and to be included in all these machinations? There was no logical explanation.

He certainly believed that everything had been orchestrated and was definitely beyond his control—he hadn't had a hand in any aspect of this series of events.

Fine. If the whole affair was already scripted and he had absolutely no way to evade it, he needed to decide what to do now, before it was too late. Should he contact the police? But what would they do? There was no way they could thwart or prevent a crime. The problem with the police was that they would start an investigation only *after* a crime occurred—not before. They could only pursue a criminal once a crime had been committed. Though they were currently searching for the man who had killed Rahima and her maid, they hadn't arrested anyone. Again, George tried to organize his thoughts: *What good will it do me if the police arrest their killer after he has killed me? My actions must be far more proactive than merely informing the police. I need to protect myself. I mustn't give up or relax, because any slip on my part will allow the criminal to behead me.*

George sat in his room wondering how to handle a crime that wasn't connected to him, even though he might now be a target. He brooded about the murderer, picturing an inscrutable man locked inside a room with a knife, a revolver, and a rope.

George Haddad's concerns were not unfounded. They were real, and violence lurked in every direction—the violence of people with arrogant faces, haughty laughter, and merciless behavior.

On Saturday morning he awakened at dawn to the sound of hotel workers having a debate about some matter—they sounded nervous. Initially, he paid no attention to their argument. Then his ears gradually picked up Shukri Jamil's name. George approached a janitor, a gray-haired man he hadn't seen before, who was seated by the gate.

"What's going on?" George asked, as the cleaner got up to leave.

"Haven't you heard? The police found the body of Shukri Jamil in the river."

George got very upset when he heard this. He had convinced himself that Shukri Jamil had in fact requested leave. Several times he had tried to reassure himself that the affair posed no real threat. Now someone had actually found the accountant's body in the river.

The noon news broadcast said that Shukri Jamil had committed suicide—apparently, he'd shot himself in the head on a bluff beside the Tigris River, on the Utaifiya side, and his body had fallen into the water. Before his suicide, he had sent the police a letter confessing responsibility for the Baghdad House murders, including that of Ted Lancaster, whose body was then found buried in a ruined building on the outskirts of the city. The police had found incriminating evidence in Shukri Jamil's residence at Utaifiya.

Later, when George arrived at the office, a dumbfounded Edith confirmed these reports. Out on the street, the Communists were demonstrating against the allegations. They accused the security forces of killing Shukri Jamil and attempting to conceal that fact by claiming he had killed himself.

Waheed shared his opinion when he saw George in the hotel corridor: the educated classes typically mistrusted the government and imagined an imperialist conspiracy behind almost any miscarriage of justice. George, however, discounted the possibility that these were political crimes. If Shukri Jamil was the true target, why were the others killed?

Moreover, did this mean the string of killings had ended, or would it continue? Until he learned the true motive, why shouldn't he think his name was on the list too? Now that the killer had begun, he wouldn't just stop, and killing would become a sport he needed to perfect. Such perfection could only be achieved through repeat performances.

George's sleepless night was spent staring into the dark while he tossed and turned, his mind racing. At one point he imagined that someone with a knife was leaning over him, and he leaped out of bed.

Even the most ordinary thing terrified him now, like the soft ticking of the clock on his bedside table. At times the croaking of frogs in the garden resembled muffled moans, and the clanging of pots in the kitchen were like metallic gunfire. Peering through the window, he mistook a stack of wooden planks for a man with a knife in his hand—a polished knife that looked red. Another time he thought he heard a woman being stabbed in the street.

George decided to try to solve the riddle of the numbers. Only this would guide him to the truth.

Seated on his bed, George gazed at the numbers he had copied from the budget ledger. *If you separate the numbers into single digits, that still means nothing. How about dividing them into pairs?* He scrutinized the new combinations. *Perhaps this will provide me with a clue. I'll have 12, followed by 75, and then the number 3.*

He wondered aloud, "But what could 12 refer to around here?" He had a hunch, but wasn't positive, so he continued his musings: *Suppose there's a bus number 12 that goes through here. I'll try this out and ask Saleem the grocer.*

George headed out to see the grocer, and immediately asked, "Uncle Saleem, what's the bus that passes by here?"

The gray-haired man, who wore glasses with thick lenses, was bagging groceries for a customer, and didn't bother to look up at George as he replied, "There are two buses: the 12 and the 15."

"Where does number 12 go?"

"Its final stop is in the evacuated zone, beyond al-Waziriya . . ."

George felt he was close to a solution. At least he had a hypothesis. He decided to ride the 12 bus that morning to the evacuated zone.

* * *

When George disembarked, he wasn't the only person leaving the bus at its terminus. Two men in blue suits set off toward the gardens and old groves. George walked straight ahead toward a cluster of deserted houses, allowing his feet to guide him. Suddenly, a seemingly abandoned white house caught his eye. An old Rolls-Royce was parked in front, covered in dust. He headed toward the dwelling, which was surrounded by trees.

It was noon, and the pavement in front of the deserted house glinted in the sunshine. There was an old, dry, and dark stone fountain at the center of the front courtyard, and it was so large that it partially blocked his view of the wooden door, which looked like a prison gate.

He proceeded cautiously across the courtyard, seeking shade next to the massive walls. His footsteps echoed against the house's stillness. He carefully scrutinized the walls and eerie-looking windows. At the right of the doorway was a metal plaque with the number 75. Here was the evidence—this was definitely the place Shukri Jamil had in mind when he wrote that number in the ledger.

He pushed against the door, and it swung open. He was hesitant about entering but sensed that no one was inside. The floor was covered with mats, and two shelves facing one another held brass vessels. Below these were numerous statues arranged like stage props. Large leather drums stood to their right; to their left were wooden blocks wrapped with ropes, which he imagined were intended for use in some unspeakable ritual. When he walked past the statues he found that some had anxious faces and others wore expressions contorted by pain. They represented slain people with funereal veils and hands bound behind their backs. A tree trunk resembling a butcher's block suggested that people had been beheaded here.

The sun's rays coming through the window illuminated the dust on a small-framed portrait of a woman being whipped. Next to it, he spotted a photo of Rahima with her daughter on one side and her husband on the other. The names *Abdul Rahim al-Agha, Rahima,* and *Ikhlas* were inscribed beneath the picture. *What is a photo of Rahima doing here?* George wondered in dismay.

He heard a movement behind him. When he turned, the person facing him was the man beside Rahima in the photograph.

"I've been waiting for you," Abdul Rahim al-Agha said. He held a glass of whiskey in one hand and a knife in the other.

George regained his composure, determined to escape by any means. "I knew we would meet," he replied boldly.

"Tell me: how did you find this place?" Abdul Rahim asked.

"Shukri Jamil left a clue in the budget ledger," George said, his voice calm now. "Why did you kill him?"

"Because—like you—he knew too much," Abdul snapped. "Have you heard about Icarus, who soared too close to the sun? He died. You've also moved too close to the sun . . . much too close. That's why you've earned this honor. Being killed is a special honor. I will enjoy it, and so will you. The entire world runs on blood and semen. You may ask why I killed Ted Lancaster . . . You might as well ask Cain why he killed Abel. Blood and semen are the foundation of this world. Bloodshed is essential for life. Death and suffering are sacrosanct."

"But you killed Rahima too," George said.

"She had to die with her lover. We agreed on that! When she betrayed me, she accepted her death. I killed her in the Baghdad House while she was kissing my hand. I tortured Ted Lancaster in this place until his spirit gave up the ghost."

George said: "You entered Barwis's room—or it was you and Barwis both, because Sargon heard a woman's voice. You killed the two women . . . and you and Barwis entered her room . . . I heard a door slam while I was descending the stairs. Then the two of you left through the ground-floor window. Later, you killed Shukri Jamil to frame him, placing evidence in an apartment you rented in his name. You murdered him so he would appear to be the sole killer. Sargon and Reem are certainly complicit too."

"Splendid! Now you know more than you ought to."

Abdul Rahim al-Agha advanced from the bottom of the stairway through the large room. Detecting an opening, George Haddad ran desperately toward the stairs, but Abdul Rahim didn't follow him immediately. Instead, he calmly poured himself a glass of whiskey and placed two ice cubes in it. Still holding the knife in one hand, he drained the whiskey from the glass and removed a rope from a drawer, which he then placed on the table. Grasping the knife, he calmly followed George, who was now on the upper floor, searching for an escape route from the dwelling.

George thought that jumping from the window onto the roof was the only way out. He found a window in the parlor; through it he could see the shingles, but this window had been nailed shut. He was struggling to get it open when Abdul Rahim appeared. Sweat poured down George's forehead, and he saw that the entire window frame was moving. The rusty old nails in the rotted frame were giving way, and after another strong pull, the window opened. Just as he heard Abdul Rahim panting before him, George slid outside. As soon as his feet touched the roof, he carefully hurried across it. He knew that if he jumped to the ground, he'd break some bones. Looking to the side, he glimpsed a column that led down to another area of the roof, so he scrambled lower.

Abdul Rahim stayed right behind him, and followed him down the same column, though his hands lost their grip. A terrifying scream broke the silence as he slipped from the roof—and fell into the stone fountain, slamming his head.

As George approached Abdul Rahim, the man was taking his last breaths as a trickle of blood flowed from his ear. His skull was crushed where it had struck the fountain. George ran off as fast as his legs could carry him.

The next day, George went out to the street, where he found a brilliant morning. He plunged into the bustle of Baghdad. Various vendors displayed their wares on the sidewalks: delicious fruit scrubbed clean, glistening vegetables, an amazing block of russet-colored sweets, and twisted wands of scrumptious caramel. There were fishmongers and people selling iced treats and juices. Amid the cacophony, George soon realized that someone was tailing him. A man with an umbrella in his hand was watching him. Whenever George turned back, the umbrella man would look the other way.

His pursuer eventually disappeared in the market, and after a few days George's life gradually returned to normal. His hours at the hotel were untroubled, and Madame Reem and Sargon showered him with what appeared to be genuine affection. After he returned from work at the end of a day, he would sometimes go to the movies, where occasionally he would doze off, depending on the film. Other evenings, he would return to the hotel, bathe, and—after window-shopping on nearby streets—dine quietly at the Abu Johnny Restaurant, have a drink in a bar run by a slim black bartender, and then return to sleep at the inn.

* * *

On the final day of his Baghdad posting, as he was returning to the hotel after work, George heard footsteps behind him. The street by the Shahrazad Hotel was deserted except for drunk woman standing by the streetlamp. A man holding a cigarette approached her. George walked past a gloomy bar with a brawl going on outside. The street was growing darker. Then he sensed that a car was following him, and his heart skipped a beat. He turned, and found two men behind him. One asked him for a light. George pulled his lighter from his pocket and lit that man's cigarette. Then a large knife, held by a firm hand, stabbed George from behind. He slid to the ground, gasping for breath, and looked up to see the stars slowly dim.

Translated from Arabic by William M. Hutchins

TUESDAY OF SORROWS

BY LAYLA QASRANY

al-Andalus District

Baghdad, Summer of 1978

"**Y**ou have a long journey coming up, with many obstacles," said Hasmik, the Armenian fortune-teller, as she swirled the coffee grounds in Youssef's cup. "All the doors will close to you. There is evil in your path," she added in clumsy Arabic, before murmuring a few prayers in Armenian.

He was not happy about her prediction, given the nature of his upcoming plans. He paid the woman her fee and left her house with his mind in a state of confusion.

Youssef did not want to believe everything that the fortune-teller read in the coffee grounds, since he was a man of science and didn't subscribe to what he called *khurafat*, or superstitions. He was a successful engineer and contractor for the country's largest air-conditioner company, and much of Baghdad knew him. But he had sought out this soothsayer because he wanted some sign about the journey he had planned for himself and his family.

That night, Youssef's wife Hala was waiting for him at the Mashriq Club for dinner with some friends, after which they would play bingo. This was their summer ritual: every Thursday they would leave the little ones to be babysat by the housekeeper and spend the evening with friends at the same club where Hala took the children every Monday morning for swimming lessons.

"Baghdad is no longer a safe place . . ." said Youssef, stopping himself before he mentioned to his friend Fouad that he was planning to move to London with his family within the next two weeks.

Youssef and his friend would often use code words and insinuations to refer to the dictatorial Baathist regime, fearing that someone from the secret police was planted among them, eavesdropping at the neighboring table.

"I know exactly what you mean," his friend agreed. "We used to sleep with our house unlocked, but now we've started securing our doors with a dozen chains."

Despite her attachment to her family and to Baghdad, Hala did not mind the idea of suddenly leaving. She loved her husband to the point of agreeing with almost all of his careful decisions. She loved him so much that she could not hide it from her friends, who envied her when she spoke about him. Once she said to two of her closest friends: "My two kids, Nadir and Dalia, look like their father because I love him so much." Youssef laughed at this theory of hers.

Hala had met Youssef in their third year at the Polytechnic and they had married after graduation at Mar Gorgis Church in Baghdad al-Jadida. They baptized their children there as well. And now she would follow her husband to London.

Hala always believed that Tuesday was a day on which evil spirits emerged from the earth to abduct people's souls. "I don't want to travel on a Tuesday—I hate Tuesdays! My uncle and grandfather both died on that day."

"My darling, I cannot change the tickets now," Youssef

replied, sounding remorseful. "I have paid for them and it's all settled."

He then opened the drawer of the study table and took out a folder holding the four tickets and the green passports. He showed her one of the tickets. "Look, the departure is for five minutes after midnight, which means that it will be Wednesday morning. For now, we have more important things to worry about." He put the folder back in the drawer. "We have to think about how to smuggle the jewelry out with us—you know the rules. Maybe we can split it up among the four of us."

"You wear the thick necklaces and the crosses under your clothes, and I'll wear the rings and bracelets," she said. "And I will attach some of the other rings to the necklaces."

That night, riddled with fear, Youssef could not sleep. What if the secret police and airport security prevented him from leaving? What if they were blacklisted or if the jewelry was confiscated from them? Furthermore, he had sold the factory and transferred large amounts of money to England by way of a friend who worked in the British consulate; he would only recover those funds upon his arrival in London.

The day before their scheduled departure, Youssef suggested to Hala that they take the children out one last time, to eat burgers at Abu Yunan's in the heart of the capital, and from there they could go say goodbye to her parents, who lived in the al-Baladiyyat District.

As they passed by one of the security service headquarters, Youssef's stomach tightened. "It is because of these butchers that there is no place left for us in Iraq," he told his wife. "This regime does not want to see anyone have a successful career unless they can profit from it."

Hala did not know about Youssef's problems at work; he did not want her to worry about his tension with the Baathists, who had been paying him visits at the factory, asking him why he was late responding to the interior minister's order to install air conditioners in one of his houses in the Mansour District. Youssef always tried to evade their questions by saying that the factory was busy with contracts or tourism companies in Erbil or something similar, but answers like these did not appease the regime. Youssef complained about this to his older brother: "The Baathists want me to play the game with them, and they won't let me be if I don't become one of them. Emigrating is the only way out."

Hala cried on the way to her mother's house in al-Baladiyyat; the children in the backseat were silent, but they could not understand why she was upset. Hala had only ever left Baghdad on short trips to Beirut and Istanbul. She wished she could say goodbye to their kind neighbors, but their departure had been kept secret for reasons even she didn't know.

The family sat for a while with Hala's parents. "You must come visit us in London," Hala said, crying in her mother's arms during their final goodbyes. After they left the house, her mother poured a bucket of water on the ground behind them for good luck.

The next morning was a scorcher. While Hala busied herself packing the last of the children's clothes, Youssef told her that he was taking Nadir for a haircut, and that they'd be back shortly.

"Don't be late, Youssef. I won't start lunch without you." Hala was very wound up, especially since she was so attached to their house in al-Andalus District. It was her whole life. She loved its furniture—she had picked out each piece carefully. All her memories with her husband and children were here, and leaving was a huge loss for her.

The housekeeper, Maryam, was the only one outside the family who knew of their plans. She was the only one Hala trusted, as she had been living with them since Nadir's birth. A woman of few words, she had devoted her life to serving her mistress and running the house, having taken a vow never to marry.

Maryam was fixing lunch when Dalia, the younger child, became sleepy and started crying. "Madame Hala, I'll put Dalia to sleep in my bed one last time before you leave," Maryam said as she lifted Dalia into her arms. "Oh, my darling, I'll miss you so much," she whispered to the child, as she took her to her room off the kitchen.

Maryam returned to the kitchen to finish preparing a final lunch, per Hala's request: okra with garlic, lemon, and fresh tomatoes. She had also prepared a pot of amber rice on the side, the smell wafting out into the street.

While Maryam was cooking, she heard a knock on the kitchen door. She opened it, thinking it was the gardener. Instead, a masked man appeared with an ax in his hand. He struck her with it and she fell to the ground. The man made his way into the house and up the stairs.

Hala heard a sharp yell followed by hurried footsteps, but it was too late for her to escape. She found herself face-to-face with a tall man, and was unable to defend herself. The man struck her on the shoulder with the ax. She fell, letting out a scream, but he caught her by the neck and struck her again on the head. Then he went to another room to look for Youssef. Unable to find him, the killer ran off after a few minutes.

* * *

When Youssef approached his house two hours later, he immediately smelled the smoke from the burned rice. He rushed in and found Maryam lying in a pool of blood. Nadir tried to scream, but Youssef put his hand over his son's mouth.

Youssef grabbed a knife from the kitchen and, believing the attacker was still inside, went cautiously up the stairs. He called out to his wife. She did not reply. He discovered her body in the bedroom, bathed in blood. But then he heard his daughter's cries coming from Maryam's room downstairs; he rushed down and took her into his arms, while his son pounded on the kitchen door in a panic.

He brought both children outside and then returned to the house, quickly climbing the stairs to the top floor, where he found the door to the roof open. Youssef realized that the killer must have fled this way. He did not know what to do. He sat down and sobbed next to his wife's body. Soon he heard the voices of neighbors gathering outside the house. He went down to find them gathering around Maryam's body.

"Look!" Abu Ahmad yelled. "My God, she's not dead, she's moving. Let me take her to the hospital."

The other neighbors helped him carry Maryam to his car, and he and his wife, Umm Ahmad, drove off to the nearby hospital.

Meanwhile, Youssef went back upstairs, where Hala's body remained. A few of the other men from the neighborhood went up with him. He hugged his wife's body, still hoping she was alive, but she did not stir.

"There is no God but God. Let me call the police. They will be here very quickly," said one neighbor.

Youssef asked him about Nadir and Dalia; he was told that one of the neighbors had taken them to her house.

* * *

Maryam lost a lot of blood and remained comatose in the hospital for weeks while undergoing several operations. The doctors said that she would live, but would never be as she had been prior to the assault.

Youssef buried his wife in the Mohammed Sakran Cemetery outside Baghdad—along the old road to Kirkuk. He and the children went to his brother's place to grieve and stayed there for a few weeks.

As for Maryam, once her condition improved, the Baathists questioned her and recorded her statement. On one of their visits to the hospital, the investigator explained what the next step was: "Listen, we want to hear your testimony at headquarters. We will arrange a lineup of suspects and tell you what you have to do, got it? The party will also give you some money as compensation for this incident."

Maryam, shaking in fear at the intimidating police officer, only managed to nod her head while clutching the cross hanging on her chest and praying silently, as if beseeching it to rescue her from herself, from the party, and from this awful predicament.

After being discharged, Maryam had to follow up with the security service. She took a taxi to the headquarters, where they led her to a room to wait alone. An officer and his aide came in after a while. "I will take you to see the perpetrator," the officer said, "and I want you to sign this document after you identify him for us. We think the second man from the right is probably the one who committed the crime."

They took her to another room guarded by two policemen. One of them opened the door and Maryam entered along with the officer, not daring to raise her head. She murmured a few simple words and pointed to the second man from the right.

He was a tall young man with a dark complexion. He stood rigid as a palm tree, even though his eyes were red, and he did not seem afraid of Maryam's false testimony.

Before leaving the building, Maryam signed a document that read: *Mahmoud Kadhim Musa, 28 years old, criminal with prior convictions. On July 25, in a cowardly act, he broke into the home of an Iraqi family, killing the mistress of the house, Mrs. Hala Habib, and injuring Ms. Maryam Toubia, but God kept her alive to witness the crime of this degenerate culprit.*

After signing the document, Maryam cried bitterly. Outside, her nephew was waiting for her in a taxi. When they reached her sister's home, Youssef was there drinking coffee, unable to conceal his shaking leg. Her sister brought her a glass of cold water. She drank it and sat down opposite Youssef. He asked her how the interrogation went and whether she had seen the perpetrator. Maryam did not answer him directly. "They asked me so many questions, as if I weren't unconscious that day," she muttered.

Youssef leaned forward and asked her, "Were you able to recognize the killer?"

She did not have the courage to tell him that she had given false testimony. Instead, she said: "It was easy to identify him—I remembered his face."

"Are you certain it was him?"

"It couldn't be anyone else," she lied. "His face was the last thing I saw before I lost consciousness on that terrible day."

"What I mean is, could you recognize him the moment your eyes came upon him without the help of anyone else?" Youssef pressed.

"Yes, he has a distinctive face. He has bushy eyebrows and—"

"But you told me when you came out of the coma that he was wearing a mask," Youssef challenged. "And now you're saying this about his eyebrows. You're talking nonsense!"

Maryam excused herself, saying she was tired and needed to take a nap. "Please, I have a headache . . . let me rest a little," she begged, putting her hands on her temples.

"Tell me, what's his name?" Youssef said.

"Whose name?"

"The man, the killer, what's his name?"

"I'm not sure . . . I think his name is . . . Mahmoud Musa," she said, and then left the room.

Maryam's sister tried to console Youssef. "We cannot argue with the will of God in these matters of life and death. Death is unavoidable, and we will all walk on this path," she told him. "Your loss has been great, but you are a man of faith and you cannot keep mourning your wife forever. You must be strong, for the sake of your two little children. They need you. God, not us, will avenge this heinous crime."

Youssef left enraged with Maryam—with himself, with Iraq, with God. He didn't really need to know who the killer was because he was certain that the Baathists were the ones who had murdered his wife. He returned to his brother's house, where the children awaited him. He took them to a nearby shop and bought them ice cream.

Every night he cried, asking himself: *How can my children grow up without Hala? How badly will they miss her? How can I raise them alone?*

"I lost everything in a single day. If I leave now, people will say that I am not mourning my wife. But should I listen to what people say?" Youssef wondered aloud. "People talk, then they go silent, but no one except me can guarantee my children's future. I have to take them abroad or else the Baathists will kill me too, and my children will become orphans."

He knew that he was the one the Baathists wanted dead on that ill-fated Tuesday.

He reminisced about when he had gone with Hala after their wedding to the jewelers' market on al-Nahr Street to have their names engraved on each other's rings—by the same Mandean jeweler from whom he'd bought the gold for her, including the necklaces with gold coins and the bracelets that were twisted into thick chains.

That day, he'd told her: "Hala, choose whatever pieces of gold you like. Let them be my first wedding gift to you."

"Darling, you are everything I could ever want," she had replied. "What will I do with this metal, when I have everything I could wish for in you?"

That day, he had realized how much she meant to him and thanked the Lord for bringing them together.

A few days later, Youssef decided to take the children back home.

"I don't want to be a burden on your wife," he told his brother.

"Don't talk like that, Youssef," his brother said. "Your children are my own."

Youssef thanked him again but headed back home with the kids. It was the first time they had entered the house since Hala's murder—desolation and gloom filled the space. The children ran up to their rooms while Youssef stood at the bottom of the stairs and recalled how he had found his wife on that summer day, drenched in a pool of blood, her face bloated. He could sense her spirit was still in the house, but he was quickly distracted by his children's voices. He bathed them and then tucked them into bed. He slept out in the living room after checking all the locks on all the doors multiple times.

The next day, Youssef went to visit Abu Ahmad. He did not give his neighbor a chance to ask questions about the incident, and tried to make him believe it was just a burglary gone wrong. The children played and ran around in the garden while the two men sat outside drinking tea. There was sorrow written all over Abu Ahmad's face. At first, Youssef thought that he was putting on such a serious face out of politeness and formality. Then he noticed that Umm Ahmad was wearing black.

"Why is your wife wearing black? Is everything okay?" Youssef asked. "Is she mourning someone?"

"Yes, her nephew died."

When Youssef asked how it happened, his neighbor said: "What can I tell you, my dear neighbor? He was just a young man . . . he died in a car accident."

"May God rest his soul, Abu Ahmad. What a shocking piece of news." Hearing this after Hala's murder made Youssef anxious, but it also made him feel like he wasn't the only one in the world subject to misfortune.

"I hadn't heard about your nephew," Youssef told Umm Ahmad as she brought them more tea. "May God's mercy be upon him."

"We did not want to upset you, dear Youssef. You have troubles of your own. It breaks my heart—Mahmoud was a lovely young man, an ambitious pilot who worked hard to make something of himself. I wish he had never come back!" she cried.

As Youssef finished his tea that evening, a cool breeze started to blow gently. He called for the children and went back home to put them to bed before nightfall. Sorrow weighed down upon him all night, but something else was troubling him. Then, just as he was drifting off to sleep, he remembered the name of Umm Ahmad's nephew: *Mahmoud!* The same name as Hala's "killer"! Was it a coincidence?

At ten o'clock the next morning, Youssef went back to Abu Ahmad's house.

"Good morning, Youssef! Is everything okay?" his neighbor asked.

"I need to speak with you. Will you come over to my place for coffee?"

"Of course, my friend. Just give me a few minutes to get ready."

Youssef soon sat down with Abu Ahmad. "Umm Ahmad said her nephew Mahmoud was living abroad—but then you said he died in a car accident. Tell me the truth, Abu Ahmad."

His neighbor became flustered and started to stammer: "No, not at all . . . He was returning from the airport after a trip abroad . . . and died in an accident . . ."

"I have known you for years—you are not telling the truth."

Abu Ahmad shifted uncomfortably in his seat. "Why do you ask?"

"I want to know the truth."

"Okay, my friend," Abu Ahmad replied. "No one knows the truth. He was a pilot in the Iraqi Air Force, but had escaped to Havana and had been there for a few years after receiving asylum. He married a Cuban woman but began to yearn for Iraq, so he came back under a false passport and brought his wife with him. But he was recognized and taken in by state security, and they executed him and deported his wife back to Cuba. That is the truth. We were afraid to say he was executed. But why are you even questioning me about this?"

"It's not that . . . I just want to know what happened because maybe the Baathists who killed Mahmoud are the same ones who killed Hala," Youssef said, his voice beginning to crack.

"Unfortunately, we all know they're killers, my friend," Abu Ahmad said as he lit a cigarette.

"I was their target that day when they murdered Hala," Youssef explained. "They know I oppose their regime and that I wouldn't do business with them, so they wanted to kill me. Instead, they killed my wife to humiliate me."

"You have to save yourself and escape. You are lucky; you have the financial means to leave the country."

"Leave? Where would I go, Abu Ahmad?"

Yet Youssef knew exactly what he would do.

That evening, he took the children to their grandmother's in al-Baladiyyat, then drove to the house of Hasmik the fortune-teller. Hasmik's young daughter offered him a cup of coffee. She tried to show him how to swirl it, but he reminded her that he had been there before and knew the ritual well. He drank the coffee, swirled the cup, turned it over, then waited for it to cool. After a little while, Hasmik entered and sat down next to him.

She looked at him, remembering his previous visit. She murmured some prayers. There was compassion in her eyes as she read the coffee grounds with great deliberation.

This time he fully believed her. He paid Hasmik the fee she asked for and left her house. He went to the travel agency on Saadoun Street and bought three tickets to London.

Translated from Arabic by Suneela Mubayi

Acknowledgments

I would like to thank my wife Margaret Obank for always being there when I need her. A special thanks to my friend Alenka Suhadolnik, who lent me her cottage in the Slovenian countryside so I could wrap up the editing of this volume. And big thanks to my friend and editor at Akashic Books, Ibrahim Ahmad, for his patience and support. Finally, my deepest appreciation to all the authors for this wonderful collaboration.

—S.S.

ABOUT THE CONTRIBUTORS

Fereshteh Shoalani

SALAR ABDOH was born in Iran, and splits his time between Tehran and New York City. He is codirector of the Creative Writing MFA Program at the City College of New York. His essays and short stories have appeared in various publications, including the *New York Times*, *Guernica*, *BOMB*, and *Callaloo*. He is a recipient of the National Endowment for the Arts award and a NYFA Prize. He is the editor of *Tehran Noir* and the author of *Tehran at Twilight*.

Bassam Haddad

SINAN ANTOON was born in Baghdad in 1967. He has published two collections of poetry and four novels. His translation of his own novel, *The Corpse Washer*, won the 2014 Saif Ghobash Prize. His novel *Ya Maryam* was short-listed for the Arabic Booker and was translated to Spanish, French, and English. His novel *Fihris* was short-listed for the International Prize for Arabic Fiction. He codirected the documentary film *About Baghdad*. He is an associate professor at New York University.

Samuel Shimon

ALI BADER was born in Baghdad and studied Western philosophy at Baghdad University before working as a journalist for Arab newspapers and magazines. He has written fourteen works of fiction. His Arabic novel *Papa Sartre* was awarded the State Prize for Literature in Baghdad in 2002, and his novel *The Tobacco Keeper* was long-listed for the International Prize for Arabic Fiction in 2009.

NASSIF FALAK was born in Baghdad in 1954. He is a poet, playwright, novelist, and journalist. He graduated from the Academy of Fine Arts, Baghdad, in 1979. In the early 1980s, he fled Iraq. When he returned home, he was arrested and sentenced to life imprisonment—but was released after the fall of Saddam Hussein. In 2003, he published a collection of short stories, and since 2006, three novels. His first novel was serialized in Baghdad's daily newspaper, *Alsabaah*.

MOHAMMED ALWAN JABR was born in Baghdad in 1952. He has published short stories and literary essays in Iraqi and pan-Arab newspapers and magazines since 1975. His first collection of short stories, *Statues Depart and Statues Return*, was published in 2000. His debut novel, *The Memory of Aranja*, was published in 2013, and has been followed by three more. He currently lives in Baghdad, where he works as a legal expert in the fields of real estate and taxation.

Hatif Farhan

DHEYA AL-KHALIDI was born in Baghdad in 1975 and began publishing his work in literary magazines in 1992. His first novel was published in Baghdad in 2006, and the second, entitled *Killers*, was published in Beirut in 2012. He has worked as an editor for several magazines, and has written more than one hundred episodes of documentary programs for television. He has been living in Turkey since 2013.

Samuel Shimon

HUSSAIN AL-MOZANY (1954–2016) was born in al-Amarah, Iraq, in 1954. He grew up in Baghdad, but left the country in 1978 for Lebanon. He later moved to Germany, where he studied German literature. He has published two collections of short stories, two novels, and a book of essays. He was awarded the Albert von Chamisso Prize for his second novel, *Mansur oder Der Duft des Abendlandes* (*Mansour, or the Scent of the West*).

LAYLA QASRANY was born in the Anbar Province of Iraq and studied French literature in Baghdad. After the Gulf War in 1991, she left Iraq for the US, where she currently resides. Her first novel, *Sahdoutha*, was published in 2011, and her second, *Blind Birds*, was published in 2016 by al-Mutawassit. She writes frequently about travel, visual art, and music for newspapers and online.

HAYET RAIES is a Tunisian writer who has published three collections of short stories. She received an MA in philosophy from Baghdad University, and a PhD in French language and literature from the Sorbonne in Paris. Raies is currently president of the League of Tunisian Women Writers. The president of Tunisia awarded her with a medal for cultural achievement in 2001 and 2006. Her stories have been translated into English, French, German, Danish, and Spanish.

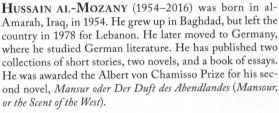

MUHSIN AL-RAMLI was born in northern Iraq. He has lived in Madrid since 1995, and earned a PhD in philosophy and Spanish literature in 2003. He has translated several Spanish classics into Arabic, including Cervantes's *Don Quixote*. He has published eleven works of his own in various genres. He is the cofounder of *Alwah* literary magazine. The original Arabic edition of his novel *The President's Gardens* was long-listed for the 2013 International Prize for Arabic Fiction.

Safaa Alwan

AHMED SAADAWI is an Iraqi novelist, poet, and screenwriter. He is the author of a collection of poetry and four novels. His third novel, *Frankenstein in Baghdad*, won the International Prize for Arabic Fiction in 2014. In 2010, he was selected for the Hay Festival Beirut39 project, as one of the thirty-nine best Arab writers below the age of forty. In 2016, he published his fourth novel, *al-Tabasheer* (*The Chalk*).

HADIA SAID is a Lebanese writer who was born in Beirut. She has worked at *Sayidaty* (*My Lady*) magazine for many years as an editorial manager. In London, she was a weekly panelist on the BBC Arabic cultural program *Papers* from 1998 to 2005, discussing short stories by emerging authors. She has published several best-selling novels, including *Artist* and *Transparent Hijab*, as well as short stories, and has written scripts for TV, radio, and documentaries.

SALIMA SALIH was born in Mosul in northern Iraq. She studied law at Baghdad University and journalism at the University of Leipzig where she obtained her doctorate. She worked in the Iraqi press, publishing articles defending women's rights. She has published five short story collections and four novels, and she has translated the works of Ingeborg Bachmann, Christa Wolf, Angela Grünert, Christa Wichterich, and others, from German to Arabic.

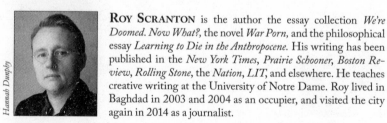

Hannah Dunphy

ROY SCRANTON is the author the essay collection *We're Doomed. Now What?*, the novel *War Porn*, and the philosophical essay *Learning to Die in the Anthropocene*. His writing has been published in the *New York Times*, *Prairie Schooner*, *Boston Review*, *Rolling Stone*, the *Nation*, *LIT*, and elsewhere. He teaches creative writing at the University of Notre Dame. Roy lived in Baghdad in 2003 and 2004 as an occupier, and visited the city again in 2014 as a journalist.

SAMUEL SHIMON was born in Iraq, into an Assyrian family, and settled in Paris as a refugee in 1985. He cofounded *Banipal*, an international magazine of contemporary Arab literature. In 2000, he and Margaret Obank edited *A Crack in the Wall*, poems by sixty contemporary Arab poets. In 2005, he published a best-selling autobiographical novel, *An Iraqi in Paris*. In 2008, he chaired the judges for the inaugural International Prize for Arabic Fiction.